I0699081

ALSO BY AMY YORKE

The Wilderise Tales
The Good and the Green
The Bright and the Blue
The Ancient and the Amber
The Silent and the Silver

The ANCIENT and the AMBER

Book Three of the Wilderise Tales

Amy Yorke

GLASSLOOK
PRESS

For the people whose entire existence revolves around a few chilly weeks in autumn

WILDERISE
HEROT'S HOLLOW
Weldan House
FOSSHOLM
Gull Bay
SUDPORT
SALLIN SEA
LANDSEND
High House
NORGATE
RODAZ MOUNTAIN
LOEGRIA
ARCAS DYRNE
Castle Corycus

Pronunciation Guide & Glossary

CHARACTERS

Alison Lennox: AL-ih-son LEN-nox. A human woman of Herot's Hollow, originally Arcas Dyrne.
Keir Ainsley: KEER AINS-lee. A human man. Doctor of Herot's Hollow and Alison's partner.
Rinka: RINK-a. An orc woman. Alison's former roommate and partner of Prince Idris.
Gwenla: GWEN-la. A dwarf woman. Alison's neighbor.
Lady Sibba: LAY-dee SIB-ba. An elf woman. Schoolteacher of Herot's Hollow and partner of Weyland Gilroy.
Weyland Gilroy: WAY-lend GIL-roy. A human man. Blacksmith of Herot's Hollow and partner of Lady Sibba.
Prince Idris: PRINCE ID-riss. A dragon man. Crown prince of Loegria and Wilderise and partner of Rinka.
Princess Ceridwen (Ceri): PRINCE-ess KAIR-id-wen (KAIR-ee). A dragon woman. Princess of Loegria and Wilderise.

King Derkomai: KING DER-ko-mye. A dragon man. King of Loegria and Wilderise.

Yordin: YORE-dinn. A dwarf man. Gwenla's cousin.

Dean Whittaker: DEEN WHIT-tah-ker. A half-elf man. Dean of Winwold College.

Mircalla Marin: meer-CAL-la MAHR-inn. A human woman. Professor of 'Lectrics, Winwold College.

Leorias (Leo): lee-OR-ee-ahss (LEE-oh). An elf man. Professor Marin's graduate student.

Polliana (Ana): PAHL-ee-AH-na (AH-na). A Halfling woman. A student of Winwold College.

Harry Charlton: HAIR-ee CHARL-ton. A human man. A student of Winwold College.

PLACES

Wilderise: WILL-duh-rise
Loegria: LOW-gree-uh
Arcas Dyrne: AR-cuss DERN
Landsend: LANDS-end
Sudport: SOOD-port
Herot's Hollow: HAIR-uts HOL-low
Sallin Sea: SAL-lin SEE
Caernock: KAIR-nok
Weldan House: WELL-dun HOUSE
Rodaz Mountain: ro-DAZ MOUNT-ain
Norgate: NOR-gate
Winwold College: WIN-wohld COL-ledge

Fulling: FUL-ling. The full-height races of the world: humans, elves, orcs, dwarves, mermaids, sirens.

Halfling: HALF-ling. Not a separate race; rather, the offspring of a Fulling and Quarterling or Eighthling.

Quarterling: QUART-er-ling. Races that come up to knee-height on humans: korrigans, hobgoblins, goblins, selkies.

Eighthling: EIGHTH-ling. The smallest races: fairies, pixies.

Magimeter: mah-GEM-ih-ter. A device for measuring magic.

Chapter One

WELCOME TO WINWOLD

Ceri

It was the autumn of Princess Ceridwen's reinvention.

The summer had been a disaster. Her father had dragged the entire court out to the middle of nowhere, and what was worse, she'd lost just about everyone she cared about.

The breakup with Isaac had set the whole thing off, but as she had realized in the weeks since, it had been a long time coming.

Ceri hadn't known how her ladies-in-waiting really felt about her until she watched them abandon her one by one. It was the loss of Jerta, her closest confidante other than her brother since childhood, that had hurt the worst. Their final argument out on the terrace of Weldan House had struck Ceri to the core, and not just because of the cruelty of Jerta's words.

No, like all of the best insults, Jerta's words had hurt because there was, within them, an undeniable kernel of truth.

Ceri had dismissed it at the time, but Jerta was right about her.

She was selfish. She was spoiled. She was manipulative and, at times, cruel, and she was a terrible friend.

It hadn't always been that way.

Ceri hadn't had the easiest upbringing in the castle. Her mother was in and out for most of her childhood, unable to bring her children with her due to the iron will of her husband: Ceri's father, King Derkomai. Prince Idris, her only brother, had left her alone there when he went to university. She'd been raised by a series of nannies, governesses, and tutors, but none of them could keep her from her father's influence once he set his sights on her as his potential heir.

Ceri learned quickly how to adapt to her father's mercurial moods. She let him spoil her when he wanted to, she stayed out of his way when he didn't want her around, and she learned to talk to him in such a way that he allowed her to do what she wanted at least some of the time.

She was just pretending to be the person he wanted her to be, but perhaps if you pretend to be someone else for long enough, you can't help but become someone else in the end.

Ceri didn't notice herself slowly turning the skills she'd learned to survive her father onto her friends, but once it was pointed out to her, she knew it was true.

It was done now.

She was starting fresh at Winwold College. Her father hadn't understood her sudden change in attitude towards attending university. She'd fought him on it the previous year when she had finally been old enough to enter, but, if she was being honest, she hadn't wanted to go not due to a general lack of interest but because Isaac wasn't going to be there.

She would be making no further decisions based upon the location of a man, no matter how handsome he was.

King Derkomai had been even more baffled when Ceri had told him she didn't wish to attend King's College, his alma mater and the nearest university to the castle.

No, she would be going to Winwold. Its primary advantage, other than being as far as from the castle as one could get while still being in Loegria? Idris would be working there this autumn as a guest lecturer, while the friends he'd met over the summer worked with a professor about that sun-powered 'lectric machine she'd helped them "invent" a few weeks earlier.

Fine, so she supposed that was one final decision she made based on the location of man, but that man was her brother, and she had missed him terribly.

Ceri's carriage conveyed her from the town of Norgate along a narrow, wooded path into the mountains. Winwold College's campus was mainly in the town below, but the first-year students, colloquially known as "freshers," were all sent to High House, a former manor which overlooked Norgate. High House was visible in the distance from the town, but it vanished from view the moment the carriage reached the tree line.

Indeed, in this dense forest, there was little to see at all. Ceri had never experienced a wood this deep and dark. The sun was so thoroughly and perfectly blocked from view that it had managed to fool an owl, which hooted softly in the distance even though it was still hours until nightfall.

At last the carriage reached an ancient bridge. Ceri leaned out the window, grateful to feel the sunlight on her pale skin and silver hair for a moment before being plunged back into the darkness of the forest.

Gods, it took so long to travel this way. Ceri had insisted on the carriage: arriving by air in her dragon form wasn't exactly conducive to her goal of blending in. Finally, after what felt like hours, the carriage took a steep turn up a hill, emerging from the woods.

The road rose sharply to cross another bridge which led to the gatehouse, its filigreed iron emblazoned with the school motto: *SIC ITUR AD ASTRA*. Behind the gates stood High House.

It wasn't exactly a manor house, but it also wasn't exactly a castle. Ceri could see the similarities with a real castle, the King's castle, Corycus, where she spent most of her childhood, mostly in the lower levels of stone. But there were additions in stone and wood and plaster, spires and towers and turrets which served no apparent function. They had been added during the manor conversion for aesthetic purposes alone, Ceri figured. She knew exactly what her father would say about them: "Waste of bloody coin."

It was hard to deny the picturesque charm of it though, standing as it did on its own with the mountains rising behind it and the yellowing trees of the dense forest nestled up against it.

The gates opened at the royal carriage's approach, and a man burst out a door from the gatehouse. He was wearing academic formal attire just like Ceri: knee-length robe, white shirt with black tie, and a black mortarboard hat, although his robe was crimson while hers was black to indicate his higher degree.

The carriage stopped before him. "Your royal highness," he said, bowing so low to the carriage Ceri thought he might kiss the dirt.

"Rise, sir," said Ceri. "Are you the dean of students?"

"Dean Whittaker, at your service," he said.

Dean Whittaker was a half-elf of roughly middle age. His hair had gone grey, and his belly had gone round, but his nose and jaw were still fine and sharp. Winwold College had had just one other dean in its four-hundred-year history, Dean Whittaker's mother, a full-blooded elf who had run the college for most of that time.

"May I show you to the royal suite? I'd be happy to take you on a tour of the grounds once you're settled in."

"That won't be necessary," said Ceri.

"The tour?"

"No, the suite." Although she'd agreed to arrive a day earlier than any of the other students, she had not agreed to the royal suite. "While at Winwold, I'd like to be treated just as any other student. You understand, don't you?"

Godsdammit. There was that manipulation again. It wasn't enough just to make her wishes known. Ceri had added that little innocent question at the end: *you understand, don't you?* Those were the words she used, but she knew what the question conveyed: *you know who I am, don't you? Will you dare to defy me?*

"Of course, of course. Ms. Asher, see to it that Ceri's things are brought to a room. Yes, one of the ordinary rooms."

"Right away, sir," said a human who stood in the doorway. She hurried up the road to the main building as if she were being chased.

"If you wouldn't mind, we can start with the tour to give Ms. Asher time to make the new arrangements," said Dean Whittaker.

Ceri nodded, and the Dean gave instructions to the carriage driver, who dropped them off at a pair of grand double doors that marked the entrance into High House.

The Dean led Ceri through a series of rooms that were both familiar and peculiar to her. The great entry hall was lined with statues, busts, suits of armor, and so many paintings and tapestries that it gave the room a claustrophobic feel, as if the amount of space required far less than whoever had decorated it could allow. There was more variety here than in her father's castle and various estates, but the contents were largely the same.

The scale of the accommodations was familiar as well, though the later construction meant there were more hallways than were present in the royal castle and palaces. The style had once been to connect rooms directly, but here at High House, there were long wood-paneled corridors, the weak 'lectric lanterns too few to illuminate the entire lengths such that they appeared to fade into shadows, giving the illusion that they went on forever.

There was something eerie about this place, but Ceri couldn't quite put her finger on it.

"And around this corner is the library. If I recall from your letter, you're considering a course of study in Comparative Literature?"

This was a surprise to Ceri, who hadn't exactly written the letter requesting her admittance far outside of the ordinary admissions window. Truthfully, she didn't know what she wanted to study.

"It's one option I've considered," she said. "I understand that Winwold doesn't require choosing a concentration until the second year of study? I'm hoping to keep my options open."

"Very wise, your highness," said Dean Whittaker. "Of course, Professor Sandak runs an excellent program in the Literature department, but there are no bad courses of study here. Now, let's see if Ms. Redclaw is here—"

From beyond the closed library doors, there came a terrible crash.

And then a scream.

All the color drained from Dean Whittaker's face.

"Oh," he squeaked. He coughed and cleared his throat. "I'm sure it's nothing, but I better go see if Ms. Redclaw needs—"

Dean Whittaker reached for the door just as it swung open with such force that it clattered against the wall, shaking some of the hallway paintings.

"How many times have I told you?" yelled a woman's voice from within.

"But Ms. Redclaw—" began a man. Ceri tried to look inside the door, but Dean Whittaker blocked her view.

"Excuse me, Ms. Redclaw, are you quite all—"

"There's been an incident," said the woman, who must have been Ms. Redclaw, to the Dean. "The library is closed."

"Ms. Redclaw—"

"*Closed.*"

Glancing around the Dean, Ceri caught glimpse of a small, grey-haired woman in a wheeled chair. She didn't seem particularly intimidating, but Dean Whittaker backed away immediately, pulling the door closed behind him.

He took a moment to readjust his tie. "I'm sorry about that. Ms. Redclaw is very particular about her library. We'll have to come by at another time."

Ceri agreed, but the truth was, she was intrigued by the commotion. There were few things that were more tempting to her than closed doors. A lifetime of wandering the halls of the castle had taught her that most interesting things happened in the private places where people thought they couldn't be overheard.

Ceri allowed the Dean to drag her along through the rest of the halls. He showed her the various departments with their offices and classrooms, noting with special pride the fine rooms which had been given to Prince Idris during his stay, no doubt at the expense of some tenured old fellow who would resent him for it greatly. (The prince himself was out for the day to greet his arriving companions.) He brought her into the grand dining hall, which was apparently a former cathedral to the Gods of Loegria, though the iconography and stained-glass windows had been replaced with depictions of scholars and significant moments in history, including the conquering by Ceri's own ancestors.

Finally, the Dean led her through a pair of doors into a cloistered courtyard.

"Destroyed in the Great Fire, but the east wing remains intact. It's handy for avoiding the cold when walking to the dormitories during winter, but on a fine day such as this, it's nice to walk outside, don't you think, your highness?"

It was a fine and sunny day here in the courtyard, the oppression of the halls forgotten in the open air. Ceri could imagine groups of students lounging out here on the grass, reading books and discussing important things. She hoped she'd find a way to be among them.

"I said go away!" Someone was yelling in the far corner of the courtyard near the lone stand of trees.

Dean Whittaker once again put himself between Ceri and the commotion. "On second thought, it might be best to show you the way you'll walk in winter," he said, attempting to steer her back into a doorway.

"Go on! Get! I said GET!"

The distant figure seemed to be arguing with a crow.

"Who is that?" asked Ceri.

Dean Whittaker looked pained. "Groundskeeper Tomasar is…passionate about his work. Nothing to worry about."

Particular and passionate. The staff at the college were much more daring than Ceri had expected. The staff and servants of the castle operated under the strictest code of conduct. Her father would have fired anyone who behaved as the librarian and the groundskeeper had done, but Dean Whittaker seemed almost afraid of his staff. Almost as soon as she had thought it, he delivered a warning. "Just don't mess with the old yew there, whatever you do."

"The yew?" At the base of the group of trees, a small cast iron fence had been erected with a sign that said *KEEP OUT*.

"That's the Norminster Yew," said the Dean, gesturing to the trees. "It's all one very old tree; the middle part has rotted away. Tomasar is quite attached to it."

Tomasar, an elderly dwarf in overalls with a scarred face and a long, grey beard, waved the rake he was using to frighten away the crows to Dean Whittaker and Ceri. The Dean waved back weakly as he led Ceri past the trees, through the breezeway beyond, and into the dormitories.

There, the human from earlier was waiting. "Your highness, your rooms are ready." They followed her up a flight of stairs to a nondescript door with a set of small brass numbers: 213.

The room was small—no, tiny. Ceri's dressing room at the castle was larger. Somehow, they'd managed to cram two single beds, two wardrobes, and two writing desks with chairs into the narrow space. Ceri passed the furniture and her trunks, which filled almost the entirety of the open floor, and headed to the window.

Through the heavy leaded glass, Ceri had a fine view of the courtyard, including Groundskeeper Tomasar's continued fight with the crows.

"It's perfect," she said.

"I'll leave you to get settled in," said the Dean. "Dinner begins at six; there aren't many here on campus yet, so we'll all be eating at the head table. Generally, it's rare for students to be invited to the head table, but of course, you are always welcome to do so."

"That won't be necessary," said Ceri. "Thank you for the tour."

The Dean fidgeted with his tie, looking around the small room as if he wanted to say more about Ceri's choice of accommodations, but he didn't dare to do so. He bowed a little less low than he had the first time and took his leave.

Ceri pushed her trunks to the side of the room that had a little less space. Truly an unselfish choice—she hoped her new roommate would appreciate how generous and accommodating she was.

Her new roommate. Ceri had never shared a room with anyone before. She had dreamt as a child of having a sister; not that she didn't love her brother, but Idris was nearly an adult in Ceri's first memories, and she'd always longed to have someone her own age to play with. She'd had a number of friends, but they had been required to keep their distance on account of her station, and they frequently were sent away along with their parents at the king's whims, no matter how much Ceri cried and begged for them to stay.

But now, she would share her space with someone else. Someone who would know her on a level that none but the servants did.

It was thrilling. And also terrifying.

Ceri began to unpack some of her things, brand new clothes in scholarly styles: straight skirts in dark wool that reached to the knees, finely starched shirts, warmed knitted jumpers, and ties in the college colors of crimson and black. There were new undergarments here too, lacy Gallic designs that could be put on without the help of a servant. (Her aunt Chloe had helped her procure those without the king's knowledge.)

The wardrobe was filled with the contents of just the first trunk, with four more to go just like it.

That was a problem for another time. Ceri looked out the window to see the Dean reentering the dining hall on the other side of the courtyard.

Perfect.

She slammed shut the wardrobe, leapt over the trunks, then forced herself to slow down to pull the dormitory door closed quietly behind her, looking up and down the corridor. No one was there to stop her.

She headed back to the library.

Outside its double doors, she could hear nothing within. There were no voices, no crashes or bangs or any sounds of movement whatsoever.

Perhaps she had missed it.

She gently turned the right-side door's brass knob, a creaking sound escaping from the hinges as she pulled it open.

The room was dark beyond, pitch black even compared to the poorly lit hallway she'd come from. She felt around, trying to orient herself but reaching into nothing but open air.

She considered stepping back out into the hallway and returning with a candlestick, but the door snapped shut behind her, engulfing her in darkness.

Something drew her further in.

She took another tentative step forward, her hands reaching into the darkness and the silence. The air in here was unnaturally hot, a stifling, oppressive heat that made it hard to draw air into her lungs.

Her hands found a bookshelf, old worn wood bowing under the weight of countless volumes. Her fingers grazed their exposed spines, feeling the variety of textures: stiff modern cloth with cool patches of neatly inked lettering, smooth leather with deep grooves where the titles and authors had been burned in by ancient hands, fraying linen with thick threads which caught under her nails and seemed to pull at her, almost in invitation.

A droplet of sweat formed on her forehead as she moved along the shelf and further into the library, entranced.

She reached the end of the shelf, keeping one hand on it as she stretched to find the next one. Then there was a crash off into the distance to her right, and the sound of thundering footsteps rapidly approaching.

She backed away, letting go of the shelf in her haste and reaching behind her for the door she'd just come through.

It wasn't there.

She felt something moving to her left. Something, or someone. She panicked, twisting backwards away from the noise to her right and the movement to her left, desperate to find the door, to find her way back into the hallway and back to her room where she should have just stayed and minded her business, far away from whatever was moving here in the dark.

And then it collided with her, sending her to the ground as something else moved in.

Chapter Two

UNDER RODAZ MOUNTAIN

Alison

"**W**ell, that settles it then. I'm coming, and that's final."

The tabby cat pawed at a phrase in the letter sitting on Alison's desk:

Of course we'd be happy to accommodate your cat. Many of our students opt to bring pets of their own.

Alison sat back in her chair, sighing and running a hand through her dark hair. They had been over this already, but Alison knew she was unlikely to persuade the cat to stay behind.

"They'd be 'happy' to accommodate me. Not that I particularly like being called 'your cat,' but that matter can be corrected when we arrive. And before you start, no, I'm not going in that basket."

"Willow, it's not like I want to carry you in the basket. It's for your own safety. There may be dogs on the railwheeler."

There also might be fairies or pixies or any of the other small folk that Willow could just barely avoid chasing, but Alison knew better than to add that.

Truthfully, it would be nice to have Willow along for the journey to Winwold College. Alison knew from her time living at the College of Numbers that university accommodations tended to be somewhat messier than the average adult block of flats, and having the cat along would mean fewer dealings with mice and other such scurrying creatures that loved to chew through 'lectric cords.

Ah, 'lectrics. It would be nice to be somewhere with working 'lectrics again. And with any luck, by the time they returned, much of the wiring work would be finished in Weldan House and Fossholm, with the extension into Herot's Hollow not far behind.

Of course, much of the success of that endeavor depended on the conversations she and her friends would be having during their journey.

Gwenla, Alison's dwarf neighbor, had managed to arrange a meeting with her cousin Yordin, an industrialist who made his fortune on the manufacturing of some sort of 'lectric machinery. At first, he had been skeptical of the design of their solar-powered machine, and he was reluctant to commit to the project. When Gwenla explained the king's involvement, his mind suddenly changed, and now he was begging them to stay longer to see the first machines come off the lines.

But that wasn't possible. The designs weren't exactly finalized: the machine produced 'lectricity, but only in the brightest sunlight, and even then, not consistently. And so they'd written to the originator of the design, Professor Mircalla Marin of Winwold College, for help.

Professor Marin was thrilled to hear of her design in action, and she agreed immediately to help resolve their issues. But, for reasons that were kept somewhat mysterious, she refused to come to Herot's Hollow to see the prototype. She insisted that they travel to her instead. She had arranged their accommodations at the university, arranged the transportation of their entire group and the prototype, and had even worked with the dean to have Idris brought in as a guest lecturer for the term.

It was quite a bit of fuss just for one little invention, although Alison had to admit that it had a lot of promise. Maybe it really could change the way 'lectrics worked all around Loegria and Wilderise, and maybe even beyond.

And so she wasn't terribly surprised to hear that they'd be able to accommodate Willow. It surely wasn't much of an ask after all else that had been arranged on short notice.

The day before their journey, Alison stopped by Keir's house to see his sister, Charlotte. She would be caring for their homes and gardens while they were away, and she had also become the neighborhood expert on cat care, having befriended Willow and Dinah instantly on account of her skills as a fisherwoman.

"Willow prefers the trout, although you can let her have some tuna on occasion as well. Not too often though," said Charlotte, handing Alison a stack of tinned fish. Charlotte was tall like her brother, but her hair had remained a pale gold even now that she no longer lived among the korrigans that had raised her. "Don't let her boss you around."

Dinah purred and brushed against Charlotte's legs, clouds of creamy tan fur floating into the air. "Treats," said Dinah.

She had learned a second word under Charlotte's tutelage, and Willow had been most impressed.

"After dinner, sweet girl," said Charlotte. Dinah playfully nipped at Charlotte's hand, earning her a nice stroke and some cheek scratches.

Alison thanked Charlotte for the fish and for taking care of everything while they were gone.

"You're welcome to come too, you know," said Alison. She enjoyed Charlotte's easy-going company and had hoped she would change her mind about joining them.

"School was never really my thing," said Charlotte. "But thank you."

Alison returned to the cottage and finished packing her things into the great green trunk she'd first carried to Herot's Hollow just a few months earlier.

It would be strange to return to Loegria. It didn't feel like going home—not just because Winwold College was on the opposite end of Loegria from where she'd lived most of her life, but also because Herot's Hollow was her home now. She never would have believed it to be possible in such a short amount of time, but it was true.

Still, they were only going to be gone for a few weeks at most, and half the town was coming along: Gwenla, Alison's elderly dwarf neighbor and champion of all things related to saving Herot's Hollow; Keir Ainsley, Alison's human partner who was out bringing the doctor who would be covering for him up to speed on his current patients; Lady Sibba, the elf schoolteacher who couldn't pass up the opportunity to meet with fellow scholars, and Weyland, the human blacksmith who didn't really want to go, but he'd made the prototype so he had little choice. They'd be meeting Rinka, Alison's former roommate, and Idris, the crown prince of Loegria and Wilderise, at Winwold.

And, of course, there was Willow.

Alison used Willow's basket to carry her fish and some blankets. "Just in case," she said to Willow, who looked indignant but did not protest.

◦•◦

The journey to the headquarters of Rodaz Mountain Industries near Landsend had been thankfully uneventful. They managed to cross the Sallin Sea without any pirate encounters, and once they made it to Loegria, Alison was pleased to reunite with the orc who had brought her to the dock from Landsend Station in the spring: Hyruk, whose highwheel carrier taxi operation had expanded from one vehicle to five.

"It's been quite a summer," said Hyruk as he loaded their trunks into the carriers. "The king brought the entire court through here. I've never seen so many people coming and going. They're saying Wilderise is where everything's happening. The next time you see me, I might be on the other side of the sea. Hey, wait a minute," he said, spotting Alison.

"I remember you. You were supposed to be coming back months ago. What happened?"

"It's like you said. Wilderise is where everything is happening. At least it is for me." Alison smiled at her friends. "We're just here on a short business venture. We'll be heading back there in a couple of weeks; I'd love to meet you here again when we return."

"I'll hold you to that," said Hyruk with a wink as he dropped them off at the station.

The rail-wheeler journey to Rodaz Mountain took less than an hour. The station appeared to be in the middle of nowhere. It sat in an empty field of browning grass, the only sign of nearby civilization being the 'lectric wires that ran high on poles, vanishing into the mountainside.

"Home," said Gwenla, brushing the grey hair from her eyes as she surveyed the seemingly empty land.

A dirt path wound down the hillside, leading to the wide mouth of a cavern. Several sets of rails, thinner than the rail-wheeler's tracks, extended from the cavern's entrance. Gwenla pulled a lever on a nearby podium, and a minecart thundered from the cavern, coming to a stop before them.

Gwenla glanced at the crew: perhaps if Weyland hadn't been there, they would have fit in a single cart. But the blacksmith was large enough to practically require a cart of his own, never mind all their luggage.

Gwenla lifted the lever and pulled it again. "The carts navigate themselves," she explained. "If we get separated, just wait until we reach the Central Plaza. You'll know it when you see it."

Alison climbed into the first minecart with Keir, who regarded the device with some trepidation as he lifted their trunks inside. "No safety belts or bars," he murmured so that only Alison could hear him. "I've seen more than a few amputations—keep your arms inside. You too, Willow."

The cat jumped from the ground and came to balance on the thin metal side of the cart. She looked down the tracks with displeasure. "You don't have to tell me twice."

For all her bravado, Willow had not enjoyed the voyage so far. Except for a stretch on the ferry, she had spent much of the time in the basket. "It's not natural to move this fast," she had said.

Alison couldn't help but disagree. Although she found carriage rides uncomfortable, she loved the rail-wheeler, and she thought the minecart seemed like it would be good fun.

She was right.

Alison pulled the lever on their cart, sending it rocketing into the darkened cavern. She found it difficult to follow Keir's well-intended instructions to keep her arms inside: the urge was to put her hands up into the air and to scream with joy at the thrill of the ride. Even Keir couldn't help but laugh as they came around a corner and went soaring down a slope, the wind whipping through his dark hair.

(Willow, on the other hand, had crawled back into her basket, growling softly when the cart's movement shifted it a fraction of an inch between Alison's feet.)

Alison's eyes took a moment to adjust to the cavern. The only thing she could make out was the trail of Lady Sibba's golden curls just ahead as their carts whizzed through narrow passages, crossing over intersecting rails and descending into cooler air. On more than one occasion, the passage opened, bringing them into an open cavern with a crisscross network of elevated rails suspended in the air, thin streams of water falling beyond sight into the depths below. Sometimes a shaft of light pierced the darkness, revealing ancient carvings in the stone and boarded up mineshafts, some still blocked by the kind of heavy machinery Gwenla's family was known for.

It was incredible. There was an entire world hidden down here. Alison had known it, had heard about the ancient dwarven cities from the dwarves she'd known in Arcas Dyrne, which was itself built over something that had once been like this but was now unrecognizable, lost to generations of progress and sharing the land with the other races. But experiencing a true dwarven mine—flying through it in the cart, feeling the drop as the world fell out from beneath her as they went over a rise—was something else.

Soon they entered a different series of tunnels. These looked more familiar to Alison, more like the underground rail-wheeler stations she knew. They were lined with polished stone and decorative tile in modern designs, and they were filled with dwarves coming and going, some in carts like theirs, others walking on dedicated paths. Their cart stopped to accommodate crossing traffic and to allow other carts in ahead, a complicated symphony of motion controlled by countless levers pulled by unseen hands.

Finally, they arrived at the Central Plaza—Gwenla had been right; it was easy to recognize. The cavern itself was the largest one yet with an enormous number of buildings carved right into its walls, layers and layers stacked on top of each other, reaching right up to the top. There were dozens of bridges crossing over the open spaces between them, some intricately carved grey stone, some gleaming brass reflecting the 'lectric lights which illuminated the space in a warm, hazy glow.

Alison's cart pulled to a stop at a busy station behind Gwenla's, which had arrived moments before. A crowd had gathered there. As Keir removed their trunks and a somewhat shaken Willow in her basket, she saw the familial resemblance among them.

"Gwenla!" The dwarves that greeted Gwenla shared her stout stature, but most of them were a good bit younger than her: nieces and nephews, cousins and second cousins and third cousins once removed, all come to see the legendary old woman who had left the mountain for a life under the sky decades earlier and had seldom returned since.

"Where's Yordin?" asked Gwenla to a dwarf woman who looked to be near to her age as others loaded the trunks onto carts and wheeled them up a ramp with the rest of the party following behind.

"He's up in the dwelling," said the older woman. "He wanted to greet you but—well, you'll see why he didn't in a moment."

"There's a surprising amount of greenery," said Lady Sibba as she came up alongside Alison. As an elf, Lady Sibba stood out perhaps the most of anyone in their group except for Weyland, whose sheer size kept him apart from the dwarven crowd even though he shared some of their features. Though there were others around with dark skin and golden hair, none had Lady Sibba's long limbs or pointed ears. Few elves enjoyed spending long in the deep places of the earth where the dwarves preferred to dwell.

Few humans either, but Alison couldn't really see why. It was noisy here in the cavern with the sounds of a great number of people at work and play echoing on the stone walls, but no more so than the city where she'd grown up, and there was a comfort in the darkness and the cool, a refreshing feeling like walking into her bedroom after a long day toiling under the sun.

Lady Sibba was right about the greenery as well—quite a few of the homes and buildings had window boxes filled with shade-loving vegetation: ferns, mosses, and a variety of edible fungi, too. "Good for the air quality, probably," said Alison, though she wondered how the plants made do with so little light.

Just as Alison began to wonder how much more her poor little legs could take, they arrived at a large pair of brass doors.

One of them creaked open slowly, but no one was there.

Inside, high-pitched voices were raised in confrontation. Gwenla hesitated at the door, a question in her look as a collision deep inside shook the walls, causing the door to once again slam shut.

"They're overrun," said Gwenla's relative. "It's been this way since little Mari was born."

The door burst open again, and this time, a small dwarf girl with pigtails greeted them. "Dad says you should come in. He's gotta pick the 'frigerator back up, then he'll be right with you."

Before Gwenla could respond, the girl had vanished inside once more.

Alison noticed that she wasn't the only one who had vanished. The dwarves that had carted their luggage up had gone as well, leaving her friends with just the sole relative as a guide, and even she refused to enter. "I'll leave you to it," she said to Gwenla. "It's good to have you back again. I hope you'll stay awhile. For Yordin's sake as much as anyone's."

Alison, Lady Sibba, Keir, and Weyland followed Gwenla inside. Willow, sensing the commotion and perhaps imagining the pulling on her tail that would ensue if she entered, opted to look around the neighborhood instead.

The interior gave Alison the vague impression that some kind of explosive had gone off. Though the furnishings were clearly finely made, they were all askew: chairs toppled over, carpets curled into dangerous trip-hazards, picture frames with shattered glass hanging precariously by wires at strange angles that surely hadn't been intended. There were lines of wax crayon running the length of the hallway, red and purple paths at waist height leading them into the current center of the chaos: the kitchen.

Inside, a large dwarf man with greying hair was struggling with the 'frigerator. He'd managed to get it upright again, but the door would no longer close.

"Let me take a look at that," said Weyland.

The dwarf simply nodded, too exhausted to ask any questions about the giant, red-headed human who offered him help.

"Gwenla," he said, rubbing his neck with a wince. "So glad you could make it. I'd offer you an ice-cold ale, but I'm afraid the 'frigerator is out of commission."

"That's alright," said Gwenla. "What's going on here, Yordin? Where's Marna? What happened to your nanny?"

Yordin laughed at the word "nanny." "Marna's up there somewhere with the rest of them," he said, gesturing vaguely behind him to elsewhere in the house. "The nanny quit this morning. It's the third one this year. This one only made it two weeks."

Gwenla shifted uncomfortably. Yordin gestured at her to take a seat at the kitchen table. "Well, I'm sorry to hear that," she said. "Won't they need you in the office?"

"The brothers can handle it. Dad would've had a fit if he knew I was skiving off on account of the youngins, but he's six hundred feet under out there down in the shaft. I reckon he'll be rolling in his grave a long time before we hear him up here."

Gwenla had told Alison of the dwarven tradition to bury their dead deep within abandoned mineshafts, the depth correlating to the esteem with which they were held by dwarven society. Yordin's father must have been quite esteemed indeed.

"You must be Gwenla's associates. Which one is the prince?" Yordin gestured to the others to join them at the table. "That one, I reckon." He pointed at Keir, who smiled and shook his head.

"I'm only a marquess, I'm afraid," he said. "Prince Idris is busy at the university."

"I never could keep all of those titles straight. Prince, marquess. It's all the same to me. How'd you lot manage to get tangled up with Gwenla?"

Alison explained how she'd joined in Gwenla's schemes to save Herot's Hollow when she moved there from the city, omitting the part about reuniting Keir with the town following his accidental imperiling of it through a magical vine he hadn't realized he'd unleashed upon it. And also the part of how she'd helped play matchmaker for Lady Sibba and Weyland. She explained the chance meeting of Prince Idris by her former roommate, and how his sister Princess Ceridwen had forced them to come up with an alternate power source on the spot when they sabotaged a hydro-'lectric dam demonstration by Andsaz, a rival dwarven industrialist.

"Oh boy, I bet Andsaz was furious. He probably fired his whole engineering team. I need to have someone reach out—there could be an opportunity there," said Yordin.

It was funny to hear this man, dressed as he was in stain-covered pajamas (stained with both sweat and some kind of reddish sauce) talk about business over a kitchen table.

Gwenla then explained her idea about harnessing the power of the sun, and how they'd turned it into a nearly working prototype with the help of a journal article published by the very professor they were going to see next.

"It was a good idea to use magic to make it seem like it was working," said Yordin. "If you're looking for a job, let me know. The number of times we've had a prototype fail during a live demonstration—magic could be a game changer." He nodded approvingly at Alison.

Alison smiled back but said nothing. She wasn't sure she felt using magic for fraudulent reasons was the best practice in general, but maybe if it were for a good purpose like saving the town, she'd consider it.

"You brought the plans?" asked Yordin.

Lady Sibba retrieved the schematics drawn up by Weyland from her satchel. She had annotated them with the terminology from the original journal article, and Alison had provided some calculations based on formulas Professor Marin had provided.

"I'll need to have my number-checkers take a look, but this looks like good work. And you say Professor Marin will sort the power-saver issue?"

The professor had written back with promising news regarding the issues they'd had with the prototype, including an issue that even Yordin wasn't able to solve: none of the current power-savers, the devices used to store 'lectricity long term, had high enough capacity to be used in the 'lectrical grid. His engines and machinery used power-savers, but there was an issue of scale.

"Professor Marin has several experimental technologies she'd like us to test. We're hoping to have the final designs within the month," said Gwenla.

"Good, very good," said Yordin. "We've got the line running components now. It'll just be a matter of assembly and power-saver production. We should be able to meet your timeline for the first delivery. I wanted to talk to you about the coin."

Gwenla glanced at Alison. They'd agreed to split their new venture nine ways: one part each to Gwenla, Alison,

Keir, Lady Sibba, Weyland, Idris, Rinka, Professor Marin, and Yordin, with Yordin receiving a double share due to his production costs. (They'd offered the same to Professor Marin, but she'd refused.) But Gwenla had been worried that her cousin would think they were trying to cheat him and might demand more.

Gwenla had been wrong.

"It's too generous of an offer. I'll accept my share, but I won't let you double it. I've had my solicitor draw up a new contract; it's at the office so it doesn't get covered in soup. But there's just one more condition I have."

"Name it," said Gwenla. "I'll do anything to keep the king from stripping Herot's Hollow."

Yordin laughed at that. "There are worse things than a mine, you know. Most dwarves know that. But you've never been like most dwarves, have you?"

"I suppose not," said Gwenla. "Name your price, Yordin."

Yordin took a deep breath in, drawing his pajamaed body upright into as dignified of a position as was possible. "Take Finnli with you."

Gwenla scrunched her grey eyebrows together. "Finnli? Who's Finnli?"

Chapter Three

THE MONSTER

Ceri

Ceri could see nothing in the darkened library, but she could feel something reaching for her on the floor.

It grabbed her by the arms.

"Don't move," said a voice.

Ceri screamed, trying to back away.

She heard the *snap* of a switch behind her, and the room was flooded with light, bright and blinding.

Ceri whirred around, squinting, looking for whatever had pursued her, but there were only the two people from earlier: the librarian Ms. Redclaw, who was wheeling away from the light switch she'd just turned on, and the young elf she'd been yelling at, who was with Ceri on the floor.

"Now look what you've done," said Ms. Redclaw.

Ceri and the elf sat in the middle of a real mess: shards of ceramic (formerly a teacup, Ceri guessed) littered over scattered books and scrolls, which were drenched with a dark liquid. The elf was picking up a metallic instrument Ceri did not recognize, bending a rod back into place with a frown.

"Are you alright?" he asked, only then glancing up at Ceri. His voice was soft with the hint of an accent she couldn't quite place, his tone seemingly unconcerned, as if this sort of thing happened to him every day.

She nodded slowly, her heart still pounding in her ears. "Tea?" she asked, her voice high-pitched and breathless as she touched the cool, dark patch soaking into her brand-new shirt.

"Oh dear." He sighed, reaching for a handkerchief. "I'm sorry; that's going to stain. It's coffee. Well, it was coffee. And tea. I steep my tea in coffee."

Ceri regarded this bizarre, highly caffeinated stranger she had taken for a monster moments earlier.

As far as monsters went, she had to admit he was fairly non-threatening. He was tall—she could tell just from the proportion of his limbs even as he continued to gather up the things on the floor—and quite thin. His golden hair was disheveled by the collision and his tie was askew, but his clothes had been generally well-kept apart from their current mishap. As she watched him, he slid his wire-rimmed spectacles up his freckled nose and back into position. The color in his face seemed to drain from it as he looked through them at Ceri.

There was a version of Ceri that would have lashed out at him or mocked him for his clumsiness. It's what her father would have done. But she could see there was nothing monstrous in the elf. And honestly, now that she saw the threat for what it was, she found the whole thing somewhat amusing. "At least it wasn't hot," she said.

Ceri shifted backwards to pull herself up, but the elf cried out, "Be careful," reaching for Ceri's hand just before she put it down on a shard of broken mug.

Ceri froze under his touch.

It had been ages since anyone had touched her so casually. Doing so was a grave offense—wait, didn't he recognize her?

"You're not from Loegria, are you?" said Ceri. He took her hand and helped her to her feet. She could still feel the shadow of his fingertips when they parted.

"Is it so obvious?" He laughed. "I've been here for a while now."

Not long enough to recognize Loegrian royalty, clearly.

"Who's there?" asked Ms. Redclaw. She had retrieved some kind of grabbing stick and wheeled over to help sort out the rest of the mess. "My eyes aren't what they used to be. Are they alright?"

Ceri turned her back to Ms. Redclaw to prevent the old human from getting a better look at her.

"I'm fine," she said. "Not a scratch on me."

Ms. Redclaw reached around Ceri with the grabbing stick, picking up an undamaged book and sliding it back onto a shelf. "Leorias, I've told you time and time again. It doesn't like you. It doesn't want you here."

Leorias. That must have been the elf's name. But what did Ms. Redclaw mean by "it" not liking him?

"I know," said Leorias. "But I need the library for my research. I've tried to let it know I'm not a threat."

To let what know?

"But you are a threat. Just look what you've done to these books," said Ms. Redclaw, picking up a drenched volume titled *A History of Astronomical Curses.*

"I'm sorry," said Ceri. She looked between the two of them. "Are you talking about the library?"

"Are you a new student?" asked Ms. Redclaw. "You're a bit early, aren't you? Unless—"

Ceri could see the idea dawning on Ms. Redclaw. Perhaps Dean Whittaker had told her she was coming. "A new student, yes," she said, hoping to interrupt Ms. Redclaw's thoughts. "I took the wrong rail-wheeler and arrived a day early."

They didn't know who she was. They really didn't know.

"The library has a mind of its own, dear," said Ms. Redclaw. "You'll get to know it well during your time here, Ms.?"

Ceri glanced around and picked two names off of books on the nearby shelves at random: "Ms. Ethel Higglebottom."

Ethel Higglebottom? Oh Gods, what was she doing?

"Higglebottom? Is that a gnomish name?" asked Ms. Redclaw.

"Er, my father was adopted into a family of gnomes," said Ceri.

She sighed. Yes, she'd wanted to start over, but she hadn't intended to pretend to be someone else entirely. She was just intrigued by the idea of not being recognized, of being treated just like an ordinary student for a bit, but things were already getting out of hand.

Just then, something fell from a shelf to the floor, narrowly missing the wet patch left by the tea coffee. It was a book, although Ceri couldn't see where it could have come from.

"*The Royal Family of Loegria and Wilderise, Past and Present*," said Leorias, reading the title.

He glanced up at Ceri. "Is this one for you? Were you planning to study history?"

Ceri snatched the book away from him before he could look inside—who knew which portrait of her they used? Any of them were problematic at the moment, anyway. "Yes," she said. "History. That's right."

It took her a moment to understand why he'd asked her if the book was for her. "You said the library has a mind of its own. Did it give that book to me?"

"Yes," said Ms. Redclaw, smiling and patting a nearby shelf. "No one knows why, exactly, but I like to think of it as an old friend that knows what you need. Sometimes it knows better than even you do. Unless, of course, you've done something to upset it." She glared her clouded eyes in the rough direction of Leorias.

"I swear I've done nothing to it, Ms. Redclaw," said Leorias.

Ceri believed he was telling the truth. Or at least he believed his own lie.

She was, unfortunately, something of an expert when it came to lying.

She retrieved the book on royalty from under her arm and thumbed through the pages. Is this how she really wanted to start things out? With more lies?

Near the back, she found the portrait of the current royal family. It was an old portrait, taken with a picture-taker five years earlier on the last of her mother's visits to Loegria, back before she'd given up on maintaining the charade of the marriage with Ceri's father for once and for all.

King Derkomai sat in the center, tall and grand in his crown and royal regalia, the piercing blue of his eyes coming through even in black and white. Queen Yuling sat to his left, her face joyless, her hand gripping Ceri's arm tightly. Prince Idris sat to the right of their father, but he was exactly a mirror image of their mother, both in features and in his tense posture. Only the fifteen-year-old Ceri, seated in front of her mother, looked relaxed in the picture. Her face was a bit rounder then, but she looked much as she did today: she had her mother's almond eyes and gently sloping nose but her father's coloring—blue eyes, pale skin, and hair that had been silver since birth.

Ceri remembered the day of the portrait well. She had been convinced that her mother was coming back to stay for good, or that this time, she'd take Ceri with her when she left.

Neither of those things was true. But to be fair to Queen Yuling, it wasn't for a lack of trying on her part, as Ceri had come to understand only recently.

"This is me," said Ceri, handing the book to Leorias. "The message was for you."

She watched Leorias as he read the names and looked at the portrait, putting it together. "Princess Ceridwen, second in line to the throne," he said. He looked down at her through his spectacles. "This is you."

"Yes," said Ceri.

"Princess Ceridwen?" asked Ms. Redclaw. "Forgive me, your royal highness." She bowed her head forward as best as she could in deference. "I didn't recognize you. Why didn't you say?"

"Probably because of that reaction," muttered Leorias. Ceri caught his eye, and he startled. "I'm sorry," he said. "I don't know why I said—"

"No, you're exactly right," said Ceri. Perhaps he hadn't meant to say it, but for a moment, she felt seen. "I'm sorry for the deception. I'm accustomed to being recognized. It was nice, for a moment, to be whoever I wanted to be."

"And you chose Esther Higglebottom, student of history," said Leorias, amused. Ceri noticed then that even after she'd told him who she was, he hadn't bowed.

"Ethel," Ceri corrected. "Where are you from, Leorias? Is it 'Lord' Leorias?" Ceri had known few elves that couldn't claim some sort of title. Most were styled "Lord" or "Lady," although some had higher titles, either in the Loegrian court or within their own elvish courts.

"Not 'Lord' Leorias, no. 'Leo' is fine. I'm from Gallia."

Well, that explained the lack of courtesy. Gallia, the country across the southern sea, famously removed their monarchs and their courts more than a century earlier.

Removed their heads, to be precise.

Ceri rubbed at her neck involuntarily. "Gallia? I hope my presence doesn't offend you. I've heard your people don't care much for royalty."

"*Au contraire*," said Leo. "Most Gallic find royalty quaint. Charming. A relic from a bygone era. Not that you're a relic, per se." He looked down, blushing. "Not that you're quaint."

"Charming, then?" offered Ceri.

Another book fell to the floor. Leo went for it, but Ceri got there first.

"*Courtship in the Modern Era: An Etiquette Guide for Young People,*" she read aloud. As soon as the words left her mouth, she regretted them.

She contemplated hurling the book across the room. This library had some nerve. Just what was it suggesting with that offering?

She hadn't been thinking anything of the sort. Not that Leo wasn't handsome. He was an elf—of course he was handsome. But that also meant he was many years her senior, although they did say elves matured more slowly, and he seemed to be a student still of some kind, so he couldn't have been too much older than her in mental age if not actual age.

But none of that mattered because she was here to study, not to court men. No matter how incredibly handsome and slightly awkward and somewhat charming they might be.

Ceri looked at Leo, who immediately tore away his glance and began to contemplate the binding on the book about royalty with some intensity.

Ms. Redclaw cleared her throat.

"Right," said Leo, purposefully not looking at Ceri or the book. "I better be going. I've got a lot to do to—and first, I've got to get these books dry enough to even know where to start."

"Oh," said Ceri. "I guess since you know who I am, I can help with that."

Ceri looked down at the stain on her shirt and removed it, pulling the dark liquid from it and into a ball in the air. It was one of the few uses of magic King Derkomai tolerated: although he generally hated magic, he permitted his own family to use it to avoid embarrassment.

Then she held out her hands, gesturing to the books, papers, and handkerchiefs they had used to clean up the mess on the floor. The droplets of tea coffee flew out of each object, joining the ball suspended in the air.

"*Incroyable,*" said Leo.

"I can't do anything about the cup, I'm afraid," said Ceri. "That's beyond my skill."

Ms. Redclaw showed Ceri to a sink in the back behind the library counter, where she dropped the floating ball of liquid down the drain.

When they returned, Leo was still there. He'd taken a leather-bound journal from the now-dry stack of books and papers and was scribbling furiously with a pen.

"Would you be willing—" Leo began as she approached him. "No, never mind."

"What is it?" asked Ceri.

"No, it's too much to ask. You've already done enough. Thank you for cleaning up my mess."

"Yes, thank you, your highness," said Ms. Redclaw. "I hope to see again soon."

Ms. Redclaw wheeled back behind the counter, leaving her alone with Leo.

"Tell me what you wanted to ask me," said Ceri once Ms. Redclaw was out of earshot.

It was purely out of curiosity that she insisted on hearing it. Ceri couldn't stand unanswered questions any more than she could stand unopened doors. It had absolutely nothing to do with the library's suggested reading. Nothing at all.

"It's just…your magic," said Leo. "I research magic. It's why I'm here at Winwold and not back at one of the renowned Gallic universities. They have discarded magic for reason, for science. They claim the time of magic has passed."

"My father holds the same opinion of magic. 'Useless and unreliable superstitious nonsense.' Unless one of the royals needs it, of course," said Ceri.

Leo shook his head. "But what if magic and science are the same thing? What if they're two sides of the same coin? I've been trying to study magic as a form of energy, as a potential power source. Perhaps magic and science need not be at odds at all. But the universities in Gallia think it's best if we leave magic behind us in the past, and even here, there's an idea that magic is different from the rest of the natural world, and that it can't be understood by the same means. I think they're wrong. There's so much still to learn if we're open to it, just so much untapped potential—"

Leo's face had animated when talking about his research. His lovely green eyes were dancing with energy behind his spectacles. Golden strands of his hair fell onto his cheeks from his movement, highlighting their symmetry. He had leaned forward without realizing it, his hands gesturing so enthusiastically that he brushed Ceri's arm again.

"Sorry," he said, backing away with a shy smile. "I get a little too passionate about my research."

Why are elves so beautiful? It's really unfair of them, Ceri thought. It was very distracting.

"What do you need from me?" she asked. She tried to ignore that phantom feeling where his hand had touched her again.

Here to study, she reminded herself.

"Well, I have an instrument here," said Leo, holding up the little brass device that he'd picked up from the ground when they collided. "It's my own design. I've been using it to measure magical potential. I was preparing to take readings tonight. It's the peak of a meteor shower; I have some enchanted objects I was hoping to measure during a celestial event. But if you'd allow it, I'd love to measure, well, you. Your magic." Leo looked meekly at Ceri. "It won't hurt," he said, reaching out a hand to her and quickly withdrawing it. He used it to brush the hair back from his face instead, which Ceri thought was a shame.

"During the meteor shower?" she asked.

Leo looked surprised. "I was thinking of later this week, but if you'd be willing to come along tonight…it will be late though, and it's a bit of a hike up to the observatory. I understand if you're not up for it."

"Would it help you?" asked Ceri.

This was her chance to be the new Ceri. The kind, selfless Ceri who didn't lie or cheat or manipulate anyone. She could help Leo purely out of the kindness of her heart.

Or, not her heart, per se, not that there was anything going on with her heart, other than the near heart-attack she'd had earlier when she thought he was a monster.

"It would help me very much," said Leo.

"Then I'll do it."

"Wonderful! Meet me after dinner by the Norminster Yew. The old tree in the courtyard."

Ceri nodded, and then she turned and fled from the library before she could say anything that might embarrass her. She left in such a hurry that she went the wrong way and had to walk around half of the school to get back to her room.

Safely behind her closed door, she removed her shirt. The stain was gone, but the wrinkles remained, and she wouldn't show up to her first dinner looking untidy.

As she spotted herself in the bathroom looking glass wearing her new white lace brassiere, she remembered that it was Gallic in design. Leo's bright, excited face crossed her mind, along with the shadow feeling of his hand on hers.

"Godsdammit," she said. She didn't know much, but she knew it wasn't a great sign to be thinking of him in her underwear already if she was trying to focus on her studies.

This boy was trouble.

Chapter Four

FURTHER JOURNEYS

Alison

The kitchen table in Yordin's house was tense as they waited to hear more of the mysterious Finnli.

"He's one of the youngins," said Yordin. "Now I know what you're going to say—"

"No," said Gwenla. "Absolutely not. Are you insane?"

"Gwenla—"

"No, Yordin. Yes, I enjoyed babysitting you when you were little, but those years are long behind me. I'm in no condition to pick up 'frigerators off the floor."

"It's fixed," said Weyland, swinging the door closed once more.

"Good man!" said Yordin, shaking Weyland's hand. "Say, do you need a job? I could use a man of your size—"

"Would you stop offering my friends jobs for a minute and listen to me?" Gwenla stood to face her cousin. He was quite a bit taller than her, though nowhere near the size of

Weyland or even Keir, but he looked small before her, defeated.

"There are seven of them, Gwenla. Seven. The manufactories have been good to us, but it doesn't matter how much coin you have when you can't get the nannies to stay. We paid the last one three times the going wage up front."

"Well, no wonder she left if you paid her up front," said Lady Sibba. Gwenla gave her an icy look, and she realized her mistake. "I'm sorry," she said. "I didn't mean—"

"No, you're right. That was foolish. The new one is starting tonight, and we won't make the same mistake. The truth is, we're desperate."

"I understand that," said Gwenla, "but I don't know why you think I'll have any more success. I haven't taken care of children in decades, and never full time. And we have a business venture to take care of."

"I'm not asking you to take care of children. Just one child. He's a good lad. Quiet, studious. Just turned eight. He's the best behaved of the lot."

"Then why him? Surely you'd want me to take on one of the more difficult children."

Yordin sighed, looking off into the next room towards the sounds of laughter and tears, which were punctuated by the occasional crash or dread-inducing crunch. "He's not like us. I can't give him what he needs. He's like you. Always sneaking off to the surface, running around up there alone. It's dangerous up there. I only go up when I have to. He needs someone to guide him. Someone who can teach him what things up there are. Someone who can keep him safe."

Yordin looked at Gwenla, his tired grey eyes touched with tears. "Please, Gwenla. Do this for us, and I'll build you any type of machine you want."

Just then, a little blonde dwarf boy stumbled into the room. He was watching something moving in a jar, paying so little attention to where he was going that he would have collided with Lady Sibba had she not seen him coming. Instead, she gently reached for his shoulder, guiding him around her.

"We have room in the school," said Lady Sibba. "The term is starting when I get back. It's good timing."

Gwenla scowled at the elf.

"What's that you have there, boy?" said Gwenla. She held out her hand.

"Finnli, show it to her. There's a good lad," said Yordin.

Yordin had so much love in his eyes for the child despite his exhaustion that Alison couldn't imagine saying no to him. But Gwenla's face was impassive.

"This is my green critter," said Finnli, holding up the glass jar. Inside was a caterpillar of impressive size. It was nearly as long as one of Alison's fingers and at least twice as fat. "He likes to eat green stuff."

Gwenla took a quick look at the caterpillar and nearly tossed the jar. "It's a hornworm. Terrible pest. They nearly destroyed my tomatoes the year before last. Take that thing out of the jar and step on it."

"No!" shouted Finnli, snatching the jar back from Gwenla. "I will not! He's my friend."

The little boy's face was going red. He jutted his chin out at Gwenla, defiant.

Gwenla gave Yordin a stubborn look as if to say, "This was your best idea?"

But when she turned back to Finnli, something changed. There was something so sweet about his little face, as angry as it was. Alison could see what Yordin had meant—he did have quite a bit of Gwenla's determination in him at the very least.

Gwenla's expression softened. "What's his name?"

"Mortimer. It's from a human story I read once."

"If Mortimer is coming with us, he has to stay in that jar. I won't have him ruining my plants. But we should put some holes in the top so he can breathe."

"Oh, thank you, Gwenla. Thank you," said Yordin. He reached out to shake her hand, but she held her hand up.

"*If*," she said. "I think I ought to stay here for a few days. Let's see how we get on before we make any major decisions. That is, if the rest of you think you can manage without me?"

"Of course," said Alison. "We'll handle the rest of the plans." Alison recognized what Gwenla was doing for Yordin—how she had seen that she was needed, and it wasn't Gwenla's way to refuse someone who needed her help.

And while Gwenla may have left the mountain for a reason, Alison knew that she had been missed, and she was glad for her friend to have the opportunity to spend time with her family.

It also gave her a pang of guilt. She didn't have a large family left in Arcas Dyrne, but she owed her mother more than the couple of letters she'd sent so far.

That was a problem for another time, though.

"Come, everyone," said Yordin. "We'll get you settled for the night in the guest rooms—don't worry, the kids don't have access to that floor. Marna and I are making our special roast supper tonight, assuming the new nanny arrives."

Alison followed the others upstairs, dodging toy railwheelers and looking forward to finding out what made the roast "special."

❧

The answer had been copious amounts of butter, an unbelievably hot grill, and a beautifully marbled cut of beef that had been raised by human farmers in the valley beyond. It was just as special as Yordin had promised.

In the morning, they thanked Yordin for his support and accommodations and headed back to the minecarts to catch the rail-wheel to Winwold, a box of sample materials as requested by Professor Marin in tow. Alison had thought Willow might have wanted to stay with Gwenla in order to avoid any further transit, but the cat's first encounter with the children put a quick end to that idea.

"Get this thing off me," she said. One of Yordin's daughters had tied a frilly pink bonnet around her neck.

It was extremely cute, but Alison knew better than to admit it. Instead, she bent down and untied the laces, freeing Willow.

"Completely undignified," said Willow. "I spent all night trying to evade those little monsters."

"Well, you can get plenty of rest on the rail-wheeler," said Alison.

The journey to Norgate, the mountain town where Winwold was located, was not far as the crow flies, but unfortunately, it seemed that there was a tiny town with a tiny station on the other side of every mountain they went around and every tunnel they passed through. The scenery was beautiful though, all snow-capped peaks and green valleys shifting to amber with the cooling of the weather, but Alison was eager to get to the college. She didn't know how much time it might take Professor Marin to sort out the issues with the solar device, and the looming threat of the king giving the order to raze the town hung over all of their heads.

The light had begun to fade by the time they pulled into Norgate Station. Norgate was the largest and busiest town they had been through since Landsend, though most of that was the college and its just arriving students, many of them on the very same rail-wheeler. A line of carriages awaited to bring the freshers and their families up to High House, and Alison and her remaining companions would be taking one of those as well.

Although they wouldn't be alone.

"Alison! Over here!"

Alison nearly didn't recognize Rinka, her former roommate and dearest friend. The orc was wearing a prim suit in a studious gray, and she'd cut her red hair stylishly short and curled it neatly. She stood with Prince Idris, looking dapper in his school attire, in front of an expensive-looking carriage.

Alison noticed the carriage lacked the royal insignia. Prince Idris didn't like to make a fuss.

Alison waved to them as Keir touched her shoulder. "I'm going to run to the post office across the street." In his hands was a small brown package tied with white string.

"For Charlotte?" Alison guessed.

"It's a puzzle I bought from the dwarves while you were sleeping this morning. A funny little metal contraption. She always loved that kind of thing."

Alison smiled. "I'll tell them to wait for you."

She crossed over to the carriage and was greeted by one of Rinka's biggest hugs.

"I missed you," said Rinka.

"How was Princess Chloe?" asked Alison once she could breathe again: the orc had one hell of a grip.

"Amazing. I'll tell you all about it on the ride up."

"Boys and girls?" said Lady Sibba, gesturing to the two carriages.

"Of course," said Rinka, linking arms with her and climbing into the front carriage. "How else are we meant to gossip?"

Alison felt bad for Weyland—he was, despite his size, one of the girls more than one of the boys.

"Don't worry," said Lady Sibba, sensing Alison's concerns. "I'll catch him up on it all once we're there."

As the carriage traveled the path to High House, Rinka told them of her travels the past couple of weeks. First, they had gone to see Princess Chloe at her country home.

"We told her the truth," said Rinka. Rinka had posed as a noble from the continental principality of Paistos during the summer in order to convince Loegria's courtiers to save Herot's Hollow from the construction of a dam. It had worked, but primarily due to her befriending of Princess Ceridwen, who had the ear of the king.

"How did she take it?" asked Alison.

"She was very surprised," said Rinka. "I think we really fooled her. But she was great about it. She had ideas for how to tell the rest of the court. Some of them were completely wild, like saying that my father had been eaten by sea lions and that in Paistos, it meant I had to forfeit my title."

"Highly plausible," said Alison.

"Do they even have sea lions in Paistos?" asked Lady Sibba.

"Not a one," said Rinka. "But her last suggestion was the best one. She has a friend who works for a women's magazine in Arcas Dyrne, and she likes to write stories about the court. Apparently the court likes to 'leak' information to her as well."

"Of course they do," said Lady Sibba.

"Princess Chloe thinks we ought to do an interview with her and tell her the real story of how we met on the ferry, the pirates, all of it. The king will be happy to have the pirates back in the news to drum up support for his military buildup. And if he publicly disapproves after it's already been announced, it'll look like he doesn't have control of his own son."

"Which he doesn't," said Alison.

"Which he doesn't," agreed Rinka, "but he'd die before admitting that."

"When is the interview?" asked Lady Sibba.

"We're going to meet with her at the end of the term," said Rinka. "It will give us a bit more time to enjoy each other's company in case…"

In case it all turned into a disaster. Rinka and Idris could be forced to split at best. At worst, she could be imprisoned for impersonation.

"I'm sure it won't come to that," said Alison, squeezing her friend's hand reassuringly. She meant it—she had seen Idris in action, and she couldn't imagine him letting anything happen to Rinka.

Alison listened as Rinka told them of her short trip to Arcas Dyrne, where they had visited Rinka's father, and the trials and tribulations of packing up Idris's office at the King's College. As the carriage entered the forest, she was surprised by how dark it became. It was so dark, she could barely see Rinka sitting next to her.

"What trees are those do you think?" asked Alison during a lull in conversation.

"Hmm, some kind of pine," said Lady Sibba. "Different from the ones in our forest, I'm fairly certain."

The forest was certainly different here. Alison knew the woods around Herot's Hollow well, but even the dense tangle of the spriggan's grove didn't compare to this. She was reminded of something Aras had said when she'd gone looking for the fairies about fouler things lurking in the woods.

In these woods, she could believe it.

Alison was relieved to reach the gate of High House. But when the servants led them inside, she found it was nearly as dark as Gwenla's home had been without any of the comfort. There was something unsettling about the sheer number of paintings in the place covering every inch of wall space. It was as though a hundred pairs of eyes followed her every move as she walked down the long corridors. She was grateful her friends were here—she wouldn't want to be in these hallways alone.

They'd been given several rooms divided by gender, but Idris assured them no one would mind if they switched as long as they didn't make too much of a fuss about it.

"I'm going to make a quick trip outside," said Willow once Alison and Keir had settled her into their room. The cat seemed completely undisturbed by their strange surroundings, but Alison was reluctant to let her go by herself.

"I'll come with you," said Alison.

She hurried along behind the cat, trying to shake the feeling that she was being followed. Willow chattered away happily, glad to be back on stationary ground once again.

"And we'll need to find the kitchens soon as well," said Willow. Alison had missed the first part of what she said. She agreed with her nonetheless.

"What's the matter with you?" asked Willow as they exited the building into a large courtyard, which was empty except for a single grove of trees in the far corner.

"I don't know," said Alison. "I'm tired from our travels, I suppose." It seemed silly to mention whatever vague sense of wrongness she felt to the cat.

She and Willow headed to the trees to give Willow some privacy, but as they approached, Alison saw that it wasn't a grove of trees at all.

"It's all one great tree," said Alison. She could tell from the way the bark was different in the center—there had been something in the middle that was gone now. It must have been hundreds of years old. She'd need to get Weyland out here to sketch it so she could show the spriggan when they returned to Herot's Hollow.

As they approached, she saw a small fence had been erected around it. "Don't go into the middle of it," she told Willow. "We don't want to do it harm."

"What are you doing?" came a voice from beyond the tree.

Alison nearly jumped out of her skin. She hadn't seen or heard any movement.

She was relieved to see it was merely an elderly dwarf in overalls. The skin on his face was deeply scarred, but it looked like whatever had happened to it had happened long ago. The groundskeeper, she presumed.

"We were just admiring the tree here. Do you know how old it is?"

The groundskeeper's deeply scarred face was stern. "Don't go inside that fence there. It's fragile."

"Of course we won't," said Alison. She took a closer look at the short needles on the low-hanging branches. "It's a yew?"

"The Norminster Yew," said the groundskeeper. "Three thousand years old, at least, according to the Dean Whittaker. The former Dean Whittaker, not her son."

"It's remarkable," said Alison.

The groundskeeper smiled. "Aye," he said. Something ginger and white dashed out from between his legs. "Oy, Barney. Get back here!"

Barney was a dog with long, silky fur and big floppy ears. He had caught the scent of Willow.

He ran up to her, tail wagging, tongue panting, eyes bright and watery.

Willow turned to the side, arching her back and hissing fiercely.

"Willow!" shouted Alison, stepping in between the pair.

"Barney!" shouted the groundskeeper. Barney ran back to the groundskeeper obediently.

"Keep that thing away from me," said Willow.

Barney and the groundskeeper turned to her in surprise. "Well, I'll be," said the groundskeeper. "I haven't heard a cat talk since I was a boy. Barney, stay."

The dog did as he was told. The groundskeeper slowly approached Willow.

"Sorry about that, miss," he said to the cat. "The name is Tomasar, and that's my dog Barney. He loves cats. He won't hurt you, but he sure would like to give you a sniff. If you'd let him, that is."

Tomasar had clearly known cats to be asking for permission.

"He may sniff," said Willow, holding herself up as much as she could. "But no licking."

"You heard her, Barn. Don't lick," said Tomasar. The dog approached again, this time considerably more cautiously.

Willow allowed him to sniff her, and she even snuck in some sniffs of her own.

To Alison's surprise, she rubbed her head against him.

"See? He's a good boy," said Tomasar. He bent and scratched the dog behind the ears. "We'll be on our way. It was nice to meet you both."

Alison realized he hadn't truly introduced himself to her, but she didn't correct him. She figured the positive encounter with the cat was enough.

"His fur is very soft," Willow admitted to Alison once they were out of earshot. "He'll need to be kept in his place, of course. But I could see him making a good pillow while we're here."

Trust the cat to find something soft to lay on the moment they arrived.

Alison waited for Willow to take care of her business behind some bushes near a ruined cloister. A cool breeze blew through it, sending a chill up her spine. She'd need to make sure she kept a jumper with her here. Autumn was well on its way this high in the mountains.

When Willow and Alison returned, plans had already been made to head back into town. Lady Sibba had forgotten to bring some kind of salve, and Idris wanted to avoid dinner with Dean Whittaker.

"He's far too eager to please," said Idris.

"But what about Ceri? Don't you want to say hello?" asked Rinka.

"We'll see her soon enough, I'm sure. The last thing she wants is her brother hanging around while she meets new people. Which means I won't let her out of my sight, but I'm sure she can manage one night on her own."

Alison didn't admit it to anyone, but she was grateful to have an excuse to leave High House again.

There was something about it that wasn't quite right.

Chapter Five

A STARRY NIGHT

Ceri

Ceri's arrival in the dining hall wasn't heralded by trumpets, but everyone at the long table at the head of the room stood as if it was. They were her soon-to-be professors, but they treated her as the honored guest, bowing and curtsying to her as she approached.

She had arrived on time, but there were only a few seats remaining at the table—a couple near Dean Whittaker near the center, and one at the end across from Leo.

If there was a feeling of her heart skipping a beat when she spotted him, it could surely be explained by the fact that he'd given her the fright of the century on their first encounter. It was a perfectly plausible explanation, and she would be entertaining no further thoughts.

Leo bowed to her, smirking.

No. Further. Thoughts.

She would not be thinking about where, exactly, she felt that smirk. She definitely would not be taking that seat across from him.

Ceri turned back to Dean Whittaker and addressed the table. "Thank you, but please don't feel like you need to stand on my account. I plan on being here for quite some time, and I'd rather we dispense with the royal protocol."

"But your majesty—" began Dean Whittaker.

"I'm not 'your majesty' yet," said Ceri. She saw his embarrassment at the mistake; he was unaccustomed to dealing with all of these rules and formalities. In front of her father, she would have mocked him. Instead, she chose to soften the blow. "I do appreciate the courtesy. But while I'm here, I'd rather just be Ceri. If that would be alright with you, sir."

Dean Whittaker sat upright, straightening his tie and reminding himself who he was. "Of course," he said to Ceri. "You may be seated," he said to the rest of the table. He gestured to Ceri to join him at one of the empty seats, and she accepted.

A servant filled her glass with a deep red wine as Dean Whittaker began to introduce her to the professors seated near them at the table. He spoke at length regarding their departments and research, and Ceri did her best to listen, trying to imagine herself studying Numbers or Loegrian or Philosophy. Her many tutors had equipped her well to at least follow the conversation, although their lessons had often come with a frankly unnecessary amount of corporal punishment. Ceri was looking forward to learning without fearing the smack of a ruler, truth be told.

The first course arrived with the clatter of a great number of silver serving dishes. Out of the corner of Ceri's eye, she caught movement at Leo's end of the table and then a louder crash—his chair had fallen backward.

Dean Whittaker stood to see what the commotion was about. "I say, are you alright—"

As the dean spoke, something fell from high above the table. It crashed into the exact spot where Leo had been seated earlier. A chandelier.

Several of the professors cried out. A serving dish was dropped, the echo of it rocking back and forth ringing through the room as the servants ran over.

Dean Whittaker rushed to Leo, with Ceri trailing behind.

"My Gods, you could have been killed! It must have come loose when they were installing the new upgraded 'lectrics last month. I'll have that builder's neck, boy, don't you worry."

Dean Whittaker pulled Leo upright. He looked shaken, his spectacles crooked on his nose again, but he was unharmed.

"Thank you, sir. No harm no foul," said Leo.

"Come, sit with us in the middle. There's no chandelier over our heads, at least," said Dean Whittaker.

The servants removed the busted chandelier as the people at the table took their seats once more.

Leo took the seat directly across from Ceri.

"Hello, again," he whispered to her.

Ceri drew in a deep breath. It felt as though this school was conspiring to put them together. She was looking forward to the arrival of the other students. Maybe once the school was busy and crowded, it would be easier to avoid him.

Not that she needed to avoid him. There was nothing between them to be avoided.

Dean Whittaker began to talk about his experience with the builders and the doubts he'd had when they were working. Ceri recognized it as the sort of thing one says to save face after a humiliation. Of course he'd seen the problems coming all along. If he'd just trusted his gut and fired them at the beginning, none of this would have happened.

She wondered how much of this song and dance was on her behalf—did he worry that Ceri would leave the school if it seemed as though it was falling apart?

Leo, to his credit, seemed to take his near-death experience in stride.

"Professor Marin and I could make use of the old chandelier in our laboratory, if it's going to be replaced," he suggested.

"An excellent idea," said Dean Whittaker. "Your highness, Leorias works for Professor Marin as a graduate researcher in the 'Lectrics department. Professor Marin herself regrets that she hasn't been able to greet you yet. It's her understanding that you, like your brother, have some interest in 'lectrics?"

Just my luck, thought Ceri. *He works for the professor everyone is coming here to see.*

There was going to be no avoiding Leo. If she wanted to keep her studies on track, she was going to have to find another way to fight whatever it was that had come over her since meeting him.

"Ceri has already offered to assist me with my research," said Leo.

Dean Whittaker beamed at him and Ceri. "Excellent, excellent. Professor Marin does extraordinary work. I'm pleased that it's finally receiving the attention it deserves."

Ceri imagined that Dean Whittaker was pleased on behalf of the entire school, which would certainly be boosted by her family's involvement.

The rest of the dinner passed without further disruption. Ceri kept finding ways to keep the dean talking until long after almost everyone else had left. If Leo noticed her stalling tactics, he gave no sign.

She didn't know why she was trying to delay their evening plans. It was purely research—nothing else would be happening.

Finally, the dean gestured to a servant to take his wine glass. "I'm afraid it's past my bedtime. Do you need someone to help you find your way back to your room, your highness?"

Leo looked at Ceri. *Stop it,* she told her heart. *No fluttering allowed.*

"I'll manage," she said to Dean Whittaker. "Thank you for allowing me to sit at the high table."

Leo nodded his head towards one of the doors that led into the courtyard.

Ceri followed him.

The sun had set while they ate; the night air was cooler than Ceri had expected.

"Are you still feeling up to a hike? It's not far to the observatory, but you'll want some better shoes," said Leo, gesturing to the heels on her loafers.

"These are excellent shoes," said Ceri. She flicked her wrist towards the heels—the gesture was unnecessary, but it added a bit of pizzazz—and they shrunk, lowering her to the ground.

Leo had been taller than her even with the added inches of the heels, but now he towered over her. She wasn't surprised: pretty much everyone did.

His lips had parted. He stared from her to the shoes. "The way you do that so casually. So effortlessly. Even the others here that have studied magic tend to struggle with it, if they can even do it at all. Myself included."

Ceri shrugged her shoulders, trying to ignore how good his words made her feel. "You should see my brother. I learned what I know from him, and a little from my mother, when she was around."

"I'm sorry, is she—"

"No, she's alive." What she was supposed to say next was that the queen had been forced to return to her homeland to settle a disagreement over her inheritance, and that she had to remain there until her uncle died or forfeit everything.

She couldn't bring herself to lie again. "Are you ready to leave now?" she asked him.

"I need to collect some things from my lab," said Leo. "You should grab a jumper as well. It's colder at the top of the mountain."

Ceri met him back in the courtyard a few minutes later. He was carrying a large rucksack and a metal container of some kind, and he'd also brought a quilted blanket. Ceri felt underprepared with just her Winwold jumper in her arms.

"Do you need help with anything?" she asked.

"I've got it," said Leo, right as he dropped the metal container. It rolled on the grass and landed near Ceri's feet. "Well, maybe if you could grab the tea."

Ceri picked it up cautiously, expecting it to be hot. "There's tea in here?"

Leo smiled. "It's a vacuum flask. One of the chemistry fellows is testing them out. They keep drinks warm for hours."

Ceri could have warmed the tea for them with her magic, but she didn't feel the need to point it out. It felt like showing off.

"There's no coffee in here, is there?"

"Only tea," said Leo. "Although if you'd like to try my tea coffee, you need only ask."

"I'd prefer to be able to sleep at some point this week."

"Sleep is overrated," said Leo. He cleared his throat, then quickly pointed at a path extending into the woods beyond the ruined cloister on the west side of the courtyard. "Shall we?"

He strode off for the path before Ceri could respond, leaving her wondering what she had missed.

She followed behind him as they climbed a bare dirt path under the trees. Leo retrieved a 'lectric torch from his rucksack, which lit a narrow beam of light onto the path ahead. Ceri had to stay close to him to see the ground in front of her.

"This is an experiment too," he explained, waving the torch. "A new type of power-saver. I would have brought one for you, but I'm not certain if it's safe."

"What could be wrong with it?" asked Ceri, backing a little further away.

"Well, it could always catch fire. Possibly violently." Leo said it quite casually, as if this was an ordinary hazard when working with him.

Perhaps it was.

Despite his warning, the torch continued to function without trouble. The path climbed steeply through the darkened forest. There was nothing to see aside from the beam of light; everything around them was pitch dark. Ceri knew she would have been terribly afraid had Leo not been with her. Even with him there, it was difficult not to feel the darkness pressing in, particularly in the moments when the torch's beam drifted too far ahead as Leo navigated the turns in the path.

After what felt like an hour but was probably only twenty minutes or so—Ceri regretted that her time spent flying and dancing around ballrooms had not prepared her physically for this much of a climb—they reached the observatory. It was a small building with a domed roof standing right at the top of the hill. Ceri had thought they had reached the top of the mountain after such a long climb, but a much larger mountain loomed behind the observatory.

Just as they were about to clear the last row of trees before the clearing, Ceri heard a cracking sound from overhead.

"Look out!" she shouted.

Leo turned the torch towards the canopy in time to see something dark streaking downwards towards them.

There was little time to think. Ceri reacted with a burst of her magic, sending the dark object—a large branch—careening into the trunk of a tree as Leo grabbed her by the waist, pulling her out of the way.

The torch fell to the ground. Ceri stood still, feeling her body pressed against Leo's, hearing his heartbeat next to her ear.

She couldn't move. She'd forgotten how.

"Are you alright?" he asked her. He removed his arm from her waist and bent to pick up the torch. He shined it on them and then on the branch, which had shattered at the base of a young pine.

"That could have killed us," said Ceri slowly. How many near misses had they had today? Two, three?

"That was you, sending the branch into the tree?"

"Yes," said Ceri. That one had cost her. The earlier spells—removing the tea coffee, adjusting her heels—had been minor feats. The force required to move the branch, as large and heavy as it was, had taken more out of her. She felt a bit lightheaded. "I think I need to sit down."

"The observatory is just ahead," said Leo. "Can you make it?" He offered her his arm.

She took it. She had no other choice.

Leo led her to the observatory steps and helped her take a seat. He looked her up and down, concerned. "Are you alright?" he asked.

"I'll be fine in a minute," said Ceri. "It's like sprinting up the stairs, doing strong magic out of nowhere. It doesn't help that I'm out of practice."

"Will you be alright if I leave you for just a moment? I left everything in the woods."

Ceri nodded. It was strange the way the air changed the moment he was hidden by the tree line, the sudden awareness it gave her of the darkness and a sense that although she was alone on the steps, there was something lurking out there.

A cool, strong breeze blew through, sending the hair on her arms up into goosebumps.

She felt a great sense of relief when Leo returned with the blanket, his rucksack, and the vacuum flask. He dropped the rucksack to the ground and wrapped the blanket around Ceri's shoulders. Then he took a seat next to her, pouring the contents of the flask into the attached cup.

"Sorry I dropped it," said Ceri.

He laughed. "I forgive you for dropping the tea while you were busy saving my life." He handed her the cup, warning her it would be hot.

Ceri pulled the cup to her lips, blowing on it. She could have cooled it with magic, but it would be pushing it under the circumstances. She braved a sip.

"It's delicious," she said, looking at Leo in surprise. She felt instantly better. It was amazing how much the simple comforts of a warm blanket and a good cup of tea could improve almost any situation.

"A family recipe," said Leo. "Lavender, lemon, and honey."

"Are you close to your family?" asked Ceri. In truth, she was already feeling well enough to go inside, but she wasn't quite ready to give up the comforts of the blanket and the tea.

Leo tilted his head, grimacing. "No, I wouldn't say that. They are a bit—how do you say it?" He searched for the Loegrian word. "Unconventional. Different, even in Gallia, which is much more accepting of other ways of life than here."

"How so?"

Leo reached into his pocket and pulled out a smaller hip flask. "I'll need something a bit stronger if I'm going to talk about this," he said.

"You don't have to," said Ceri, but now she was extremely curious. She held out her cup.

Leo smiled at her and tipped in the flask before taking a swig. "Wilderisen whisky," he said. He started to speak but took one more swig first. "I told you I have no title. It's not because my parents aren't nobility—they are. But they've had too many children to pass on titles to each of us."

This wasn't uncommon. Like the Loegrian court, most courts gave lesser titles to the children of a noble until there were no further titles to give. Most ran out by the third or fourth child, and many couples had more children than that. "How many siblings do you have?"

He sighed. "Forty-one."

Ceri nearly choked on her whisky-laced tea. "Forty-one children?"

"Er, well, forty-two including me. Those are my full siblings. If you count half siblings, it's sixty or so still living. We think…"

He trailed off.

"I don't understand," said Ceri. "I mean, I can see you're a full elf, and I know you live a long time—"

"My parents are over one thousand years old," said Leo. "And my mother loves children. Every twenty years or so, she has another one. My parents are married, but a thousand years is a long time. There have been others. Sometimes several of them at once. Always with permission, never in secret. Sometimes it's so romantic it's nauseating."

This was so far from the world Ceri had grown up in, she didn't know where to start. "I have so many questions."

"I'm not surprised," said Leo. "Go ahead."

"You said you weren't close. Is it just because there are so many of you? Do you even know all of their names?"

"Of course I know their names. Not all of the half-siblings, but that's because some of them were gone before I was born. But no, that's not why we aren't close. Truthfully, I never quite fit in at home. My parents are all about free love and living in harmony with nature. They haven't fit in within Gallic society for several generations, not even with most of the other elves. They live in a commune for free-thinkers, and I don't know. I guess I wasn't born to think freely. They sent me to Gallic schools—the first in the family to go in centuries. But I didn't fit there either. Like I said, Gallia has turned its back on magic. But look at what you can do. It seems equally insane to me to deny the reality of that as it does to deny the benefits of science and technology."

"So you're from two worlds, but you've never fit in with either," said Ceri. "Like me."

"Like you?"

Ceri took a deep sip from the cup. The whisky made it even warmer. She didn't know if it gave her courage, but at least it gave her some comfort. "My mother left us."

Leo didn't look surprised. He'd never heard the fiction they'd spun about the queen's absence.

"It wasn't her fault, not really. She tried to take us with her when I was a baby, but my father wouldn't let her. We went to see her during the summers until a few years ago when my father stopped allowing that too."

"I'm sorry," said Leo. "That must have been hard."

"My mother is from the Far East—Formosa, they call it here. But I don't know her language. I knew some of it when I was little, but when she left and my brother went away to university, I lost it. The last time I visited, I could only speak to people who knew Loegrian. To them, I was Loegrian."

"But to Loegrians, you're Formosan."

"Exactly," said Ceri. "My father's family treated us kindly, particularly my Aunt Chloe, who was the closest thing I had to a mother. But I spent most of my life feeling like I was different. Feeling like I had to pretend to be someone else."

She left out the part about who she had pretended to be while trying to please her father. She didn't want Leo to know.

In fact, she had said far too much already. The truth of Queen Yuling's departure was a closely guarded secret, although there were, of course, a number of rumors floating around. He wasn't the first person she'd told the truth, but look at how that had turned out for her.

The people she trusted had betrayed her. She had sworn she'd be more careful about trusting, and now here she was, pouring her heart out to a stranger because he was good looking and had offered her tea?

"This was a mistake," she said, standing suddenly. "I'm sorry."

"What? Ceri, what's wrong?"

"I shouldn't have come here. I shouldn't have said any of that."

She took off down the steps.

"Ceri, wait," said Leo. "You won't be able to see in the dark. I'll take you back if you want."

He was right that Ceri wouldn't be able to see in the woods, but she wouldn't need to.

In the space of a heartbeat, she transformed into a dragon.

"*Mes Dieux*," said Leo. "Ceri—"

She turned towards him. She was much larger than him now, her pale skin now pearly white scales which glittered in the light of the crescent moon. She spread her grand wings and took flight.

Ceri rose quickly, the bare hilltop observatory and the looming dark forest shrinking beneath her as she soared towards the cloudless sky. The sky had darkened during their hike to near pitch, the first twinkling stars appearing.

Here, above the trees, she could see clearly.

Ceri looked down at the speck that was Leo still frozen on the stairs below. He had done nothing wrong. Was this kindness, leaving him like this? After she had promised to help him?

All because what—she'd let herself get too comfortable for a moment? And now she was going to punish him for it?

It was that same selfishness of hers again. He had shared with her something vulnerable about himself, and she had, unprompted, turned the conversation back to her, revealing more than she'd ever intended to. And then she got upset about it and allowed him to think it was his fault.

What the hell was wrong with her?

She dove, feeling the rush of air over her wings. She could not resist turning one flip—it helped her slow down, on top of looking really cool—before she touched back down and transformed back, her clothes transforming down to size with her. (It had been kind of him not to laugh at a dragon wearing a Winwold College uniform.)

"You did nothing," she said, speaking to him as if nothing had happened. His mouth gaped open at her, but she ignored it. "I just said too much. I don't know how to do this."

"Do what?" He was shaking. Ceri realized he hadn't seen a dragon before.

Great. She'd scared him half to death twice in one day.

"I don't know. Whatever this is. Have friends. Be normal. I don't know how to do it."

"Friends," said Leo with half a smile.

She didn't know if she could be his friend. She didn't know if she could be anybody's friend, but maybe, if she wanted to truly start over and try to be a better person, she could try. It would be simpler than being…more than friends, at least. Maybe if she could think of him as merely a friend, those pesky thoughts she'd been having since they met would go away.

Leo had continued to speak during her realization. "You don't have to be normal. Gods know I'm not. I think you're—"

He stopped himself. She wished he hadn't. She wanted to know what he thought of her: did he see the new Ceri or the old?

"You're doing just fine," he said, sighing and looking away. "Come on. Let's go up. It's going to be a beautiful night for research."

Ceri followed him as he led her into the observatory, trying to be content with her new nothing-more-than-a-friend companion. There were a handful of people inside taking turns through a large central telescope. Leo waved hello to a couple that he knew without stopping. He led Ceri up a flight of stairs and out onto a balcony with wide, sweeping views of the mountains and the valley beyond. The 'lectric lights of the college were tiny sparks in the distance.

There were others out on the balcony. They waved to them, but Leo led her down to an empty patio. There, he spread the blanket down and took a seat on it, inviting her to join him.

"It should be starting soon. You may be able to see a few even now," he said, but he wasn't looking up at the sky. He had opened his rucksack and was removing a number of items from within it: his leather notebook and ink pen; the brass device from earlier, which still looked slightly bent out of shape; a silver locket on a delicate but tarnished chain; a children's doll with a painted porcelain face; a large hollow horn with elaborate carvings; a dagger with a rusty blade; and a lighter made of dwarven steel, worn from use. "I need to take my baseline readings," he explained as he began scribbling in the journal, waving his device over the other items.

"What are these?" asked Ceri, picking up the doll. Its hair looked to be made of corn silk, and it gave Ceri a deep sense of unease looking at its smirking face.

"Be careful with that," said Leo, grabbing the doll back then smiling in apology at the hasty gesture. "Each of these objects gives off a powerful—and, more importantly, measurable—magic field. I found them in charity shops in Norgate mainly, except for the lighter. That one I found right here in High House."

"They're enchanted?"

"I believe so. What I'm trying to understand is how the magic is stored in them. How it ebbs and flows, how it recharges. I have a theory that powerful magic events, events like the meteor shower, recharge them in some way. I'm hoping to measure it tonight."

Ceri hadn't realized that meteor showers had anything to do with magic. She'd heard superstitions, but she thought they were just that. "I've never felt anything particularly special during a meteor shower."

"Have you seen one?"

"No," she admitted. The castle was in an open area, but it was so close to Arcas Dyrne that the night sky never got truly dark there. "You said you wanted my help. What did you want me to do?"

"Just something small like what you did before. The spell you used to get the tea coffee out of your shirt, or the one you used on your shoes. I'd like to measure it before and during the meteor shower to see if there's a difference."

That seemed simple enough. Ceri was curious to see the measurements herself. She'd never heard of measuring magic before. "It's your own design?" she asked, picking up the device.

"Yes," said Leo. He smiled, pleased to be asked. "I call it a magimeter. It's a modification of the devices we use to measure 'lectricity. It has a small gem inside I found from talking to a shaman in a dwarven mine. They use gems like it to find certain rare ores. Mithril, for one."

He was really quite clever, despite his penchant for attracting trouble. She watched him as he carefully held the magimeter to each object in turn, marking the readings down into a table.

"Strange," he muttered.

"What is it?"

"The locket has never read this high before. I'm worried I may have broken the magimeter during our collision earlier."

"I'm sorry," said Ceri. If she hadn't been nosing around where she wasn't meant to be, that wouldn't have happened.

"Entirely my fault," he said. "Something in these objects, possibly in the magimeter itself, interacts with the library in a bad way. It's…an opinionated place, and it likes to make its opinions known."

"By throwing books at you?" Ceri remembered the library's choice of books when she was there and blushed. Perhaps it had known her own mind better than she did.

Maybe now if they returned together, the library would offer her a book on friendship. She hoped it would, at least.

"And also by turning off the lights. Ah, that's more like it," he said, taking a third reading, this time leaning a bit away. "Perhaps it's interference." He gestured to Ceri's shoes.

"Oh," said Ceri. "I can turn them back."

"Just a moment," he said. "I'll measure it when you do. I don't want to waste your energy. Then you can flatten them again during the meteor shower."

"But those aren't exactly the same things," said Ceri. Her science tutor had been particularly insistent on valid experimental design. "I'll extend one heel now, then the other during the meteor shower. So it's the same, you see? I can sit them out of the way so you can get the rest of your measurements."

Leo beamed at her. Gods, his smile was bright. "That's absolutely right. Very good thinking, Ceri."

It felt entirely too good to hear his praise. *Friends*, Ceri told herself. *I'm only here to make friends. Or I'm only here to study. Something! Stop it. Stop melting when he looks at you.*

Ceri did as she had planned, doing her best not to notice how close he was to her when he waved the magimeter as she gestured near the heel.

"Hmm," he said as he scribbled down the readings. "More power than I'd thought for such a spell. I'll be intrigued to see how the readings change."

He moved the objects to the opposite side of where Ceri had left the shoes and lay back on the blanket.

"Don't you want to measure me again?"

"Sure," said Leo. "But there will be plenty of time for that once it really gets going. Let's just enjoy the view until then."

He gestured to the spot on the blanket beside him.

Ceri's heart began to race. How could he be so casual about this? Had he done this before? Did he invite loads of women up here during meteor showers?

Truthfully, Ceri doubted it. He didn't seem the type to use something as romantic as this setting to woo someone. She wasn't sure he saw any romance in it at all. It was just research to him. Perhaps that's why he was able to be so calm about it.

She tried to channel that energy as she lay down next to him. The blanket was so small that there were only inches between them. He was so close she could hear his breath.

Looking at the wide-open sky with her back on the ground gave her the uncanny feeling that she would fall from the earth and land right in it, taking her place among the stars. It left her dizzy and wondering once again if this was all a mistake.

Leo grabbed her arm at her side then, pulling her back to solid ground. "Look!"

With his other hand, he pointed up and to Ceri's left. Ceri just saw the trail of it, a bright streak of white.

"I saw it!" she said. And then: "There's another one!"

She saw it first this time, just to the right of where she'd been looking before.

It was funny how exciting it was to spot them. They were out here looking for the shooting stars, so it shouldn't have come as much of a surprise when they saw them. And yet there was such a feeling of joy at catching one with her own eyes that she found herself laughing.

"Right there!" said Leo, pointing a bit closer to the horizon.

They continued watching the shooting stars for a long while. Every now and then, Ceri would turn to Leo. His face was as bright and merry as her own, and she found it so nice to share in the joy and wonder together.

On one occasion, when she turned to him, she caught him looking at her. She wanted to look away, but she didn't. That dizzy feeling of falling was upon her again, only in a different direction.

"Isn't it wonderful?" he whispered. He leaned closer to her.

She thought then of what she had been trying not to think about since she'd arrived at Winwold. She thought of Isaac telling her he couldn't see her anymore. The regretful look in his eyes as he told her he'd fallen in love with someone else and that they were going to be married.

She thought of Jerta and Deepa and Elise and all the other ladies and gentlemen who had left her. Their stinging words. Their casual cruelty. The fact that she had deserved it.

The reason she was starting over.

Leo wasn't like any of them. Not because he was an elf—though she hadn't had any full elves in her inner circle before. But because he hadn't grown up here, in this world of royalty and courtiers and all of the nonsense it entailed. It was alien to him; she could see that clearly. He didn't care that she was the princess any more than he cared what color her eyes were or anything else about her.

Though, considering his proximity, perhaps he did care for some things about her.

She broke his gaze, sitting up. "It's incredible. I never thought there would be so many." Even as she said it, she spotted another. Somehow, it seemed a little less magical from up here. "I'll get the shoe," she said.

Leo coughed slightly, sitting up as well. "Of course," he said. "Perfect timing."

He measured his objects again while Ceri waited, and then he measured as she restored the heel on her other shoe. Once he was satisfied with his measurements, she flattened both heels again for the walk back.

"Anything interesting?"

"Possibly," said Leo. "I'll need to do some calculations. Understand the deviance from the baseline, compare it to previous measurements. The effect is small, if it's there, but it's a start."

Ceri yawned. It has been a long day, and she found that even the small magic she had performed had worn on her quite a bit.

"Do you want to stay longer?" asked Leo. "I have what I need for my research, but I'm happy to stay if you'd like. Did you make all the wishes you wanted?"

Ceri hadn't made a wish at all. Perhaps she should, but what would she wish for?

"Just one more minute," she said, lying back and thinking.

The sky loomed above her. In her heart, she knew she was alone underneath it. That we were all alone, really, each of us living lonely under the infinite sea of stars, rarely even aware of what's above us.

She spotted a shooting star, the brightest one yet, streaking across the sky.

She closed her eyes and wished.

Chapter Six

OLD FRIENDS

Alison

Dinner in Norgate had been a pleasant affair.

Dean Whittaker had suggested a faculty-favorite establishment with generous portions of both food and ale, and by the time they had finished, Alison was adequately inebriated enough that whatever foreboding sense she'd had about High House or the surrounding woods had gone when they returned by carriage in the early hours of morning.

In the bright—too bright; she really shouldn't have had that third pint—light of day, it was difficult to imagine anything amiss at all. Move-in had begun in earnest, and the hallways that had seemed forlorn and claustrophobic the previous evening now felt pleasantly busy, humming with the kind of excited energy Alison missed from city life. (Well, occasionally missed.)

Lady Sibba had gone with Weyland to meet a friend from the Rock who taught courses on theatre; Rinka was with Idris, helping him unpack his office; and Willow had vanished before dawn, undoubtedly hunting mice or finding the dog for use as napping material. That left Keir and Alison to wander the hallways alone until their appointment with Professor Marin that evening.

"She keeps odd hours for a 'lectrics researcher, don't you think?" asked Keir as he helped a Halfling fresher with a trunk that was as big as she was.

"Perhaps it's easier to see what's working in the dark," said Alison as she followed him. She wanted to use a tiny bit of magic to lighten the load, but she had found that her magic, which was inconsistent at best, was downright unreliable away from Herot's Hollow.

"Perhaps," said Keir. He received a grateful handshake from the Halfling as he dropped the trunk into her new room, and he and Alison continued on towards the library.

Alison shared Keir's fondness for libraries, though they had greatly different reading preferences. Keir read mostly nonfiction works in a wide variety of subjects, many of them at least tangentially related to his medical career. Alison, on the other hand, felt she had gotten to know enough about the real world by living in it. She preferred to get lost in fiction, passing her time in worlds that were nothing like hers and where anything she could imagine was possible.

And, of course, there was poetry. What had started as a coin-making venture had become something that felt as much a part of her as the color of her eyes or the way she liked her tea (one sugar and a splash of milk). It was a source of both joy and frustration, the outlet for her innermost yearnings and the imperfect medium with which to express them, limited by only her own ability to create and persist in creating.

Alison perused the stacks of poetry books, having been aided in locating them by Ms. Redclaw. She had just spotted a familiar name—Fanguk, the orc whose poetry book she had found during her first trip to Wilderise—when she heard something fall to the ground a couple of shelves away.

"Hello?" She had walked through those stacks on the way and had seen no one around, and she hadn't heard anyone come by since.

She felt the same sense of unease from the night before, but the 'lectric lights were bright in the library, and she found they gave her courage.

She checked the aisles near where the sound seemed to originate, but there was nothing.

Nothing but the tingling sensation on the back of her neck of being watched.

She had just returned to the poetry section to check if it was a new work by Fanguk, so that she could grab it and get out of there, when she heard it again.

"Willow?" she said. "Are you there, girl?"

And then again, only this time much closer and much more clearly: it was the sound of a book being dropped.

"Willow, come out of those shelves. What are you doing—"

This time, the book that fell was the very same Fanguk book she had spotted before. It dropped to the ground in front of her, falling open to a page somewhere in the middle.

Alison looked into the shelves where the book had fallen from but saw nothing.

But while there was nothing to see, there was something to feel—magic. Old magic. It was the same warm sensation as the path into the fairy woods, the same as the path that led her to the korrigans.

Perhaps this was a path as well.

Alison retrieved Fanguk's new book (*From Green to Grey: An Orc's Journey*) and walked through the stacks, collecting the others: *A Primer on Modern Poetry, Movements and Key Players* by Dr. Serena Carter; *On Commercial Writing* by Stephen Duke; and *Printing Presses of Loegria: An Updated Guide* by The King's College Department of Literature.

Alison, sensing a theme, looked around once more. Surely this must have been Willow's doing. Keir, although he technically possessed both the magic required and the knowledge of her desire to publish her poetry, would have never been so coy.

Another book fell, this time at some distance from the others. Alison spotted Keir nearby, eying a shelf suspiciously.

Alison knelt to pick up the book—*Overcoming Self-Doubt* by Dr. Elijah Goldberg—and saw that Keir carried a small handful of books himself.

"For you or for me?" she said, holding out the book on self-doubt.

Keir laughed. "Both, probably. Has the library been helping you as well?"

"The library?" asked Alison.

"Ms. Redclaw came by around the time my first book dropped and explained. It's alive in some way. It can sense thoughts and feelings—I thought that sounded like utter nonsense, but, well…"

He held up his books to Alison. *Innovative Techniques in Perinatal Care* by Dr. Andre Jackman; *The Journal of Pediatric Medicine: Vols. 54-55;* and *Staffing a Medical Practice: Guidance for the Modern Physician* by Dr. Erica Lopez.

"I didn't know you were thinking of hiring someone," said Alison, spotting the last book.

"I didn't either. The idea occurred to me in passing when I was asking Dr. Marten to fill in for me while we were away. I haven't mentioned it to anyone. I suppose, after everything we've seen, it doesn't seem that outlandish that the library is sentient in some way."

"Perhaps not," said Alison. The books it had suggested to her were undeniably useful, and she wondered if maybe the presence she'd felt watching her that she had taken for something malevolent had, in fact, only been the library trying to help her.

She wanted to believe that to be true, at least.

⋅෯ⓐⓞ෯⋅

Alison and Keir spent a lazy afternoon lounging on the grass of the courtyard near the Norminster Yew, reading their books and watching the students coming and going. Willow stopped by to say hello and to chase the last butterflies of summer and the first yellow leaves of autumn.

After a noisy dinner in a half-full dining hall alive with first meetings, faculty reunions, and a recounting of summer adventures, Alison and Keir met the others and headed to a small, isolated building to the northeast of the main campus near the woods.

To the right of the door, there was a small plaque:

Professor Mircalla Marin
Chair of the Department of 'Lectrics
Office Hours: Sunset to Sunrise
Closed Saturdays

"Sunset to sunrise?" muttered Keir. It was just now sunset, and the 'lectric lamps that lined the paths through the campus had begun to flicker on.

"Oh, you don't know about Professor Marin yet?" asked Idris. His face was carefully blank, but there was a hint of humor in his dark eyes.

"Know what?" asked Keir.

"I'll let you see for yourself," said Idris. He knocked on the door.

Or he would have. The door was already open after his first light rap.

"Come in," said a rapturous voice.

Professor Marin, Alison presumed.

Alison couldn't get a good look at her: the reception area they entered was dark, and the professor herself did not stop to make introductions. She led them into a corridor and through a labyrinthine series of hallways, moving so gracefully it was as if she was floating.

Alison supposed she must be an elf to move with such grace, but her ears weren't visible beneath her long, dark hair to confirm her suspicions.

Finally, they arrived at a set of double doors.

"Please don't touch anything when we enter," said Professor Marin without turning around. "Do you have the samples?"

"Right here," said Weyland, producing the box they'd been given by Yordin.

"Good," said Professor Marin, but she did not take it from him.

Idris chuckled, undoubtedly enjoying his private joke about Professor Marin.

They filed into the laboratory one by one. It was difficult to avoid touching anything because there were so many things in the room: wooden shelves of corked vials filled with dark powders and shimmering liquids; tiny boxes labeled with one or two letters, some with red caution labels; sheets of metal, neatly pressed from a manufactory; various lengths of wire in several colors; and a number of stands filled with strange brass instruments, meters in several different scales, and a large number of switches.

Sitting on a stool near one of the stands was a young, blonde elf with round spectacles and a nervous disposition. When Professor Marin approached him, he stood abruptly.

"See to the samples," said Professor Marin.

The elf took the box from Weyland, smiling nervously at the much larger human. "Thank you. Professor Marin has high hopes for the mithril in particular—"

"Not yet, Leo," said Professor Marin. "First, let's show them their machine."

They followed Professor Marin and Leo through another set of doors onto a covered patio of sorts. It was somewhat like Weyland's forge, open on the sides with a covered roof, although there were a number of large shades against the walls and a number of platforms extending out into the darkened field beyond.

Professor Marin flipped a switch, and one of the platforms was retracted back under the roof. On it was their prototype solar machine. Its large metal cone had been modified to be somewhat less round, and there was a different box attached to it than the one that had held the 'lectric generator they had purchased, but it otherwise looked about the same.

"Let me show you what I've done," said Professor Marin.

She flipped another switch from something connected to the back of the prototype, and the bright light of an exposed lightbulb came on.

Professor Marin finally turned around.

Something about her appearance immediately unsettled Alison, but it took her a moment to figure out why. At first glance, she had seemed like an orc. There was a greyish cast to her skin, and she had fangs visible when she smiled, but only on the upper teeth. But her features were unmistakably human, except for one thing: her eyes were blood red.

"Vampire," said Lady Sibba. Her voice was laced with fear.

Surely not. Alison had come to accept that many of the things she had been taught were make believe were very much real, even more so after hearing about mermaids from Rinka, but vampires? Surely those were the invention of gothic novelists from the previous century.

(Had any writer ever actually created any of their fiction, or was it all in some way tied back to a reality that some people were happier to have forgotten?)

"You didn't mention an elf was one of your number," said Professor Marin, not denying anything. "They harbor unfounded prejudices against my kind."

"Your kind?" said Lady Sibba, reaching backwards for the door without turning around. "Your kind is an affront to nature. A twisting of the order of things—"

"An order in which only elves are granted near limitless life? What kind of order is that? Elves speak of order, but have you ever noticed that all orders they're involved with feature them at the very top?"

Alison regretted that Gwenla wasn't here for this conversation; she had similar feelings about certain elf societies. But she also wasn't one to tar all elves with the same brush.

"Is Leo not an elf?" asked Alison, gesturing to the young man who was staring very intently at his shoes. "Professor Marin, forgive us. We were simply surprised to find out what you are. Surprised, and perhaps a bit frightened. I, for one, believed vampires to be myth."

"I apologize for the outburst. I know that your people teach that vampires are born of dark magic and that you must be quite afraid." Her voice was velvety smooth and alluring. Alison looked at Idris at the mention of dark magic; it was his area of study. No wonder he already knew Professor Marin's secret.

"Debatable," said Idris. "Dark and light magic are still the accepted divisions, but as you pointed out, there's some debate about who defines what the natural order is or should be. There's even debate about if the divisions should exist at all."

"I don't mind the dark magic label," said Professor Marin. "I think it fits." She gestured to the workshop.

It was clear now to Alison what the purpose of the shades and platforms were: to prevent Professor Marin from having to go out into the sun during the day.

"Wait," said Keir, realizing something about the same time that Alison did. "You're a vampire trying to harness the power of the sun?"

"I'm the vampire that did harness the power of the sun," said Professor Marin. "Can you blame me? It's my greatest nemesis. Who understands the power of the sun more than the vampire?"

Alison looked back at Lady Sibba, who had shrunk against the door. Weyland had put his arm around her waist. Rinka joined them, whispering to Lady Sibba to ask if she was alright.

"Tell me what you eat," said Lady Sibba, her voice shaking. "And tell me how you eat it."

Alison could hear Lady Sibba trying her best to understand. The schoolteacher was obstinate at times, but she wasn't unreasonable.

"Blood, of course. Human blood, preferably, since I was once human, but any blood will do."

This admission sent a chill through Alison. Perhaps she had read one too many of those gothic novels. The vampires in them were murderous, filled with insatiable hunger.

But surely someone with that condition couldn't last long as a university professor. And from her status, she had been here for a long time.

"There's an infirmary here at the college. It receives a supply of blood," said Professor Marin.

It was Keir's turn to object. "That blood is needed. It's a matter of life and death—"

"At times, yes," said Professor Marin. "On those nights, I must go hungry. It doesn't kill me to do so, but it does exhaust me. And worse, it sets back my research. But fresh blood has a limited period of usefulness. I'm given what remains once that period expires."

"Does it taste bad?" Alison couldn't help but asking.

"Like stale bread," said Professor Marin. "Once every few weeks, with permission, I drink from the 'tap,' so to speak. There's a woman in town—well, that's truly none of your business. But I take only what she can spare, never a drop more. Are your curiosities sufficiently satisfied?" She surveyed the group. "Did you come here to talk about me or the machine?"

"So you don't hurt people?" asked Weyland, unperturbed by Professor Marin's desire to change the subject while Lady Sibba was still frightened.

"Never. Not once," said Professor Marin. "All that nonsense about insatiable hunger is just that—nonsense. If finishing your slice of pie meant killing a sentient being, would you do it?"

"Well," said Rinka. "What type of pie is it?"

There were laughs all around, some of them more nervous than others, but even Lady Sibba managed a chuckle.

Professor Marin turned back to the machine. It didn't appear to be running—the water in the cylinder was not boiling—but the bulb was steadily lit.

"A power-saver?" asked Keir.

"Indeed," said Professor Marin. "I've modified the reflectors somewhat to capture light from even more angles, and I've wired in a more appropriate 'lectric generator than the type you used. But yes, the power-saver is the most critical addition. This kind powers the new motor carriages you've heard about, but there are problems with it on the scale of an entire grid. That's what I've asked you to bring the samples. Leo has been helping me research a number of power-saver alternatives, and we have some ideas that we think can greatly increase the storage capacity."

"How long will it take to test?" asked Alison.

"A week or so to go through the options you've provided," said Professor Marin. "Of course, classes begin again next week, so we may want to say two weeks. Perhaps less if you're willing to help."

"Name it," said Weyland. "This equipment—it's beyond me. But I'm good with metal. I'll do what I can."

"What can the rest of us do?" asked Keir.

"Run tests, take measurements. The bulk of the work has to happen during the daytime. This workshop has been designed to accommodate my…particularities, but I have to sleep during the day as well. I'm certain Leo would appreciate the help."

From across the room, Leo looked at Professor Marin with admiration. In his hand was some kind of brass instrument, undoubtedly for measuring 'lectricity of some kind.

Suddenly, there was a loud buzzing sound from the power-saver.

"What the—" began Professor Marin, but she stopped as she saw it: a huge flash of lightning, nearly purple, going from the power-saver to the object in Leo's hand.

"Leo!" she shouted as he collapsed to the ground.

Chapter Seven

THE ROOMMATE

Ceri

There was something wrong with Ceri's face in the looking glass, and she knew exactly what it was.

She had returned late from her night under the stars, and she'd woken late this morning to the chaotic sound of move-in day arriving. She dressed quickly, hoping her new roommate would be there soon, but as she surveyed her appearance, she knew it just wouldn't do.

She looked like herself. Or, more accurately, she looked like the version of herself she didn't want to be anymore. The version of herself that had stared in the looking glass in Weldan House, sobbing over Isaac, just weeks earlier.

"No more," said Ceri. She looked at her long silver hair, the way it fell in silky sheets over her chest, nearly touching her waist.

It was beautiful, and it had to go.

Ceri didn't have any scissors, but she guessed where she could find some: in a supply closet she'd passed on her way back in the night before. She dodged the parents and students juggling bags, trunks, and the occasional animal carrier and retrieved the scissors, along with a few spare notebooks and pens for good measure.

Back at the looking glass, she pinched the hair into a neat row with one hand as she held the scissors in the other.

How hard could it be?

She didn't think, she just cut.

A huge chunk of silver fell apart into strands and came to rest in the sink below.

She let out a high-pitched giggle, looking at the chunk that was shorter than the rest. It felt insane.

It felt good.

She kept cutting, chunk after chunk until the sink was littered with silver. Finally, she'd gotten all of it.

Her hair was just to the bottom of her neck, every strand seemingly a different length than the one next to it.

She screamed.

"Oh my Gods!" came a voice from the bedroom. "Are you okay?"

Ceri was so shaken by her ridiculous mistake that she had not heard someone come into the room. That someone, as Ceri saw when she rushed into the bathroom, joining Ceri in front of the looking glass, was a Halfling. (Only the very top of her pink bun was visible.)

Ceri's new roommate.

"Oh, you've really gone and messed it up," said the Halfling.

"Pardon?" said Ceri. She looked down at the girl, shocked to be spoken to in that way.

From her accent, the girl clearly wasn't from Loegria, although there was nothing obviously foreign about her appearance. She was of fairy ancestry judging by her shell pink hair, and her other parent was likely human, judging by her full lips and soft jawline. There was a softness to her in general, in everything except her voice.

"Your hair," said the Halfling. "Where is he?"

"Who?" Ceri was baffled by this girl.

"The guy that hurt you badly enough to make you screw yourself up like this. I know he exists. Or she, I guess, but probably he if we're being honest. Hang on, let me get my stool. I'm Polliana, by the way. You can call me Ana."

Well, Ana was right about one thing: there was a "guy."

Ana carried a short stepping stool into the bathroom and set behind Ceri. "That's better," she said once she climbed on top. Now her entire face was visible in the looking glass.

"How did you know—"

"That it was a guy? It's always a guy," said Ana. Then she held out her hand. "Scissors."

Ceri wasn't sure if this was a good idea. The hair needed to be longer, not shorter. There was magic for that, but to maintain it day in and day out until her hair grew back on its own? Ceri had never tried to keep magic going for that long.

"Scissors," repeated Ana. "Unless your mother is a hairdresser as well. But judging by the tears in your eyes, I think that's unlikely."

"Alright," said Ceri. "But don't take too much."

"Go back in time and tell that to yourself from five minutes ago," said Ana. "Still, I've seen worse. We can work with it."

Ceri watched as Ana gripped sections of hair, carving into the bottoms of them in a way that looked entirely too chaotic to produce a good result.

"Are you sure you know what you're doing?" asked Ceri. "Shouldn't you be trying to cut it straighter across than I managed, not less straight?"

"Just trust me," said Ana as she continued, completely ignoring Ceri's protests.

In fact, she ignored almost everything Ceri was doing—the sighing, the nervous tapping of her foot—everything except the movements of her head.

Ana gripped Ceri's neck firmly. "Keep still."

Ceri balked at both the touch and the command. Just who the hell did this Halfling think she was?

She was just about ready to let Ana know exactly who she was dealing with, "brand new Ceri" be damned, when the Halfling said, "Finished."

The change was remarkable.

Ceri's hair was still shorter than she had planned, but it now angled gently from the back of her head to her chin in a smooth, perfect line.

"This is magic," said Ceri.

"No magic," said Ana. "Just blending."

"Thank you," said Ceri sincerely. She awkwardly grabbed Ana's arm. She wasn't used to all this casual touching, but it seemed like people liked it, so she tried her best. "You saved me."

Ana laughed. "I'll have to tell my mom I saved someone from a hair emergency on move-in day. She'll be so proud."

Ceri followed Ana back into the room, where she spotted a huge trunk on the opposite side from hers.

It was nearly as big as Ana was. "How'd you get that in here?" asked Ceri.

"Oh, let me tell you about that." Ana leaned towards Ceri, making a hand gesture like she was conducting an orchestra that emphasized every word. "The most gorgeous man I've ever seen carried it for me. He was kinda old: probably a parent, but I'm hoping it's a professor. You should have seen me struggle on the train."

"The what?"

"The train. Oh, right. The 'rail-wheeler.' You have the silliest names for things here."

Definitely not from around here then. "Where are you from?"

"Turtle Island," said Ana. "Part of what you call the 'New World.' My dad is from here though, a fairy of the Seelie Court. Are you from Norgate?"

Another person that didn't recognize Ceri. It made sense, Ceri realized, although she hadn't considered it as a possibility before arriving. Universities tended to attract people from all over the world. There was a good chance that many here wouldn't recognize her.

She really liked that.

"No, I'm from Arcas Dyrne," said Ceri. "Well, the castle nearby. My name is Princess Ceridwen of Loegria and Wilderise, but you may call me Ceri."

She waited tensely, trying to anticipate Ana's response.

"Stop it. You're kidding," said Ana. Her voice had raised considerably in pitch. "A princess?"

"I'm quite serious," said Ceri.

"I'm supposed to be anti-monarchy on account of the fairy court interference, but...a real princess?" Ana's eyes were wide with wonder. "From a castle? It's like the fairy stories my dad told me. I can't believe my roommate is a princess!"

She hopped up onto her bed and jumped up and down on it. "Come on!" she called to Ceri.

Ceri didn't know what to do. Ana was bouncing on the bed like a child, giddy with joy. Ceri hadn't felt that kind of freedom—well, ever. If she had ever bounced on a bed, she couldn't remember it. Her childhood was basically repetition after repetition of the word "no."

"Ceri, or should I say 'Princess Ceridwen,' don't leave me to jump alone! You're pretty small. It won't hurt the bed. Come on!"

Ceri moved towards the bed. Ana paused long enough to help her up.

It was difficult to balance on the mattress, but Ceri just managed it.

"Jump!" said Ana.

Ceri bounced her heels a little, hesitantly.

"You won't hurt me. Take my hand and jump!"

Ceri did as she said. It felt odd at first, and it was hard for Ceri to fight that nagging feeling that someone was going to come in and yell at them at any moment.

But no one came, and after a few bounces, she forgot to worry about it.

"This is fun!" said Ceri through her giggles.

"No one can tell us what to do here," said Ana. "We make the rules now. If we want to eat chocolate cake for breakfast, we can. If we want to jump on the bed three times a day, no one is stopping us. We're free!"

"Free!" cried Ceri, and for the first time ever, she felt it.

⋆⟐⟐⟐⋆

Ceri and Ana spent the day unpacking Ana's things and sharing stories of their upbringings. Ana had come to Winwold to connect with her father's side of the family, who were from a nearby wood. She hadn't thought much of what she'd study yet, which gave Ceri a lot of comfort: she wasn't the only one who didn't know what she wanted to do.

They had dinner together in the dining hall. Ana was pleasantly surprised by the food options, even if they didn't quite live up to her father's fairy cooking.

"I mean, fairy food is basically cheating," said Ana. "There's this kind of grey goop that tastes like whatever makes you happy, and they put a dab of it in everything. Not too much though. There's nothing worse than having dinner and being literally unable to stop smiling long enough to eat anything. Ask me how I know."

Just as they were clearing their trays, Ceri spotted Leo coming into the dining hall.

"Who's that?" whispered Ana as Ceri waved shyly. "He's cute. Did you already meet someone cute? I can't believe they let you come a day early."

"He's an elf though," said Ceri, not acknowledging the part where Ana had called him cute. "He's probably a lot older than us."

"Even better," said Ana with awe. "I'll leave you to it." Ana darted off in the opposite direction.

"No, stay—" said Ceri, but she was already gone.

"Hi," said Leo when he reached her. He was carrying a little box in his hands. Maybe he'd brought his dinner?

"Hi," said Ceri.

"Your hair," said Leo. "It looks amazing…ly good. It looks good. No, great. It's good." He grimaced. "Sorry. I didn't get much sleep last night. Up late running the numbers."

Ceri wasn't sure how to feel about that. "Er, thanks," she said. "Anything good in the numbers?"

"They're very promising," said Leo. "Though a bit surprising. Most of the items had no change, but the horn showed a large increase, and there was a small difference with you as well." He cleared his throat. "Speaking of, I was hoping I'd see you. I wanted to thank you for your help last night—"

"It was nothing," said Ceri. "Happy to be of service."

"Still," said Leo, holding out the box. "I appreciate it. This is for you."

Ceri was taken aback. "For me?"

He'd gotten her something?

"It's not much," said Leo. "I—well—open it," he said, looking down.

Ceri lifted the lid from the box. Inside were two brownish lumps with yellow centers.

"Are these egg tarts?"

Ceri just barely recognized them. They were crudely made, to say the least.

"I found the recipe—well, the library gave me a book of recipes from the Far East. It gave it to me *eventually*, after a number of unnecessary insults…anyway. I'm not much of a cook. The recipe made twelve, but these were the best two."

Ceri pulled one of the misshapen egg tarts from the box.

"You don't have to eat it now," said Leo, holding up a hand to stop her, but Ceri had already taken a bite.

It was far better than it looked. The pastry had maybe a bit too much chew, but the custard was exceptional: smooth and creamy, with just the right amount of caramelization.

"These are my favorite," said Ceri, her eyes closed in pleasure after she finished the whole thing in two bites. "Did you eat the others already?"

"No," said Leo. He smiled in relief, and it dimpled his rosy cheeks. Ana was right: he was cute. "They're back at the lab. It's the building out on the edge of the woods. I've got to get back to work tonight to help Professor Marin. If you wanted to stop by…"

Ceri hesitated. She still hadn't managed to see her brother, and there was a chance he would be there with the Professor. And those egg tarts. It was hard to deny their appeal.

Plus Leo would be working, so it seemed like there would be little opportunity for any awkward moments. Not that the moment last night under the stars had been awkward.

Not that Ceri had thought about it at all since. That would be ridiculous.

"Alright," said Ceri. "Let me run back to my room and let my roommate know. I'll meet you there."

Chapter Eight

THE POWER-SAVER

Alison

"He's cursed," said Idris. "No doubt about it." He stood over Leo while Keir attended him on the ground.

"He's lucky is what he is," said Keir. "Lucky he's an elf. That would have killed a human."

Leo stirred on the floor, coming to in a daze. "What happened?" he said. "Ceri?"

"What did you just say?" asked Idris, his eyes narrowing.

"Are you alright?" asked Ceri. Alison turned to see that the young princess had entered the workshop without anyone noticing. "I heard screaming. What happened?"

"Of course my sister is somehow involved. I've never met anyone more attracted to trouble," said Idris as they watched Ceri bend down to help Leo up. She shot Idris a rude gesture.

"I like your hair," Rinka mouthed to Ceri when Idris's back was turned.

Ceri smiled.

"Was it the power-saver?" Lady Sibba asked Professor Marin.

"I don't know. I've never seen anything like that in our lab. We're careful with the shielding and connections."

"What did you say about him being cursed, Idris?" Alison asked.

"Oh, he's clearly cursed. Can't you feel it? There's magic all over him. Strange magic, definitely none of ours."

Alison couldn't feel it at all. She looked around, but even Ceri seemed mystified by this revelation.

"None of yours?" asked Leo. "Can you all do magic?" Whatever impact the 'lectrocution had made was clearly fading. Leo was excited as Gwenla got when she was scheming.

"Why do you want to know?" asked Rinka.

"It's related to my research. Ceri has been kind enough to help me, but if all of you can—"

"Oh she has, has she?" asked Idris, looking at her sternly. "You've been here one day—"

"Don't you dare lecture me. I've seen what you get up to—"

"It's about your safety. You don't even know him—"

Alison interjected, addressing Leo. "Not all of us. I can, though not consistently. Keir here also has some sort of ability, though we're stronger together." She looked at Rinka for help. Leo was an assistant of Professor Marin's, and she was the only one who could help them with their solar machine. If she trusted him, why should they doubt him? Maybe his inquiry would lead them to an answer.

Rinka nodded, understanding. "I also can do something with the powers of others. I'm not really sure how it works."

"Ah, you must be a conduit," said Leo.

"A what?" asked Rinka.

"A conduit. It's what I call people who can channel the magical power of other people. It's a rare gift, from what I've seen, and a particularly useful one because magic used by a conduit generally can't be detected." He turned to Idris. "To your point, you are correct about the magic you sense around me. But it's not on me. It's on the objects that I'm studying."

From his pocket, he pulled an ordinary lighter made from dwarven steel. "I was just preparing to take some measurements when you arrived. This is just one of several objects—"

"This is cursed," interrupted Idris. "It's a powerful curse at that. Highly malevolent. What in the name of the Gods are you doing carrying around a cursed object? Did you say, 'several objects'?"

"Idris, stop it," said Ceri. "He's just doing research."

"*I* do research on curses and cursed objects," said Idris. "And do you know where I keep them? Safely locked away in specially designed storage devices to ensure the curse cannot escape. It's basic dark magic handling. Really, a graduate researcher carrying cursed objects around like children's toys. I've a mind to speak with Dean Whittaker."

Ceri was furious. Even Alison thought Idris was going a little too far. She highly doubted that Leo had intended to do anything wrong.

"You're being unfair," said Rinka. Idris frowned at her but said nothing. "Half the country doesn't believe magic exists. You didn't even know the conduit thing Leo just mentioned. I'm sure now that he knows, he'll want to handle the objects correctly. Right, Leo?"

Leo nodded. "Of course. I didn't mean to—that is to say, I didn't think they were harmful. They register on my magimeter. They may not all be cursed. But even if they are, that poses another interesting research question: is there a difference in the magic storage based on the nature of the enchantment? If I could take a look at those cursed objects of yours…"

Idris glared at him, and Leo shrunk back in response. But then Idris looked from Ceri to Rinka, who both looked ready to throttle him, and sighed in resignation. "Fine. *After* you've had proper training on their handling and not a moment before it."

Leo reluctantly handed the lighter to Idris.

"Isn't it dangerous to you as well?" asked Alison. "If it's cursed, after all."

"I'm already cursed," said Idris. "If it gets me between here and my office, I probably deserved it." He gave half a smile—half an apology—to Leo.

"I'll go with you, just in case," said Rinka.

"We'll be back for the others with the proper storage," said Idris, putting his arm around Rinka. "Do *not* touch them while we're gone. Don't even go near them."

With the pair of them gone, Ceri relaxed. "Ignore my brother," she said to Leo. "He's insufferable when he thinks he knows better than you."

"No, he was right," said Leo. "Truly, it explains a lot. I thought I was just unlucky. I'm sorry I put you in danger last night."

Last night? Alison shot a look to Keir. It was a good thing Idris wasn't here to hear that.

"Well, I'm relieved it wasn't the solar machine at least," said Professor Marin. She had taken a wise step back while they argued, tinkering with the machine rather than participating. "I want to run a few more tests to be sure."

Ceri led Leo away, asking him something about egg tarts, and Professor Marin took the opportunity to talk to Alison, who likely seemed the most level-headed of the bunch.

"Keep an eye on him during the day for me, will you? Leo is a kind young man, but I worry about him. I'm glad Professor Idris is here to knock some sense into him, but I imagine it'll take more than one lecture to persuade him. I've never met someone so singularly focused. It makes him a wonderful research assistant, but I never thought I'd find myself so worried about an elf's longevity."

"Of course we'll look after him," said Alison.

Truthfully, Alison didn't know how they were meant to babysit an elf that was likely decades older than any of them, except for Lady Sibba.

But judging by the giggles coming from inside, they wouldn't have to worry about it—Ceri was already on the job.

Back in their room that night, with both of them reading their respective books in bed, Alison turned to Keir to discuss something that had been troubling her.

"I think I felt the curse earlier," she said. "But not on Leo, or even on the lighter. I feel it here, in the hallways when I walk around alone. Do you feel it too?"

"I don't know," said Keir. "I feel a sense of unease at times, but I attributed it to the darkness in the hallways and a lack of air circulation. Maybe some peculiarities in the architecture. Sometimes buildings like this that have been partially ruined and added onto over centuries have strange features. Places where walls come together at odd angles, steps that seem too short or too tall, that sort of thing. It can be a bit disorienting when you're used to well-made structures."

"My cottage is pretty wonky, and it doesn't give me that sense at all. But I do see what you mean."

Keir closed his book and looked at Alison. "Do you feel unsafe?"

"No," she reassured him. "Not really. I feel as though I'm being watched though. Not all the time. Just…I don't know. I'm being silly. It's probably just all the royal guards hanging about."

"Alison." He tucked the hair behind her ear. "I trust your instincts even if you don't. If you feel like something isn't right, we can leave. If you want to stay and try to figure it out, I'll stay with you."

"Thank you," she said and kissed him softly.

"Of course, I'm suspicious of the library, personally. Yes, it's helpful, but doesn't it seem odd to you that the library can read everyone's inner-most thoughts and feelings and no one seems to think that's unusual? Perhaps that's what you're feeling. Perhaps it's listening to us right now."

He had meant it as a joke, but the idea sent a shiver up Alison's spine.

"Maybe I'll just put these books in the bathroom for the night. Just in case."

Keir laughed, but he also handed his book over. "Just in case," he said.

⦿

It didn't take long for those of the group who weren't preparing for the autumn term to settle into a routine.

Following breakfast in the dining hall, Alison, Keir, Weyland, and Lady Sibba joined Leo (and often Ceri) in Professor Marin's workshop to run their tests. Weyland and Leo cobbled together some kind of crude power-saver from the material samples and a few of the lab's many parts, while Alison and Lady Sibba crunched the numbers from the previous experiments. Keir's official role was ensuring their safety, but in practice, he was frequently called to the High House infirmary. While there had been no further major 'lectrocution incidents with the solar-power crew, there had been an outbreak of a nasty cold during the move-in.

They continued day after day, sharing their progress with Professor Marin each night. She reviewed the results and suggested modifications, and the next day, it was back to the workshop again to try four cells in the chamber rather than two or a zinc cathode rather than one of adamant. There were countless variables and combinations tried, but by the night before the first day of school, they had narrowed down the design significantly.

"Mithril is extraordinary," said Professor Marin when they showed her the latest tests. "It's far better at handling overcharge when combined with iron than the alternatives. The answer is here if we can just solve the leakage problem. Of course, it's very expensive, but if it's the crown making the investment…"

"Gwenla says there's more mithril than the dwarves let on," said Alison. "It's sort of a false scarcity situation. Keeps the prices high."

"It's a good thing we know a dwarf," said Weyland. "I barely managed to get my hands on mithril even when I worked for Derkomai."

After they packed up their experiments for the day, Alison hesitated before opening the door to her room. The halls were filled with the nervous anticipation of the upcoming term, students coming and going, collecting last-minute supplies and books and discussing plans on which classes to try (and which ones to avoid).

It reminded Alison of her own first day of college. Her father hadn't managed to get time off from the manufactory on move-in day, so her mother had been the one to help her carry the same trunk she still used into her tiny dormitory. They had fought bitterly, as they often did when they were tired and stressed, arguing over what Alison needed to do, which Alison had felt perfectly capable of figuring out for herself.

Her mother had tried to make amends as she left, perhaps not wanting to leave things with her only daughter on the final day of her time under her parents' care on a bad note, but Alison had refused to listen. She didn't feel the weight of it at the time, the loss her mother must have felt. She didn't even feel the massive change that was happening, not really. All she felt was relief that her life was finally starting and gratitude to be free of her mother's nagging and their constant bickering at last.

That was all she felt until the night before classes began, at least. By then, the anticipation had turned into anxiety, and she found herself paralyzed with fear that it had all been a mistake, that she wasn't smart enough to go to university and that she ought to go back home right then and forget about the whole thing.

She had called home, hoping to speak with her father. They had always been close, and she knew he would know just what to say to make her feel better.

But it had been her mother that had answered.

Alison kept the conversation short, still holding some piece of resentment over the way her mother had made her feel the week before, but her mother had said something to her that had stayed with her nonetheless:

"Everyone feels the exact same way you do. None of us know what we're doing, not really. You aren't a mistake. You worked hard and you deserve to be where you are. Don't let that voice inside you keep from being as great as I know you can be."

At the time, Alison had rolled her eyes and ignored what she said. She had zeroed in on the phrase "as I know you can be" as evidence that her mother thought she wasn't great right then.

But now, watching the students in the halls, she got it.

They looked at her and saw someone grown up, someone with the answers, but she wasn't.

She never would be, and that was okay.

Her mother had never had all the answers, either.

They did the best they could. Sometimes the doubts crept in anyway, but Alison had done what her mother had told her to without even realizing it: she had learned to stop listening to that voice that told her she didn't deserve to be happy.

Alison walked down the hall. At the end, tucked between a pair of statues, was a long-talker. It was much nicer than the one she had used to call her mother all those years ago—it probably wouldn't even fade out if she talked on it too long.

She picked up the receiver and gave the party line number to the operator.

It rang five times, but finally it picked up.

"Hi, Mum," she said. "It's me, Alison."

Chapter Nine

THE FIRST DAY OF SCHOOL

Ceri

There was a knock on Ceri's door about an hour before Dean Whittaker's opening address for the autumn term was due to begin.

Ceri and Ana had already been awake for an hour, perfecting their hair and makeup for the first day.

(Ceri could not believe her luck that her roommate was the daughter of a hairstylist. Having had her dressing needs met by servants for her entire life, she was grateful to have someone with the necessary expertise to help her learn to do it for herself.)

It was Dean Whittaker. He, too, looked as though he'd been awake for some time. "I'm sorry to drop by unannounced, your highness. I was wondering if you'd like to speak at the opening address this morning."

Ceri was surprised by the request. "Are there usually other speakers?"

"Not usually, but we don't tend to have royalty around. The presence of the royal guard on campus needs to be explained, if nothing else."

Ceri had insisted on not having guards following her every minute of every day, but because of that, they'd had to secure the entire campus instead. "What about my brother?" asked Ceri.

Dean Whittaker nodded; he was getting to that. "I've asked Prince Idris to say a few words. He agreed, but he told me I'd better ask you as well. I mean, that it would be good to ask you as well, since you are also royalty."

Nice save, thought Ceri, but she knew which of the two phrasings her brother would have used. "I'd really prefer not to," she said.

She didn't want to admit that Idris was right: that if she hadn't been asked, she would have been insulted. But also, she had no desire to speak. "While I'm here, I'm trying to be Ceri, not Princess Ceridwen. Do you understand?"

"Of course, of course. How right you are," said Dean Whittaker. "Although you may change your tune after Professor Ali's Numbers exams. I've heard they often veer closer to a hazing exercise than anything else."

Ceri decided then that she liked Dean Whittaker. He was far too eager to please, but she appreciated that he did consider her opinion separate from her brother's.

An hour later, Ceri and Ana sat at one of the long tables in the dining hall meant for the students. Dean Whittaker did exactly as he promised: he mentioned the guards, he allowed Idris to speak, and he did not out Ceri's presence.

Of course, it didn't stop people from recognizing her.

There had been a few encounters during moving week, but the rumors of her attendance had grown, and by the time she reached her first class of the day (Loegrian, with Professor Proudfoot), it seemed like most of the school knew who she was, judging by the pointing and whispers.

She'd expected some acknowledgment from Professor Proudfoot, considering half the class was staring at her, but to her surprise, Professor Proudfoot simply dove straight into her lecture.

The other thing Ceri had expected was a mixture of boredom and fear. That's what education up to this point had been for Ceri: relentless memorization of names and dates and formulas and vocabulary, followed by varying forms of corporal punishment for failures. The slap with the ruler. The cane on the legs. A strap or a belt, which Ceri hated the most.

King Derkomai had not only approved of these punishments, he also sometimes performed them himself.

Ceri did feel a familiar tightness in her chest as the lecture began, but it was quickly replaced with relief. It was immediately and abundantly apparent that Professor Proudfoot was nothing like her tutors had been. She was funny and personable, mixing in personal anecdotes about her upbringing in the Ash Woods with her discussion of the syllabus and her approach to selecting the works they'd be covering. She welcomed suggestions on what they'd like to study or how to improve the course so they got more out of it—welcomed them.

In fact, all of her courses were more or less the same. Some of her professors—like the infamous Numbers professor, Professor Ali—were stricter than others, but none of them seemed to have any interest in making sure Ceri or anyone else learned "the hard way." There was a genuine sense of openness to new ideas, a desire to encourage students on a path they found both interesting and fulfilling, a hope of improving the school for future generations.

It was enough to make Ceri cry.

"What's wrong?" asked Ana, following Ceri back to the room after their final class.

Ceri was walking so fast, poor little Ana had to run to keep up. "Nothing."

"Don't lie to me."

Ceri paused. "I didn't know it could be like this."

"Like what?"

"So…nice. Everyone is so nice. And it's all so interesting. It's all of the good parts and none of the bad. I can't believe it."

"Ceri, I like you a lot, but I am not following you at all. You're crying because people are nice and the classes are good?" asked Ana. The poor girl was out of breath by the time they reached their dorm room.

Ceri told Ana about her experiences with her tutors. Ana was horrified.

"Where I come from, that's abuse. I'm so sorry you had to go through that. The worst I ever got was an 'Ana, I'm disappointed in you' from my Elvish History teacher, and that damn near broke me. You know you're really strong to have gone through what you did and to still come here."

Ceri didn't feel strong, but she was grateful to Ana for saying it.

"You'll never guess who I met in that Ancient Languages class you didn't want to go to," Ana said once Ceri had calmed down.

"Who?"

"Harry Charlton!"

That didn't help Ceri any. "Who?"

"Do you not have picture shows in the castle? News reels? Newspapers? Harry Charlton is from Arcas Dyrne, and he's a flagball super star! He led Typhon Memorial Comprehensive to their victory over the Arcas Dyrne Dragons last year to win the championship. Winwold has a great flagball team. He said he'll be going down to the main campus for practice a lot, but he really wanted to have the fresher experience, so he's living up here. Isn't that so cool? I think he may be more famous than you. No offense."

Ceri smiled. "None taken." She didn't care much for flagball; that was more of her father's kind of thing, but she didn't mention that to Ana.

"The first game is on Friday. Do you want to go together?"

"Sure," said Ceri.

Who knew? She'd been wrong about school. Maybe she was wrong about flagball as well.

Unfortunately (or maybe fortunately, for Ceri), the first flagball game of the year was cancelled.

The students reacted to the news with as much devastation as if someone had died. Dean Whittaker stood up at the head table on Thursday morning having just given the terrible announcement, and Ceri was worried that someone was going to pelt him with a tomato from their plate of full Loegrian breakfast.

"Now, I know that comes as a shock and a disappointment to us all. Especially Groundskeeper Tomasar," said Dean Whittaker with a wink. The groundskeeper had quite a pool going on the outcome of the game. "We are still hopeful we'll be able to reschedule the game after the regular season. Believe me, if there were any other choice—"

"I don't see any storm," shouted someone a couple of tables over who ducked down quickly afterwards to not be seen.

"It hasn't arrived yet, though the wind is picking up. I've been assured by the royal meteorologists that this is an unprecedented situation. Storms of this size and magnitude hardly ever hit this region. For the safety of the entire school, classes will be cancelled tomorrow so we may make preparations. Some of the students who live too near the river's floodplain will be joining us at High House tomorrow night. The plan is to board up the windows here in the dining hall, and we'll all spend the night together here until the storm clears, hopefully the next day."

Most of the school seemed to be upset, but Ceri was excited. It sounded like a great big sleepover, just like the ones she'd had with her cousins and ladies-in-waiting when she was a little girl.

"We'd better have baths before it comes tomorrow," said Ana. "Storms like this are common on Turtle Island. Sometimes the water and 'lectrics are out for weeks."

Alright, that sounded less ideal. Ceri wondered what that meant for the power-saver research. If the 'lectrics went out, could they keep working?

"There you are," said Leo, joining Ceri after Dean Whittaker had finished his announcements. Ana took it as her cue to leave; she was just the best about that. "Professor Marin wanted me to ask everyone I could if they can help move our equipment to the infirmary. Are you up for some heavy lifting?"

"You mean, can I use my magic to help make it lighter?"

"Perhaps," said Leo. "And perhaps, if I were to take a measurement or two…"

Ceri smiled. "Is that the only thing you like about me?"

"It is the least of the many things I like about you."

The frankness of his response surprised them both, but Leo did not take it back. He also could not meet her eye as he asked, "What do you say?"

"Since it's for a good cause," said Ceri. "The infirmary, not your magic obsession."

"Obsession, such a perfect word," said Leo. The way he said it—a sultry hiss in his accent—made the hair on Ceri's neck stand on end. "What is it you say? 'I have you pegged'?"

"You have me pegged," corrected Ceri. "You as in you. You are the one who is pegged. I'm not pegged."

"That's what I said, no?"

Ceri laughed at the look of utter confusion on his face. "Close enough," she said and followed him to the lab.

✦

Ceri and Ana arrived in the dining hall the following evening freshly bathed, having carried their pillows and blankets across the courtyard as a light rain began to fall and wind whipped through the branches of the yew.

It didn't seem like much of a storm, not yet at least. The flagball team seemed to agree with their assessment: despite repeated warnings from Dean Whittaker, they had remained in the courtyard tossing the flagball around until Groundskeeper Tomasar had come at them, waving his pitchfork.

Ana was staring at Harry Charlton. "Look at him. A quarter elf, they say. I can see it."

Sure, Harry Charlton was undeniably attractive in that classic, meaty sort of way that Ceri had once found appealing, all bulging muscle and closely cut hair. But Ceri found his tireless need for attention—he was currently clowning around with the ball, messing up the makeshift beds other students had made on the floor—exhausting.

"Why don't you go talk to him?" asked Ceri. Ceri was proud of herself. This was a significant sign of personal growth, keeping her mouth shut. She would've pointed out his obvious flaws to Jerta. And Ceri would still do so if she saw something that was actually concerning, but he seemed harmless enough, so she'd keep her opinions on his grandstanding to herself and let Ana like who she liked.

She was positively mature.

"Me? I'm a Halfling. He's…"

About as tall as Idris, which was to say ludicrously tall. Maybe that was why he held no appeal for Ceri. He was built like her brother.

"I'm pretty sure everyone is smaller than him," said Ceri. "I can't see why it would matter. Have you ever tried talking to him in your Ancient Languages class?"

Before Ana could answer, they were interrupted by a worried-looking Professor Marin. "Hello, your highness. Have you seen Leo come in yet? I thought he might be with you."

Ceri looked around the room, but she didn't spot the blonde, bespectacled elf anywhere. "No, I haven't seen him. Did he leave the lab yet?"

"A couple of hours ago. He said he wanted to get a few things before the storm came. I'm sure he'll turn up soon enough. He's probably fighting with the library again."

Ceri could hear in her voice that she wasn't sure if that was likely, and Ceri could guess why.

"You don't think he's going to try to take measurements in the storm, do you?" she asked. "Idris has all of the cursed objects."

"I don't know," said Professor Marin. "Knowing him, he's found *something* to measure. I'm just hoping it's inside. Please let me know if you see him come in."

Ceri waited a respectable length of time after Professor Marin left, then she stood up.

"Ceri, you can't," said Ana. "This kind of storm is really dangerous. People die on Turtle Island all the time, mostly because they go out when they're supposed to stay in."

"Exactly," said Ceri. "Leo's out there."

Ana nodded slowly, understanding. "Be careful."

"You too," said Ceri.

The guard posted at the door stopped her. "Can't let you outside, princess. Our orders are no one goes back out."

Ceri recognized this man from court. She'd never liked him much. "Let me out at once or the king will hear about it. Those are *my* orders."

The guard hesitated.

Ceri tried a different tactic. "I'm not going to be gone long. I just need something from my room. Something…ladies need."

That did it. The most reliable way to get a man to get out of your way was to mention anything particular to being a "lady." Every lady knew that.

"Alright, but hurry back here. They're sweeping up the last students."

Ceri headed out into the hallway alone.

In the distance, thunder rumbled.

Chapter Ten

A DARK AND STORMY NIGHT

Alison

The conversation with Alison's mother had gone better than expected. She was unhappy that Alison had written so little since her move to Wilderise, and she couldn't understand why Alison had chosen to give up everything she worked for to go live in a place without so much as a long-talker, but all that mattered to her was that Alison was happy and doing well.

And she was. The power-saver research was really coming along by the time the storm arrived. Weyland had managed to improve the design of the power-saver casing significantly, reducing most of the troublesome leaks and producing a design that almost met the theoretical requirements Professor Marin had outlined.

They were so incredibly close to cracking it.

It was a shame to have to delay the research on account of the storm, but it also offered them a chance to test their prototype in a real-world scenario. They'd charged each of the candidate power-saver designs to full capacity during the week and had brought them to the infirmary for use in case the 'lectrics went out.

The best of those had been brought into the dining hall along with the students who were being treated and a couple of machines required for their care. Keir had checked over the entire temporary setup while Alison helped move tables to clear the floor; the medical equipment reminded her too much of her father's time in the hospital. Still, she was grateful their research could already be put to good use.

Of their group, the two who were most upset by the storm were Lady Sibba, whose journey back to Herot's Hollow to begin the school year had to be delayed, and Gwenla, who had called Idris's office the day before, frantic with worry.

"We have pumps down here to keep the water out and plenty of coal to burn if we lose the 'lectrics. Oh, but be careful up there on that mountain! I wish you would just come back here. Under a mountain is better than on one when a storm's coming."

Alison reassured her that the college was doing everything it could to keep them safe. And even if they'd wanted to join her, the rail-wheelers were exclusively operating in the opposite direction to pull the most vulnerable people in from the coast.

It was only once they were starting to settle in, the make-shift beds made and the last stragglers arriving, that Rinka noticed someone was missing.

"I see Ceri's roommate over there, but no Ceri," she said, pointing to the Halfling girl.

"Find that Leo, and you'll find her," said Idris. He had taken the spot closest to the tables in order to continue grading the first assignment of the year while the lights were still on.

Alison looked around the dining hall. It was absolutely packed with people—and more than a few pets, including Willow and Barney the dog—but she didn't see Ceri or Leo anywhere.

"Do you see Leo? I don't see him either," she said.

"I'll bet they're right outside doing some last-minute measurements," said Keir. "Probably something about the power of the storm or some such. Do you think I should go check?"

Idris's eyes flashed up on the word "measurements."

"Hello, all," said Professor Marin, startling everyone except Lady Sibba and Rinka, whose superior hearing had heard her coming. "Have you seen Leo? I haven't been able to find him. I asked Ceri to keep a lookout—"

"Oh, Godsdammit," said Idris, shutting his grading notebook. He didn't need to hear the rest to know what had happened.

None of them did.

"You think she went to find him?" asked Professor Marin.

"Of course she bloody did. She can't help herself, can she?" said Idris, rising to his feet.

"Idris," said Rinka, joining him and placing a hand on his shoulder. "It's alright. The storm has barely started. We'll find them and bring them back."

"I know," said Idris, calming down. "Just…it's Ceri."

"I know," said Rinka soothingly.

"We should split up," said Alison. "There are a few places they might have gone. The lab, the library, the dorms."

"You don't have to help—the dorms?" asked Idris.

Alison looked to the others for moral support but found none. "Er, she might have left something there…"

Idris rolled his eyes. He wasn't that stupid. "I'm betting on my office. It's where all those damned 'enchanted objects' of his are."

"Did you lock it?" asked Rinka.

"Of course I locked it," said Idris. "But I learned to pick that kind of lock when I was eight."

"The prince picks locks?" asked Rinka, intrigued by something she had let to learn about him.

"How else are you meant to find all the secrets hiding in the castle? Look, if Leo wanted to get in, he could have. And if my sister was with him? Well, all the more likely. Come on. Let's go track down those idiots before they get themselves killed."

"We'll take the library," said Alison. Keir nodded at her that it was a good idea. "We can go to the dorms afterwards, taking the long way through the halls."

"We'll head to the lab," said Lady Sibba.

"You can't go out there," said Rinka. "It's too dangerous to go outside."

"I have a greater ability to withstand lightning than most, just like Leo," said Lady Sibba.

"Lightning maybe, but not a cyclone," said Weyland. "There's a long-talker in the lab. We can call them."

"There's one on each floor in the dorms if you wanted to check there while we check the library," said Alison.

Willow chose this moment to join the group, the new setting having been thoroughly inspected and the other pets having been greeted and assessed.

"What's going on? Who's missing?" she asked.

"Ceri and Leo," said Alison. "We're about to go find them."

"There are a lot of smells here, but I don't think Leo has been here recently at all. Ceri went this way," said Willow, her nose close to the ground. "If we had more time, we might enlist that Barney. He's cleverer than I gave him credit for, and he has one hell of a nose on him."

Idris and Rinka were already making their way to the door.

"Willow, you don't have to come. It might be dangerous," said Alison.

"For you, maybe. I'd like to see the storm try. Cats always land on their feet." Willow stretched defiantly and continued on the trail.

"Where are you all going?" asked Dean Whittaker. "The guards are out there searching for Princess Ceridwen. One of them said she was heading back to the dorm for...personal reasons."

"Classic Ceri lie," said Idris. "We think we know where she may have gone. We won't be long." He moved through the doorway without waiting to hear Dean Whittaker's response.

Alison shot a look of apology at the Dean.

"Wait!" called Dean Whittaker. "Take these at least. In case we lose the 'lectrics." He handed them each a candle and a match.

Rinka, Idris, and Willow parted from the group at the first turn, heading upstairs to his office—apparently Ceri's first thought as well, from the trail—as the rest of them continued down the corridor towards the library and the dorms.

Outside, they could hear the battering of the rain against the windows and the howl of the wind.

"It's picking up," said Lady Sibba. "The Rock gets storms like this every year. I never thought I'd see one here. We need to hurry. If the 'lectrics go out, we won't be able to call the lab."

They picked up the pace, practically running through the empty corridors. Lightning flashed through the un-boarded windows, much closer this time. Finally, they reached the turn for the library.

"Be careful over there," called Alison to Weyland and Lady Sibba as they continued down the corridor towards the dorms. "If they don't answer, come back to the dining hall. Don't be a hero."

As the sound of their footsteps faded into the distance, the creeping feeling of being watched returned. Alison looked at Keir. "Do you feel it?"

"It's just the storm," said Keir. "And the quiet now that the others are gone. The library is just ahead. I doubt they're in there. Let's check it quickly, and we can head back."

They walked down the hall, their footsteps echoing over the sound of thunder. Keir was right. It was just the isolation that she was feeling. The rest of the school was safe in the dining hall, and they were out here alone. That would be enough to make most people feel a little uneasy.

The library doors were just ahead. The lightning cast strange shadows in the corridor, the flashes growing ever more frequent as they continued. The windows rattled in their casings.

The 'lectric lights in the hallway, dim as they were, flickered once, and went out.

Alison reached out for Keir but found empty air.

He had just been beside her. She felt around the darkened corridor but only found the paintings and tapestries on the walls and the dying glow of the 'lectric bulbs in their sconces.

"Keir?" she asked the darkness, reaching in her pocket for the match.

She felt around for something rough, finding a statue of jagged stone: the one-winged phoenix just past the library, she realized as she felt it. She had wandered too far.

She struck the match against it and brought it to the candlestick.

Her heart rose into her throat as a door creaked open somewhere nearby.

"Keir? Is that you?" she asked, her voice small and frightened.

There was no reply, but she could feel it in the hallway with her. A presence, dark and unkind.

She backed away, fumbling with the match, trying to will the wick to ignite.

Then there was a loud crash in the distance: the exterior doors burst open, sending a gust of wet wind blowing through.

The match and candle blew out.

"Alison!" shouted Keir's muffled voice from somewhere far away.

The nearby door slammed shut, leaving her in the darkness, alone.

Chapter Eleven

TWISTED FIRESTARTER

Keir

The first thing Keir realized as the door shut behind him was that he wasn't in the library.

He wasn't certain how he knew it. The room was pitch dark, the air unmoving. Somehow, he could sense that the space wasn't large enough. Somehow, he could feel the walls closing in.

The second thing he realized was that he was alone.

"Alison?" he called. The sound was muffled, strangely quiet in this space.

Keir felt behind him for the wall. It was there, which came as somewhat of a surprise. He felt the texture of the wallpaper, something vaguely floral. He reached lower and touched wood paneling. This wasn't the corridor he'd come from, although he'd known that already.

He must have taken a wrong turn in the dark.

He reached the edge of a frame. He felt the inside of it, hoping for a chalkboard, but found the smooth contours of an oil painting.

There was a change in the air in the room. It was subtle, like the soft breeze when someone walks by. He felt the weight of them, the warmth.

It was not Alison.

Moving slowly, he reached into his pocket for the match he'd been given by Dean Whittaker. He knelt to the ground; the floor was stone in this room.

He struck the match.

There was the sound of muffled laughter. Male, young. From its warmth, possibly a dwarf.

A prank, Keir realized. One of the young freshers with an overactive imagination. Keir was accustomed to pranks. Charlotte had enjoyed them almost from the time she could walk: leaving sticky pudding in Keir's chair, replacing sugar with salt, even locking him into one of the many rooms of Weldan House from time to time.

"Very funny," he said as he lit the candle.

He jumped. There was movement behind him.

No, it was only his shadow. It moved with him as he turned, the candlelight flickering.

He was in a small room. An office, it seemed like. There were a pair of armed chairs facing a mahogany desk, a large shelf full of books, and a globe in the corner. The painting he had felt before hung near the doorway.

He tried the handle, but it was locked, of course.

"Alison? Can you hear me? I'm trapped in an office."

He heard movement from the hallway beyond. Probably the prankster. "It's a very funny joke, but you've had your fun. Let me out of here."

At least there were no windows in the room. As far as places to be during a storm went, it wasn't a bad option.

The issue was Alison.

She was out in the hall alone in the dark. He hoped she'd managed to light her candle; she had less experience with them, having been raised in the city. Of course, Alison could probably light it with her magic if she needed to.

He could have as well, he realized.

Keir had known the truth of his magic long before the fairy had told Alison. He could feel it in him since the vine, looking for an escape.

He had denied it. Why would it offer itself to him now and not when he needed it? Why had it denied him the chance to save an innocent child?

If the magic—the old magic, funny how quickly they'd stopped calling it "old," how quickly they had embraced it as part of the now—had a will of its own, Keir certainly couldn't understand it.

A part of him wanted nothing to do with it at all.

But then there was Alison. She was his light in the darkness. She seemed to have some intuitive sense about things that Keir couldn't comprehend. There was a way that the world just responded to her, a way it seemed to move and bend around her, that Keir greatly envied. But more than envy, he was grateful to be part of it. And he'd do anything, *anything* to protect it. To protect her.

No matter what it cost him.

Though it pained him to do so, Keir reached out into the world with the sense he knew was there, the sense that had been revealed to him in all its terrible glory by the fairies.

At first, he felt nothing, not even Alison's familiar presence on the other side of the wall.

Then he felt it.

There was something holding him here, and it was full of malice.

Keir did not scare easily, but even he was disturbed by the sudden, certain knowledge of something there in the darkness that wanted him—what, tortured? Dead? It was impossible to say, but he could feel that it wanted him, him specifically, for reasons he could not fathom.

However, and perhaps the presence couldn't understand this, this knowledge was also a comfort to him. Though the presence had no love for anyone, it seemed Alison was safe, at least from this particular threat.

The presence was in the room with him, and it was for him alone to face.

Keir turned his sense to the door: not locked, held closed by magic. Twisted, dark magic: the kind that had been bent in the way Keir had tried to bend it. Magic that endured, that had corrupted.

As he felt for some kind of opening, he noticed the painting on the wall.

It was a strange painting, unusually macabre for the setting. The college was filled with portraits of scholars and kings, paintings of pastoral settings and historic battles, mythological lovers and religious idols. The usual. But this painting was bizarre.

There was a banquet in the woods, a group of figures seated at a table under the trees. It wasn't unlike the place where they dined with the fairies. In fact, it was exactly like that place. The more that Keir looked at it, the more that he recognized. There were Mab and Genn, although that wasn't truly surprising. There were legends of fairies living forever in their fairy realms, and if Keir had learned one thing this year, it was that most legends were true.

But there was the dwarf he'd danced with. And there, was that Idris? Rinka, Alison, everyone there but him.

The plates on the table were full, but it wasn't the feast he knew.

It was a body, dismembered and bloody, each plate filled with a different limb or organ.

In front of Alison was his head.

At this, he laughed. "You should have gone with the heart," said Keir to the unseen presence. "It would have been a better choice, metaphorically speaking."

The painting ignited.

Excellent work, Keir thought. *You've angered the ghost.*

"I take it back," he said, looking around the room for something to put the fire out. Flames had covered the entire frame in the matter of seconds. "It was a very good scare. Very creepy."

Smoke was beginning to fill the room. He didn't know if this was real—he suspected it wasn't—but it wouldn't matter if he passed out before he could save himself from the fire.

"Alison!" he shouted. He searched through the door for her presence, and this time, through a hole the flames had burnt, he found it.

"Keir, I'm here," she said. Her voice was so quiet he could barely make it out. "I can't get the door open."

"It's magic," he said.

"I know," said Alison. "But I can't stop it. I can't feel you. I can't feel anything. There was something here before, but it's gone now."

"It's in the room with me," he said. "And the fire."

"Fire? Keir!"

Keir could feel her beating against the magical barrier to no avail. It wasn't here for her.

It was here for him.

"Stay there, I'm going to try something," said Keir.

The flames were consuming the floral wallpaper and crawling down the panels of wood. Everything in this room was made to burn.

Keir reached out into the hallway. Alison's magic was there, cool and calming as a mirror-still lake on a summer's day. This moment frightened him more than anything this presence, this ghost, had shown him.

He needed to do this. Not just to save his own life, although that was a powerful motivator. He couldn't leave Alison alone. He saw her beautiful face standing over him. Saw the tears spring into her blue eyes. Heard her anguished cry. He knew what would happen if he failed.

He could not fail.

He grabbed onto the magic. He felt Alison's power flow through him, felt the surge of it through his body.

He turned to the flames and snuffed them out.

He turned to the door and wrenched it open.

The air changed. The presence had gone. Keir picked up the candlestick from where he'd left it on the floor. Nothing was burnt. The painting on the wall was untarnished—a scene of an elvish ship on stormy seas.

Alison ran into the room, practically knocking the candle from his hand.

"What in the name of the Gods happened? There was a fire?" asked Alison.

He put his arm around her shoulder. "I think you were right about this place. There is something strange happening here."

Chapter Twelve

THE TRAIL OF BLOOD

Lady Sibba

Winwold College held little in common with the fine elvish institutions Lady Sibba had known.

It was the pace of it, mostly. Traditional elvish education was an exercise in patience. Few completed their studies in less than a decade, and some took considerably longer than that.

Not so at Winwold. It was a thoroughly modern place, with shortened requirements to accommodate the shorter lifespans of most of the students, and to Lady Sibba, it moved in such a whirlwind that she wasn't surprised a cyclone had spun up near it.

Lady Sibba had always known she wanted to be an educator. She had passed her girlish years forcing the other children on the island to sit in on her "lectures." She'd made them complete very important (and often impossible) assignments, like feeding candy syrup to a hummingbird by hand and counting the fronds on a palm tree. Then she'd given them marks based on their performance.

As a result, she had few friends, but that had never bothered her. She had a purpose.

Her purpose now was a foolish one. She'd seen the way the wind blew through the trees from the dormitory she and Weyland shared earlier in the day. This kind of storm was not to be underestimated. They belonged in the buttressed dining hall, not out here in the shoddily constructed corridors that connected the main halls with a much newer, and much weaker, building.

Weyland would never stand for that, and she knew it.

It was what she loved about him. Weyland was simple. That wasn't to say he was unintelligent; in fact, she had been pleasantly surprised by his intellectual curiosity once she'd gotten to know him better. But to him, the world was a simple place. People were good or they were bad. You helped good people if you could. You stayed out of the way of the bad ones.

Ceri was a good one; a young one, but a good one so far. Lady Sibba had expected Weyland to feel a resentment towards the princess and her brother. They were the king's children, after all.

He had surprised her. Perhaps he saw in them a shadow of himself. They were victims of King Derkomai as much as he was.

"Do you know how to use the long-talker if we find it?" asked Weyland.

That was a good question. They had been invented before Lady Sibba came to Wilderise, but those early models probably had little in common with what they were using now.

"I don't know," said Lady Sibba. "Did they have one in the castle?"

"If they did, I wasn't allowed to use it."

One positive thing the summer's shenanigans had given Weyland was the ability to talk freely about his time being held captive. Freely for him, at least.

Lady Sibba had written to Weyland during his captivity. She wasn't sure why she'd done it. She'd seen him grow up in Herot's Hollow, but only from a distance: his father, the former blacksmith, had kept him from the schoolhouse. When they met again after his father died, he'd grown into the mountain of a man that he was.

Perhaps that was part of it, she had to admit. What person that liked men could resist a mountain of a man?

There was also the fact that he'd been kind to her after Lady Willana had passed on. Lady Willana was the reason she'd come to Herot's Hollow at all, and with her gone, she had been ready to abandon the schoolhouse and to return home to start over. But Weyland had come by while she was packing up, and she'd never forget what he told her: "It's better with you here."

That was how she felt about Weyland, too. It was better when he was around.

They passed a pair of guards as they finally entered the dormitory wing.

"You need to get back to the dining hall," they told them. "Whatever is in your dorm can wait."

Lady Sibba looked at Weyland, amused to be mistaken for a student. "We're not students. We're visiting scholars. We're out here looking for Princess Ceridwen. She's not in the dining hall. Have you seen her?"

They hadn't, of course, but they were so preoccupied with their new task that they left Weyland and Lady Sibba to theirs.

"Idiots," muttered Weyland. These were some of Weyland's bad people. Lady Sibba didn't blame him for that particular opinion.

They climbed a flight of stairs. Ceri's dorm was somewhere around here. Neither of them had thought to ask for her exact room number, but it didn't matter: they had hands to knock with.

Weyland started beating on the doors on the right side of the hall. "Ceri? Ceri, are you in there?"

Lady Sibba took the left. "Ceri? Are you there, princess?"

They'd made it to roughly the middle of the corridor when the lights went out. Lady Sibba was prepared for this eventuality; she had the match and candle already in hand. She struck the match against the bottom of her boot and lit the candle.

Then she used hers to light Weyland's as he fumbled for his match.

"We'd better hurry," said Lady Sibba. "Those long-talkers have power-savers in them, but they won't last long."

"I'll keep trying the doors. You try the long-talker."

Lady Sibba nodded. She headed to the end of the hall.

The long-talker was somewhat like she remembered it. It had a rotary dial on it now with numbers. She wasn't sure what to do with that. She hoped operators still existed.

"Number, please."

Good. At least there was someone to speak to. "Um, hello. I need the 'lectrics lab at High House. Part of Winwold College."

"You're calling from Winwold College, ma'am. Is this an emergency?"

"Yes, I know I'm calling from Winwold. No, it's not an emergency. I just need to get to the lab."

"I can't make internal connections. Check if there are numbers on the side of the box. Have a good night."

The receiver clicked before Lady Sibba could respond.

Check the side of the box, the operator had said. Sure enough, there was a list of numbers there.

Professor Marin, 'Lectrics. 090.

Lady Sibba tried pressing those numbers in order, but nothing happened. "Come on…"

The pounding of Weyland's fist on the doors was echoed by the pounding of shutters against windows. Lady Sibba knew why they hadn't been able to board up the entire college on short notice, but it disturbed her to hear it. Those windows wouldn't hold if it continued like this for long.

Lady Sibba tried again, this time turning the round dial from each number.

That seemed to work. There was a ringing sound on the receiver.

"Sibba?"

"It's ringing," she said. "No answer yet."

The phone rang and rang. Well, at least if they weren't there, there was no reason for them to have to go outside.

"Sib, you need to see this. Sib!"

"Just a minute."

How long should she let it go unanswered before she gave up? She thought about the size of Professor Marin's lab. There were a few rooms other than the main workshop where they spent most of their time. An office, the toilets, a small classroom. The long-talker was probably in the office, meaning they'd hear it from almost anywhere—

"SIBBA!"

Lady Sibba's blood ran cold. Weyland was terrified. She rushed over to him, trying not to let the speed of her movement put the candle out but going as fast as she dared.

She saw the gleam of it, the reflection of the candlelight, before she saw Weyland.

Blood.

Unmistakably. A large pool of it, and a trail leading away.

"Ceri!" they both shouted as they followed the bloody trail.

What could have happened? The only people that should have been out here were their own group and the guards, unless...

"It can't be Professor Marin," said Weyland. "She was in the dining hall when we left. You saw her."

"What if she crossed the courtyard? She would have beaten us here."

"You think she went out in that?"

The rain crashed against the windows in waves.

"No, I suppose not."

Lady Sibba had been ashamed of her prejudice against Professor Marin, but she'd truly believed vampires to be bloodthirsty killers by nature for most of her life. It was hard to rewrite something like that in her mind, but she was trying.

"The trail ends here."

They had followed the trail down the corridor, down the stairs, and to the door leading to the woods behind the campus.

The door rattled in its casing, battered by the winds outside.

Weyland reached for the handle anyway.

"Wait," said Lady Sibba.

She knelt and lowered the candle to the bloodstain on the doormat. "This isn't right," she said.

"What do you mean?"

It had been decades, but Lady Sibba had seen violence firsthand. It had been during her travels through the eastern continent, not long before she came to Herot's Hollow. The Unified Pantheon hadn't taken in that part of the world. Out there, there were still bloody conflicts over the faces of the death god or whether it was the goddess of the hearth or the goddess of the home. The kind of fight that had plagued the peoples of the world since they'd first drawn air.

Lady Sibba had seen blood spilled. She knew the way it poured out of wounds, the way it could splatter from a violent thrust, the way it trickled from small cuts. This blood looked like it had been dropped from a bucket from several feet up.

"It's fake," she said. "These aren't real bloodstains."

"They look pretty real, Sib."

"They aren't. Look at that splash. It's like spilled milk. Blood doesn't splash like that, not even from an artery. It forms arcs with the beat of the heart."

Weyland gave her a look that said he'd ask her later how she knew this, but he believed her.

"If it's fake, who did it?"

"I don't know," said Lady Sibba. "But I'm willing to bet it wasn't Ceri. Let's go back."

They looked to the ground to follow the trail back, but it was gone.

"Impossible," said Weyland.

"Magic," said Lady Sibba. "Be on your guard. There's something going on."

She looked up at him. He nodded at her, his red face resolute. He was determined to keep them safe.

If you had to be stuck in the magically haunted hallways of an ancient college campus during a hurricane, there were worse people to be stuck with.

Chapter Thirteen

WHISPERS IN THE DARK

Rinka

The door to Idris's office had been unlocked with magic.

"Ceri's magic," said Idris. "I never should have taught her how to do that."

"Leo was here as well," said Willow, sniffing the door frame.

No surprises there.

The only real surprise was that Willow could smell them at all over all of the other smells that must have been in the corridor. Idris's classroom was right next to his office, and it had been full to capacity all week. It seemed like the whole school—minus Ceri, of course—had turned up to hear his lectures.

Rinka didn't blame them. Idris was the crown prince of Loegria, which was a novelty in itself, and while magic was generally considered a bit old-fashioned, the study of dark magic had retained a certain allure. Idris called it "sexy." She doubted him somewhat—was it the subject that was sexy or was it just him?

He had loved that she had asked him that.

It turned out to be both, as she had found out when she attended one of his lectures earlier in the week. And his lecturing style didn't hurt either. He was passionate, relatable, clear. The class held onto his every word. Dean Whittaker interrupted to ask if he'd consider moving to the music hall so that the crowd in the corridor would have somewhere to sit.

Idris was so infuriatingly good at everything, it would have been easy to hate him.

It was a good thing, then, that she loved him instead.

"Where did they go next?" she asked Willow.

"Down the hall." The tabby cat kept her nose to the ground until a rumble of thunder startled her upright.

"It's alright, Willow," said Rinka, stroking her on the back. "We're safe inside."

She looked at Idris and knew exactly what he was thinking: Ceri might not be.

"You two go on ahead," said Idris. "Stay on their trail. I'm going to check my office quickly to see if they managed to get the objects back, then I'll join you."

Rinka took Idris's hand as he was walking away and gave it a squeeze. "We'll find them."

"I know," said Idris. He leaned over and kissed Rinka briefly on the lips before going inside.

Rinka was reluctant to leave him. She knew he'd been struggling with Ceri's presence since their reunion, and this situation did nothing to help matters.

It was his guilt that was getting to him. He blamed himself for his absence from her life when she needed him, and, in trying to make up for lost time, he had overcorrected and come out on the side of overprotective.

It would be better if she or someone else found Ceri first, for both of their sakes.

"I'm not sure they were together," said Willow. "Leo's smell is weaker. Sometimes, it vanishes entirely. I'd guess it was more than a day since he's been here."

"Maybe he came here yesterday after Dean Whittaker let everyone know about the storm," said Rinka. "Or maybe Idris has it wrong and he didn't take the cursed objects at all."

"I wouldn't take that bet. That boy doesn't care about anything as much as his research."

"Well, maybe there's one thing."

Rinka had noticed the energy between Leo and Ceri immediately, and she wasn't alone.

In fact, it seemed like the only people who weren't convinced were Ceri and Leo themselves.

Rinka was confident they'd work it out eventually. Assuming they survived this storm.

The wind blowing through the leaves outside sounded like a whisper as they passed a large set of windows and descended a staircase.

"Leo's trail ends here," said Willow. It was a door into the courtyard not far from where they'd left the dining hall. "But like I said, it's an older trail. Ceri's continues that way."

"That's headed towards the library," said Rinka. "Alison may have already found them."

There was that whispering sound again. No, not a whispering sound. Whispers.

Rinka froze. "Ceri? Leo?"

"What are you doing?" asked Willow. She was already ten feet ahead, continuing down the hallway.

"Can you hear that?" asked Rinka.

Rinka couldn't hear anything herself. The whispers had stopped. Maybe it really was a trick of the wind.

Or maybe it was the way the sound carried in this old building. Rinka had been in some old elvish constructions in Arcas Dyrne. Old temples and the like, sometimes for the clothes and food they gave away when times were tough after her parents' divorce. There were hallways that would carry the sound from one end to the other and great domes used to whisper political secrets without having to stand close to the recipient. Maybe this was something like that. Alison and Keir were nearby, after all.

"I'm losing Ceri's trail," said Willow just as the lights went out.

"Great," said Rinka. "Just what we need."

She reached into her pocket and withdrew the match.

"What am I supposed to do with this?" asked Rinka. "I can't see a damn thing to strike it on, and I don't have a matchbox."

"Follow my voice," said Willow. "I can see just fine."

Well, at least there was that. Rinka tried to stay towards the center of the hallway; there were so many statues and coats of armor and random plinths to avoid on the sides.

"*Come here. Come closer.*"

It was the whisper again, clearer this time.

"Ceri? Alison? Keir? Leo?"

A door or window had come open or broken somewhere, sending a damp wind blowing through the hall. Maybe they were outside?

"You're not going to find them standing in the middle of the hallway. I could barely even hear you, and I'm right here," said Willow, oblivious to the fear in Rinka's voice.

"*Closer. I need you. Closer.*"

That was odd. "*I need you.*" What did that mean?

"You don't hear that, Willow? That voice?"

"I only hear you, and my hearing is a bit better than yours."

"*Please. You're almost there. Just a little more. Come closer.*"

"Nope," said Rinka, stopping in her tracks. "Nope, we're going back."

"What do you mean? We ought to at least see if the trail leads into the library," said Willow.

"Nope. I'm hearing strange voices. It's time to go."

Rinka had seen just about every picture show that had been made. There weren't too many that were scary, but the scary ones all had one thing in common: people who failed to take note of obvious signs of trouble and kept plowing ahead into danger.

They didn't have the benefit of an intertitle to tell them what the danger was, but Rinka didn't need it.

Strange voices in a dark, spooky manor that only she could hear? Nope, nothing good was going to come from that.

"Don't go. Come closer. Closer."

"Well, that's certainly not ideal," said Willow, "but I'm not hearing them, so I don't see the harm in going on ahead."

"Willow, please. Alison would never forgive me if I let something happen to you. Let's just go get Idris. He's probably almost here already. Then we can pick up the trail again once we have someone a bit more equipped to deal with whatever that voice is."

"Closer. Closer. Closer…"

"Fine," said Willow. "Maybe if we get you a matchbox, you'll stop stepping on my tail."

"Sorry," said Rinka, following the cat back up the stairs as the whispered voice faded away behind them.

Chapter Fourteen

THE LIBRARY

Alison

Alison listened as Keir recounted his experience in the office. There was no sign of a fire or any other presence in the room, but she didn't doubt him for a moment: she'd seen what magic was capable of.

Speaking of magic, she was wildly impressed that he'd been able to wield her magic—their magic—to put a stop to whatever it was that haunted him. As much as he tried to deny it, he seemed to be deeply connected to the old magic, and she was proud of him for facing his fear and wielding it in his time of crisis.

"Shall we keep going and try for the library?" he asked after she had finished with her questions.

"I think we'd better. Something like what happened to you could be happening to Ceri right now."

The door of the library was cracked open despite the breeze blowing through the hallway.

"It seems like this should have shut," said Keir, his voice filled with apprehension. "I don't like it."

"We'll stay together," said Alison. "We're stronger together."

Once they were inside, Keir lit Alison's candle to help them see. "What happened here?"

The floor was littered with books. It was as if the library had thrown a tantrum, emptying half of its shelves in its fury.

"There's a path through them. Look," said Alison. There was a narrow path through the shelves where the books had been roughly shoved aside. "Ceri's magic, I think."

"Ceri?" she called. "Are you in here?"

"Ceri! Leo!" Keir shouted. His voice carried quite a bit further than hers, but there was no answer.

As they followed Ceri's path, they heard a whispering sound from across the room.

"Do you hear that?" asked Keir.

"Whispers? Yes, I hear it. I can't make out what it's saying."

"It's probably better if we don't know."

They turned the corner in the opposite direction. Whatever the whispering was, it didn't seem like Ceri had gone that way.

As they came upon the next set of shelves, a couple of books fell. "Poetry," said Alison, kneeling to pick one up. "This is where I was when we first arrived. Thanks, library, but we're a little busy right now."

The next book that fell hit her in the head. "Ow! That's really unnecessary." She felt odd speaking to the empty room in the dark. "Did Ceri go this way? We're trying to find her."

As if in response, a book dropped from a shelf further down.

"Thank you," said Alison.

They continued on the path, letting the library guide them when they lost her trail. It led them to an area in the far back near to the whispering sound.

"I don't think that's Loegrian," said Keir. "I can make out some of the words now, but it doesn't sound like any language I know."

The trail through the books on the ground seemed to lead to a door, but the library was dropping books nearer to the whispers. "What do you think?" asked Alison. "Left or right?"

Keir picked up one of the books the library had just dropped. "*Grimoires of Turtle Island: A Collector's Guide.* These are magic books. *Codex Voynich. The Principles of Elvish Spellwork.*"

Alison lifted her candle in that direction. "There's a possibility that whatever you encountered in that office could have gotten to the library."

"I don't feel it here. Do you?"

"No," said Alison. The whispers didn't sound angry, but Alison had some sort of innate distrust of talking inanimate objects that was hard to shake. She sighed. "I guess we better see where it leads."

The answer was an ordinary bookshelf. It contained more whispering magic tomes—*Mystical Properties of Gemstones, Ritual Sacrifice in Antiquity,* and a book that seemed to be vibrating on the shelf.

"On the Study of Portals and Doorways—portals?" asked Alison. She tugged on the book, but she felt resistance.

It wasn't a book. It was a handle.

She heard the click of a switch, and the bookshelf swung open, revealing a hidden passage.

"Whoa," said Alison. "Do you think she went this way?"

"Only one way to find out," said Keir, leading her inside.

Chapter Fifteen

THE CURSED CHILD

Idris

The door to the storage closet was unlocked but not by magic.

The lock had been clumsily picked, likely with a screwdriver and a hairpin, judging by the scratches.

"Idiot," muttered Idris. He was thinking of himself as much as Leo.

He had been hard on Leo, but he had done it as much for Leo's own safety as for everyone else's. Curses were dangerous and often unpredictable, and the fact that Leo lacked the ability to sense the inherent danger meant he shouldn't be trusted with his "enchanted" objects.

But Idris, having seen Leo's dedication to his research, should have done a better job of locking them up. Things had just been so busy at the start of the term. The demand for his courses had far exceeded his expectations, and frankly he wasn't sure he was going to be able to manage without some help. He had hoped that his intimidation, clumsy though it was, would have been enough to deter Leo at least long enough for him to get a handle on the job he was brought here to do.

Of course, there was another possibility. It was a stone he'd rather leave unturned, but with Ceri nowhere to be found, he couldn't afford to ignore alternatives, no matter how improbable.

There were some curses that had a way of corrupting the mind. Idris hadn't had a chance to study the objects Leo had collected, but it was very possible that one of them was cursed with something that could have overtaken his conscious will. He may have had no choice but to steal it back.

This was a far more dangerous notion. A curse like that could push him far past the threshold of what he was normally capable of. It could force him to remove any obstacle in his path.

Any obstacle, including one petite dragon princess with a taste for trouble.

The storage room had clearly been disturbed. Several cases had been picked or broken open, all of them with items missing. All of the objects he'd collected from Leo— the lighter, the dagger, the locket, the doll, and even the horn, which was the only object that Idris couldn't immediately identify as cursed—were gone, as were two other items: an exceptionally old watch, with a curse Idris hadn't yet identified, and a sapphire ring, which had the power to turn nightmares real.

"Godsdammit," said Idris when he realized the ring was gone.

The ring was a particularly nasty piece of work. He was grateful that he had discovered its ability by showing up to class one day in his underwear rather than through any of the far worse things that could have happened.

Idris needed to get that ring back before Leo or Ceri fell asleep. Or sooner. In combination with the other objects, it could have done anything to anyone.

That was the other thing about curses: they liked to work together. A nightmare ring on its own was only as dangerous as the dreamer's worst nightmares. Most dreamers tended to wake up before actually dying, so the ring only did its worst in rare cases. But in combination with something else, even something relatively benign like a spoon that made you eat after you were full, the results could be disastrous. The ring could make you eat something horrific: a pie made from a beloved child, or that awful porridge they served in the dining hall, and the spoon would force you to keep eating it until you no longer could.

Just as Idris had turned to catch up with Rinka, the door slammed shut. There was laughter in the air—high-pitched, girlish giggles.

"If this is some kind of joke, it isn't funny, Ceri."

Idris felt the movement in the room as the lights went out.

"Did you take the invisibility pendant as well?" he asked as he ignited the candle with his magic.

The box containing the invisibility pendant was undisturbed, but the laughter continued.

Not Ceri, he thought. *Not unless she found an outrageously good magic teacher without Father knowing.*

This was one of the many loose curses, almost definitely. Maybe some of the college's own magic at work in there too. Places this old were always crawling with it, even if there were few left who could sense it. And there was always the chance it had been corrupted by another curse into something far worse than intended.

"Show yourself," he said. He tried the door—held shut by magic, of course.

He tried to break through it but felt it fighting back against him. It was doable, maybe, but it would leave him with little energy to face anything else that might be thrown at him.

Or anything else that might be thrown at Ceri.

"You're no fun," said a voice. It was a child's voice.

The doll, Idris guessed.

Children's curses were often unintentionally created by young practitioners of magic who hadn't gotten control of their powers yet. The curse that Keir had admitted to creating one whiskey-soaked night a few weeks earlier had a lot in common with a children's curse. They had lessons like morals at the end of a story. Idris suspected this curse had something to do with sharing toys.

"I can't play with you for long in this room. There isn't much air in here, and the candle will burn through it fast. Open the door and we can play together."

"No candle then," said the voice. Idris's candle snuffed out. "I want to play."

"We can play," said Idris. "But I need to be able to see to play. And I need to be able to breathe to play."

He lit the candle once more. The curse was unlikely to be the entire spirit of a child; he'd heard rumors of such but had never found evidence of it for himself. But even if it was a fragment of it, it might respond to the kind of parental authority that children often craved.

"I don't think so," said the voice. It giggled malevolently and put out the candle again.

Idris didn't like this. The voice was unusually confident for a child. And there was something sinister in the laughter that unnerved him.

"Alright," said Idris. "What do you want to do then?"

"I want you to play with me forever, and I know how."

Ah, there it was. A classic spirit request. The poor child that had cursed the doll may have done so as their dying wish.

It was sad, but the main issue was that the spirit wanted to kill him right now and was incredibly capable of doing so.

He was going to have to chance it and burst the door open. Hopefully by the time they'd found Ceri, he would have some magical assistance from Alison and Keir.

He focused his power on the door. It was incredible, the force that was holding it closed. It was like pulling against a crate of cannonballs.

"Where are you going?" asked the voice.

Not good. He needed to get out of here, now. He pulled with all of his power.

The door opened a crack. He grabbed onto the handle and pulled physically, inching it open.

"I don't think so," the voice said again.

It slammed the door shut.

There was another laugh, but this was a different laugh entirely. Older, male. An orc, maybe, or a dwarf.

"Who else is there?" asked Idris. He should have seen this coming. The children's curse alone shouldn't have been able to keep the door shut against the power of Idris's magic.

Unfortunately, Idris had just used a ton of it to try to break free. He was immediately exhausted to the point of needing to sit down. He leaned against the shelves to avoid collapsing.

"My friend likes to play with me. You said you wanted to see."

"Idris?" Rinka's voice was muffled on the other side of the door. The enchantment let little through. "Are you in there?"

"In here—" began Idris, but his voice was cut off.

There were hands around Idris's throat. At the exact same moment, the silk lining of the case that had held the lighter burst into flames.

"You wanted to see," said the child's voice. "Can you see now?"

Idris thrashed against the invisible hands. In the flickering of the fire, there was little to see in the room but sinister shadows. A pair of them, dwarf and human child.

"Idris? I can't get the door open," cried Rinka.

Idris heard the knob turning back and forth. Then there was a crashing sound of something colliding with the door: she was trying to break it open.

He couldn't respond. The hands were cutting off his air. He didn't have long.

He stumbled to his feet and threw himself across the room at the fire. He slammed the case shut.

The doll's case caught fire instead.

Both dwarf and child laughed.

"You'll play with us soon," said the child in a sing-song voice. "Soon…"

There was a creaking sound from the shelves Idris had just been leaning on. Something was moving.

It was likely to be whatever physical presence the dwarf or the child had taken. Idris pushed against the hands around his throat with what was left of his power, freeing himself to take one more painful gasp.

He thumbed a hidden latch on a tiny case behind him. In it was a single silver coin. The curse on the coin was so slight that he rarely even kept it in its case—the coin always came up tails, no matter how many times you flipped it.

In Idris's hands, it was no mere silver.

He had so little power left though. Could he stretch it into a sword without passing out from the effort?

The shelves stirred. There was something behind there.

He had to take a chance. He concentrated on the coin, and then—

The shelves swung open, blocking the door back into his office.

"Idris!" shouted Alison.

He dropped the half-formed sword. It hit the ground as the coin it had been and bounced, finally landing on tails.

He gestured desperately to his neck.

"He's not breathing," said Keir. "Alison!"

Keir took Alison's hand, and Idris felt the incredible power of their combined magic smack into the room.

The hands around his neck were gone in an instant.

"The door—" Idris started, gasping.

"I know," said Keir. "I was trapped the same way."

Keir pulled the shelf that had concealed the hidden passage they had emerged from closed, and he and Alison tackled the door.

Just as they were swinging it open, the blade of an axe appeared through it, cleaving the old wood.

Alison screamed. All three of them jumped back, holding each other in the far corner of the closet.

The axe came free. Its wielder stepped into the light of Keir and Alison's candles.

"Hello, all. Having a good night?" asked Rinka, slinging the axe over her shoulder.

Chapter Sixteen

THE SECRET PASSAGEWAY

Alison

Rinka rushed over to Idris, who could barely stand. "Gods, what happened to you?" she asked him as she helped him hobble to his desk in the next room.

"Curses," said Idris. "Two, at least. Are you okay?"

"Me? I'm fine. Heard a strange whisper and hightailed it out of there."

"Whispers?" asked Alison. They had followed the whispers to the secret door. To Idris. And they hadn't had a moment to spare—any longer, and he would have been done for.

"A woman's voice asking me to come closer. I've seen the picture shows. I figured if something was begging me to come closer, I ought to do the reverse."

"Clever," said Idris, coughing.

"We heard whispers too," said Alison. "But they weren't in Loegrian or any language I recognized. They were coming from books in the library. Spellbooks. They led us to the passage."

"Hmm," Idris groaned. "Perhaps—some—protective magic—of the college."

"Don't try to speak," said Keir. "Let me have a look."

"Gods, Idris, your neck," said Rinka. "It's red. You were choked?"

"Alison, can you hold the candle up so I can examine him?" asked Keir.

"I'm fine," said Idris. "Just trying to catch my breath." His voice was clearing some with each word, thank the Gods. "Did you find Ceri?"

Alison told him of the path they had found in the library, and Willow told them Ceri's trail had led there as well.

"Let's go," said Idris, stumbling to his feet.

"Perhaps you ought to wait here," said Keir. "I see no immediate signs of damage, but some of them can take hours to appear."

Idris gave him a look that told him there was zero chance of that happening with Ceri still out there.

"Let's take the shortcut at least," said Alison. "The passage in your closet should take us right back there."

Truthfully, Alison would have liked to have sat down herself. She and Keir had used an extraordinary amount of magic to free Idris, and she could see that Keir was feeling it as well.

Rinka, on the other hand, looked great. "Maybe there's something to this conduit thing," she said cheerily. "You lot burn yourselves out, and I reap all the rewards."

"Where did you get that axe?" asked Idris.

"In the hallway. 'In case of emergency,' it said. It seemed like an emergency."

Alison and Keir led them into the secret passageway. It sloped gently down, the walls stone on one side, wood on the other.

"These walls are false," said Keir, tapping on the internal wooden walls. "Built during one of the conversions. Weldan House has some passages like this for the servants."

"I always dreamed about using a secret passage," said Rinka. "I had hoped it would be under better circumstances though. Listening to the ladies gossip at lunch. Sneaking away in the night to meet a secret caller."

"You hardly have to sneak," said Idris, "but if you wanted to give that a go once this is all over…"

"I liked him better when the ghost had him," said Willow.

"It wasn't a ghost," said Idris. "It's some aspect of whoever originated these curses though."

"Take it easy," said Rinka, helping him as he stumbled. "I don't want to have to drag you out of here."

"But I'd like that," said Idris.

At least they were going downhill.

Finally, they made it back into the library. The hidden door was still open, and the mess of books looked undisturbed.

"What happened in here?" asked Rinka. "That Ms. Redclaw is going to be furious."

"It was defending itself," said Idris.

"Oh, the library," said Alison as she realized what Idris meant. "All these books—it was defending itself from something."

"I smell Leo here," said Willow. "Ceri too. Both of them recently."

"Don't tell me they went outside," said Idris.

Lightning flashed through the windows. The door where the path in the books had led definitely went outside.

"It's dangerous out there," said Keir. "The lightning alone—"

"I'll go," said Idris. "Dragon blood. It's strong."

"Not a chance," said Rinka. "What will you do if they're in trouble when you find them? All of you are dead on your feet. I'll go."

"No," said Idris. "Keir, stop her…"

It turned out they didn't need to argue. Just then, the door burst open.

Ceri stepped through, soaked to the bone.

"He's gone," she said. "Leo is gone."

Chapter Seventeen

IN THE EYE OF THE STORM

Ceri

“Gone, how?” Alison dared to ask. Ceri could see that the others were thinking it.

“Not dead. Gone. I saw it with my own eyes,” said Ceri. “He was there in the center of the courtyard. I didn’t see him at first—the lights went out, and it’s so dark out there. But the lightning flashed and I—”

She choked up. “He can’t be gone, can he? It’s not right.”

Rinka came up to her and put her arm around her shoulder. Ceri loved Rinka. She was what she imagined having a sister would be like.

“Should we go out there, Ceri? Does he need help?” asked Keir.

“No,” said Ceri. “Don’t go out there. He’s not there, I’m telling you. He’s not there!”

"Let's get you back to the dining hall and into some dry clothes, and we can talk about it," said Rinka.

"Oh," said Ceri. She removed Rinka's arm for a moment and concentrated on the water soaking her school uniform, her hair, her body. There was a lot of it, far more than the contents of the coffee up that she'd picked up right here in the library.

Leo's tea coffee.

She sobbed, and then added those tears to the floating ball of water.

"You've been practicing," said Idris, awed.

Ceri opened the door, flung the water outside with her magic, and slammed it shut again.

"What happened to you?" Ceri asked him. He looked like death.

"Let's wait to go over all of that when we get back to the others," said Alison. "I'm not sure what could be listening. Ceri, none of us have much energy left for magic after to-night. If something happens—"

"I got it," said Ceri. "Did you all come looking for me?"

"Yes," said Idris. "Lady Sibba and Weyland as well. Has anyone seen them?"

"No," said Willow. "I could smell them in the hall though. It seemed like they went to the dorms as planned."

"Should we go and find them? What if they had a similar encounter to ours?" asked Alison.

"Let's check the dining hall first," said Keir. "It's closer."

"There's a professor that practices some form of witch-craft," said Idris. "Maybe she can help if they need it."

Ceri felt bad about putting all of these people in danger chasing after Leo only to…to…

"Hold on, princess," said Rinka as Ceri cried, putting her arm around her again. "It'll be alright. We'll figure it out."

Ceri really wanted to believe her.

They traced the path back through the books—Ceri had to be stopped from trying to put them back on the shelves in order to save her energy in case it was needed—and returned to the dining hall, to the immense relief of Dean Whittaker.

"Oh, you're back! You're all back!" said the Dean. Lady Sibba rushed over with Weyland close behind.

"What happened to you?" asked Lady Sibba. "Was it the blood? Did you see it too? Oh, hello, princess. Glad you're alright."

"Where's Leo?" said Professor Marin. "Did you find him?"

"Can we have a place to sit down?" asked Idris.

"Of course, of course," said Dean Whittaker. He directed Weyland to the stacked dining room chairs and benches. He and Rinka arranged them in a circle in a far corner of the room.

"Let's start with Ceri," said Idris. "Tell us what happened to Leo."

"I went to your office first. I thought he might have gone there for his objects, but the door was locked. I opened it anyway, just in case he'd locked it back from the inside. But no one was in there. Your closet was unlocked, and I could see he had taken them back, so I thought I'd try the library."

"The objects?" asked Dean Whittaker.

Idris and Professor Marin filled him in on Leo's research and Idris's confiscation.

"Too right you were," said Dean Whittaker. "I must say, I'm not familiar with the accepted methods of storage myself. If you wouldn't mind educating me—"

"Another time," said Idris, gesturing to Ceri.

"Why did you try there first?" asked Rinka.

"Leo said the library hated him but that it hadn't always done so. I thought maybe it was the objects the library hated, not him. I mentioned that to him, and he seemed interested in the theory."

"So you thought he was going there to test it out," said Alison.

"I thought he was going to measure the objects in the storm primarily—it's a rare event, absolutely the kind of thing he'd want to know about—but if he had the opportunity to take other measurements along the way, I guessed he'd take it. And when I got to the library, I could see I was right."

"The fallen books," said Alison. "The library was defending itself against the objects."

"I think so," said Ceri.

"By the way, we'll come and help Ms. Redclaw clean up in the morning," Idris told Dean Whittaker. "Just as soon as I get my magic back."

"Yes, you'd better," said Dean Whittaker. "Or I'll never hear the end of it."

"So you followed the trail of fallen books through the library…" said Alison.

"Yes, I cleared a path. I reached the door and went outside."

"Outside? Into the storm? Oh, Gods, King Derkomai will have my head! But how? You're bone dry," said Dean Whittaker.

By way of explanation, Ceri lifted a mug with her magic from a nearby table, picked up the contents in it, and dropped them back into the mug again.

"Right, right, of course," said Dean Whittaker. "Forgive me, your highness. Please continue."

"It was hard to see in the courtyard on account of the rain, and then the lights went out, and I couldn't see anything. But when the lightning flashed, I saw him there in the middle of the courtyard. He had something in each hand—I couldn't see what they were, but I'd guess his magimeter and one of the objects. And then—"

She choked on a sob.

Rinka reached across the circle and squeezed her hand.

"The lightning struck him."

"Oh!" Professor Marin cried out. Alison took her hand—it was ice cold.

"I've never seen anything like it. It was a terrible flash, blindingly bright, so close I could feel it. The thunder happened at the same time and sent a gust of wind through the courtyard, even more than the storm. I could smell it in the air. I couldn't see him. I couldn't see anything. I ran out into the courtyard."

"You did what?" said Idris. "Are you insane?"

"Idris," said Rinka.

"Don't yell at me!" said Ceri. "Lightning can't strike the same place twice. I was safe."

Several people tried to speak at once.

"No, it definitely can."

"It absolutely does all the time."

"It hits our old building in Arcas Dyrne like five times a year."

"It's never, ever safe to go outside during a thunderstorm."

"Okay, okay, I get it!" said Ceri. "I get it. I didn't get struck, okay? I'm fine."

Ceri rolled her eyes. She needed friends her own age who weren't such know-it-alls. She looked across the room at where Ana was laying down.

"Hold on," she said.

She crossed the room to Ana. A few people whispered—she guessed the word had gotten out that she was missing.

"Ana?"

"Oh, you're okay! Thank goodness. Where's Leo?"

Ceri shook her head. "I—do you want to hear the story? I'm telling it now."

"Okay," said Ana, following her back to the circle.

"I ran out into the courtyard. The rain was pouring so hard that it hurt. It's like it was raining sideways. I got to the spot where Leo should have been. I could just see the scorch marks on the ground. But he wasn't there."

"What do you mean, 'wasn't there'?" asked Idris.

"I mean he wasn't there. Alive or not. No Leo. No nothing."

This last part wasn't strictly true. There was something there, something tucked into the waistband of Ceri's skirt. Something she had hidden when she'd dried her clothes.

Leo's journal.

If Ceri mentioned it right now, they'd make her hand it over. They'd go through it together, or they'd take turns reading out loud from it or something equally mortifying.

And Ceri needed to know what was in it first. She'd hand it over to them, but not before checking for…well, she wasn't sure what.

She knew what she'd write if she kept a journal.

It was the reason she didn't.

"Perhaps it was some kind of magic?" asked Keir.

"I don't understand," said Alison. "That's not how magic works, not to my understanding of it anyway. When we were trapped in the vine's world, our bodies were still in this one. We know it because we found Aras's body."

"That was one kind of magic," said Keir. "But we've seen others. What was that book you found when you found the secret passage?"

"Secret passage?" said the Dean and Ana at almost the same time.

Alison explained about the passage between the library and Idris's closet.

"The book was something about portals and doorways, but it wasn't a real book. I think it was just a joke by whoever made the passage. I don't think portals are real. Are they, Idris?"

"Not to my knowledge, although I wouldn't be surprised, to be honest. It would have to be extremely powerful magic though, to move objects through the physical realm."

"You think he went somewhere?" asked Ceri.

Ceri hadn't thought he was dead initially, but once she'd retold the story, she couldn't really see how he could have survived such a thing.

"Lightning doesn't disintegrate," said Professor Marin. "If it happened as you said, his body should still be there. He may have even survived it. The strike in the lab was nowhere near as strong, but this doesn't sound like ordinary lightning either."

"The strike in the lab?" asked Dean Whittaker.

This time, no one answered him.

"It's not there," said Ceri. "I'm certain."

"Could he have run somewhere in the dark?" asked Rinka.

"I would have heard it. I was close. I was almost to him when it happened."

"We'll set up a search as soon as the storm has cleared," said Dean Whittaker. "I can't risk anyone else until then."

"It sounds like it's slowing down out there," said Weyland. "Maybe we could take a look around—"

"Absolutely not," said Lady Sibba. "This is the eye of the storm. We're only halfway through."

"As soon as the storm clears," repeated Rinka. "Okay, Ceri? If he's here, we'll find him."

Ceri saw Alison and Keir exchange a look. "What?" she asked them.

"Nothing," said Alison. "Just that if it's like what happened to us in the spring, it may not be easy to find him. Or to get him back."

"I think it's likely very similar to what happened to you in the spring," said Idris. "He took two other cursed objects from my storage in addition to his own. One is a ring that makes nightmares into a reality."

"That doesn't sound ideal," said Alison. "What's the other?"

"A watch, but I'm not sure of its power," said Idris. "I've taken it out a few times to examine it. I could feel the magic on it, but it had no discernible effect. I'm not sure why he took it."

"His magimeter," said Ceri. "It would have read high on it. That's why he's taken it."

Ceri was surprised Leo had taken things that weren't his, but she was sure that he was only borrowing them. He probably thought Idris wouldn't even know they were gone.

"You didn't see anything on the ground near him? None of the objects?"

"Nothing," lied Ceri, once again omitting the notebook. "But it was dark and pouring with rain. The wind was so strong I could barely walk."

"We'll check in the morning," said Idris. "Did the lightning strike happen just before you went inside?"

"Yes," said Ceri.

"The things that happened to the rest of us tonight. If it's like Ceri said, that may be over, at least," said Idris.

"Are you sure?" asked Alison. "I don't sense anything here, but I'm so drained of magic, I'm not sure I would."

"No, I'm definitely not sure. Dean Whittaker, while we discuss the other goings on tonight, would you find us anyone in the room who feels comfortable practicing magic? Witches or sorcerers or healers. Any magic practitioners of any kind. There may be a threat to the school, but none of us are in any condition to help."

Dean Whittaker rose awkwardly, making his chair squeak on the wooden floor. "Of course. A threat, you say? You know what? Don't tell me yet. Let me go find some help first."

Dean Whittaker looked shaken, to say the least.

"I'll go with him," said Professor Marin.

"Some tea would be nice, too," said Idris.

Ceri rolled her eyes.

"Now then," said Idris. "Who wants to go first?"

⚜

After hearing all the horrible stories about what Idris and his friends had been through that evening to find her, Ceri felt even worse about everything.

"I can't believe I was so foolish," whispered Ceri to Ana when they lay down on their makeshift beds later that night. "I should have just told them where I was going. Maybe if Idris was there, he could have stopped Leo."

This was a big admission for Ceri and something she never would have told Idris himself. But she trusted Ana to keep her secrets.

"I can't believe all of that stuff happened here," said Ana. "I know I have a bit of magic in me on my dad's side at least.

Would you be willing to teach me some? Once we find Leo, of course."

Ceri liked that Ana was certain they'd find Leo. Everyone was, in fact. Listening to the rain beat against the roof and the boarded-up windows, she just hoped that wherever he was, he was safe.

Ceri waited for Ana to fall asleep and then slipped away, carefully stepping around the beds and tables, heading for the toilets.

The lights were still out, but Ceri had taken Alison's candle, which she had left behind after their meeting. She lit it with her magic and headed into a stall, pulling the door shut behind her.

She carefully balanced the candle on the floor, pulled out the journal, and began to read.

Journal of Leorias of Gallia, Doctoral Candidate in 'Lectrics Summer–Autumn, Year Three

If found, please return to Professor Marin's Laboratory

Ceri snapped the journal shut again. Could she do this? Ceri knew that he recorded the numbers in the journal when he took his measurements, but did it contain any of his private thoughts as well? She assumed so; it's why she didn't mention it yet to the others. And if there was anything in there about her, she wanted the chance to read it first.

But to do that, she needed to actually read it. It felt like a violation.

It was also really, extremely tempting.

They had only known each other for a couple of weeks. There was a decent chance she wasn't mentioned at all.

But if she was mentioned, what did he say about her? Would he have written anything about the night they met? The night they watched the shooting stars?

Would he have written about that moment when he looked at her before she sat up and ruined it?

She thought about that moment. A lot.

Or what about the things he'd said he liked about her?

She wanted to know.

But that wasn't the reason she was going to read it. She needed to read it because he might have mentioned what his plan was tonight, and it might be the key to finding out where he had gone.

And if she found out anything else incidentally, well, that couldn't really be helped, could it?

Ceri opened the journal again, this time flipping through pages until she found the last entry.

Friday, Day 5 of Autumn Term

The items were reacquired from PI's storage with minimal effort, but I was forced to leave prior to cleaning up the mess. Here's hoping he doesn't check his storage prior to joining the others in the dining hall.

The dining hall matter poses some concern, but there will likely be too many people to do a thorough accounting. I have no means of preventing my discovery other than hiding until the storm begins in earnest. It would be

*ideal to take all measurements in the exact same loca-
tion, but I'll have to assume that some taken in the
cloister won't impact the numbers too greatly.*

*I remain convinced that the exact center of the court-
yard has some degree of impact on the readings,
especially considering the final reading from the horn
prior to its confiscation.*

*I have considered bringing LBB into this plan. She
would no doubt be of use. But as there is some degree of
hazard from the storm conditions, I cannot risk it. She
is—*

There were lines marked out here. Ceri pondered the ac-
ronyms as she tried to read the struck text: PI was clearly
Prince Idris, but who was LBB? She could think of no one
at the university with those initials. Lady Blue Blood? Lady
SiBBa? Little Book Brat?

Did he mean her?

She squinted and tilted the text at all angles, trying to
make it out.

*extr——ary. All plans — her front have failed,
mise—. She can— be —ided. The feel— —not be rea-
soned —. She is inevi—le.*

"Godsdammit," she muttered. Perhaps once she'd read
some of the other entries, she'd know his handwriting well
enough to make better sense of it.

One additional note: as I searched for my objects in PI's storage, I found two other items of interest. The first gave average to below average readings with the magimeter; see table above as "Ring—Sapphire." The second, however, gave the highest readings I have ever seen from any object, including the horn. See "Watch—Gold." I would have liked to ask PI permission to study these items in particular, but I did not feel it would be granted in time for this unprecedented event. As the conditions cannot be replicated later, after I have convinced PI of my intentions, I have borrowed them temporarily without permission.

It weighs on my conscience to do so, but with any luck, I'll be able to return them before he even realizes they're gone. This, I know, is a considerable risk. Should I fail in this endeavor, PI will likely be hostile towards me for the foreseeable future. This could pose a problem if—

More scratched-out text, this time so thoroughly inked over that it had bled through to the next page.

Well, so far this hadn't told her anything she hadn't already known. And if there was anything of a personal nature regarding herself or LBB, or whether they were one and the same, it hadn't been revealed in this entry.

She flipped back through the pages, noting a number of mentions of "LBB" in most of them.

She might as well start back at the beginning.

Chapter Eighteen

LBB

Leo

Leo had planned on being better prepared on the day of the meteor shower, but something—someone—had crashed into his life and derailed everything.

Having passed his qualifying exams during spring term, he had finally been given the right to start his own research rather than simply teaching tutorials and assisting Professor Marin with hers. He had spent the entire summer cataloging and measuring the enchanted objects he'd managed to obtain, fighting with the library over the books he needed, performing tedious calculations by hand, and then repeating the entire thing again the next day.

It had been glorious.

There was hardly anyone on campus. This was part of why Leo had chosen 'Lectrics in the first place; it was one of the few concentrations not located on the main campus in

Norgate. Leo valued the peace and quiet, having never experienced it for himself before leaving his parents' village. And considering his desire to study magic, these ancient buildings felt like a more appropriate setting than the new construction in town. There was magic in the history of a place, in ancient echoes and forgotten secrets.

It was his: not for the taking, but for the understanding. He sought not to control what he found, merely to observe it. To measure it. Record it. To learn about the principles that made it work.

Then, perhaps, he'd find a way to put those principles to use, but such endeavors, as important as they were to Professor Marin, truthfully mattered little to him.

The quest for knowledge was pure. It was perhaps the only pure thing in this world.

Leo had been in the library again, this time reading historic and religious records of "miracles" and "supernatural events" that happened during meteor showers, when the 'lectrics had gone out.

It wasn't a particularly unusual occurrence, although Ms. Redclaw's absurd overreaction each time it happened made it seem as though it was. Professor Marin had offered to come take a look at the library's circuits—at night, of course—after Leo himself had failed to identify a problem. (The breaker box had zapped him for his effort, despite the fact that he'd cut power to the main breaker before doing anything else.)

But she hadn't had the opportunity to do so yet, on account of being busy making arrangements for this solar project that was undoubtedly going to take away from Leo's time for his research. He tried not to interrupt her too often; doing so resulted in taking on responsibility for some tiresome task or other related to the accommodations of the visiting entrepreneurs.

He'd decided to give it up and take the books with him, which annoyed Ms. Redclaw because books he borrowed had a peculiar habit of going missing before he could return them, only to show up later at the door of the library as if they were cats asking to be let back in, and he figured he'd hit the light switch on the way out in case it decided to work this time, when—*BAM!*

There she was.

Leo didn't hit his head when they collided, but it felt like he had.

She was…stunning, and not just in the literal sense.

Growing up surrounded by his nearly infinite number of siblings and his parents' companions had left Leo with little room or privacy to consider matters of the heart. There had been a woman or two during his undergraduate years, Loegrians that had found his accent and foreign sensibilities charming, but they had moved on to pursue their research with nearly the same fervor as he himself possessed.

That was the trouble with other academics. The pursuit of knowledge was often a lonely and consuming quest, and if two people were on different ones at the same time? Well, there was little to tie them together.

Leo's immediate interest in Ceri was not purely academic. It was not pure at all.

He had been ashamed of the impulse, the lust that practically knocked him off his feet again as he saw her more clearly through his spectacles.

Gods, had she seen it? Could she see it on his face?

His heart had pounded so hard in his chest he'd felt like it might explode. Could she hear it?

He felt ridiculous. He felt out of control. He had come completely unmoored from his careful, meticulous existence in one single moment.

He spent the next several minutes doing his best to hide it. Going along with her obvious lie about her name, trying to focus on why whatever he was feeling was a bad, bad idea that needed to be put down before it consumed him.

She was too young. That was the key. He was sixty-six, and she was—what, eighteen? Nineteen, maybe?

Of course, eighteen for a human was quite different from eighteen for an elf. At eighteen, Leo had just been learning to read. The age of majority for elves was sixty, and relative aging slowed down even further past that threshold. There were tables comparing developmental milestones he could consult. Or there was always that formula his parents used: a fifth of your age plus seven prior to age 111, then a sixth of your age plus eleven prior to age 222, and on and on.

No. He was supposed to be coming up with reasons this was a bad idea, not rationalizing it.

Then she'd given him the answer herself: she was a princess. The princess of this very country, the country he'd hoped to make his home.

Well, that was taken care of. There was simply no possible way a Gallic son of elves so eccentric that their noble status wasn't even certain among the elvish courts could possibly be a match for a Loegrian princess, not even a temporary one.

Problem solved. Crisis averted. Reason had, once again, won out, just as it was always meant to.

And then she had showed him her magic.

Oh, Gods, he was done for. How could he possibly stay away from her when she was capable of *that*? It would be unthinkable. It would be academic negligence to ignore such an avenue of inquiry.

No, he had to find a way to study her. He couldn't let such an opportunity pass him by—not just magic, but dragon magic, forbidden magic that she practiced in secret, in quiet moments alone in her room—*no, stop it; don't think of her alone in her room.*

Merde.

She walked away from him, cleaning up the mess he'd made (how humiliating), and he began scribbling down everything that had happened in his journal:

Friday, 9 days before Autumn Term
Entry 2

Managed to find book, but library 'lectrics on the blitz again. Collision on the way out. A young woman of extraordinary magical ability—could be fascinating to measure. Strong, near-effortless grasp of magic.

He paused. He didn't want to include too much information about her or anything identifying in case he ended up publishing extracts from the journal at a later date. He typically used initials when describing people: hers would be PC, he supposed, for Princess Ceridwen.

But that didn't feel right. He didn't allow himself to journal his thoughts and feelings; he was trying to be objective as a researcher, after all. But he thought if he didn't put something down on the page that acknowledged what he felt, he might go crazy and try to express it some other way.

Hereafter "LBB." Will ask LBB if I can take some measurements.

LBB: lovely beyond belief. It was the first thing that came to his mind.

Chapter Nineteen

RIPPED PAGES

Ceri

Ceri was growing increasingly frustrated with this journal.

She had gone all the way back to the beginning, but the entries over the summer had been inscrutable. It was all tedious observations about the objects and more numbers and calculations than seemed strictly sane. The script was incredibly neat, but that was about the only thing that kept if from looking like the ravings of a madman.

She finally found the first mention of LBB on the day of their library collision. It was definitely her, then.

But infuriatingly, there was no explanation for the initialism.

What could it possibly mean? Lonely Book Boy? No, she was a girl. 'Lectric Back Burner? What did that even mean?

And then there were strange calculations in the margins. In all the other pages, the calculations were done in line, generally with explanations of their reasoning and meaning.

But here they stood alone. Far simpler calculations without all the strange symbols Ceri didn't recognize:

$$66/5 + 7 = 20.2$$
$$66/6 + 11 = 22$$
$$66/3 = 22$$
$$66 - 50 + 7 = 23$$

There were "X"s next to each equation.

Did that relate to her in some way? Was this part of some kind of code, tied to the Gallic alphabet or something? Oh, what if LBB was Gallic? *Le Beurre Blanc*? Why didn't she pay better attention to her Gallic tutor?

She was losing it.

"Ceri, are you in here?"

Ceri snapped the journal shut, hoping Ana hadn't heard it.

"Ana?"

"Yeah, it's me. I woke up and saw you weren't there. I figured I'd try to find you before they sent out the search and rescue team again."

"I'm okay," she said. She hoped no one else had noticed she was gone yet. "Just a little indigestion. I'll be out soon."

Godsdammit, she was lying again.

"Oh, I'm so sorry. I'll leave you to it," said Ana.

Ceri heard the door swing shut.

She opened the journal again. She had made it to the night of the meteor shower.

Her pulse raced as she read.

Friday, 9 days before Autumn Term
Entry 3

I've just returned from one of the most remarkable experiences of my life. But hold on. I'm getting ahead of myself.

LBB agreed to assist me with my research this very evening. I couldn't believe my luck—to be able to record observations not just of the enchanted objects, but of a magic wielder themselves on the same night? I couldn't have asked for more.

The night, however, was almost over before it began by two separate circumstances of objects nearly falling on me. That makes twelve total over the summer. I'd say we've gone from strange coincidence to unmistakable pattern at this point. After some trial and error, I seem to have narrowed the culprit down to either the doll or the locket. I haven't been able to identify any pattern in the falling objects themselves, nor can I make any determination about how or why the objects fall, just that they seem to invariably do so on days where I've interacted with the doll, the locket, or both.

The second circumstance afforded a rare opportunity: LBB saved me (and perhaps herself) with her magic. Oh, but if I could have measured it! The force of it was astonishing. The branch practically disintegrated when she sent it careening from us.

(Of course, the danger to LBB was unforgivable. I must be careful to avoid handling the doll or locket in her presence or when her presence is anticipated. The idea that something could happen to her on my behalf? No research is worth such a cost.)

When we reached the observatory, I had expected to be most excited about the meteor shower or measuring the objects, but the promise of LBB—the potential of her power, of course—was on my mind more than anything else. I must have said something clumsy to her because she took off, quite literally! I'd heard of the Loegrian monarchs, of course. (Who hadn't heard tales of the dragons of Loegria's court?) But to see it in the flesh? I'm convinced if Gallia had been ruled by dragons rather than elves, the monarchy would not have been abolished at all. No one would have dared defy such power.

She returned to me with little explanation, but knowing myself, I was not owed much of one.

That stung to read. She hated that he felt he was at fault for her little outburst. She would have to find a way to apologize for it once they found him.

I began to realize my error as I set out the blanket. I had planned to make my observations alone, and with no time to secure more materials, I had to make do with what I had on hand. The blanket was far too small for us both. I should have offered it to her, but I didn't. I know why I didn't—no need to document that here.

"Yes, you did need to document it here!" Ceri muttered. "Stupid elf."

We took the initial measurements per the table above. Note how high the reading is for even such a small bit of spellwork. Perhaps the trick to the enchantments is that they are sustained by a low level of magic over a great period of time.

The entry went on about his magic theory for some time. Ceri skimmed ahead.

When we went to lie down on the blanket, well. How should I put it? As a student of 'Lectrics, I feel equipped to say there was a spark between us. Perhaps it was merely the camaraderie of doing important work together. Despite my efforts to be objective, research can bring out a great deal of emotion in me. I undoubtedly read too much into that moment—

He hadn't.

—but it had quite the impact on me. It is difficult to describe LBB.

Here it was. Ceri's heart was in her throat.

She's clearly brilliant. Even without undergraduate studies, she already has a firm grasp of experimental methods. I imagine if she went into research, she would be a force to be reckoned with.

And the name I have given her. The abbreviation which I dare not reveal here. It is apt.

The next few phrases were marked out, but poorly. Ceri could make out every word.

She is perfect, starlit and stunning. A miracle.

Ceri could barely breathe. This was the first day they met. She had felt the attraction—there, she admitted it. She had hoped he returned it—there, another truth. She had lied to herself in the moment, but she knew.

But to read it here in his own words? It was a degree of intimacy she had never shared with someone.

She hoped he would forgive her for this violation. Because she knew right then she was going to read every word in the rest of the journal.

And she hoped he'd forgive her for what she had to do next.

Ceri ripped the page from the journal. It was simply too revealing. If it had been her journal, she would have wanted him to do the same before showing it to the others.

She hoped he'd understand.

She folded the page and placed it into the pocket of her skirt for safekeeping.

Then she read on.

There were four more folded pages in her pocket by the time she reached the end of the journal. The afternoon when he'd given her the egg tarts, the same night after he'd been 'lectrocuted, and two other moments in the laboratory that Ceri hadn't even noticed but that Leo described in a level of detail that was charged, no pun intended.

It took everything she had not to pull the pages back out and reread them immediately.

The candle was burning low by the time she'd finished. She must have been in here for an hour or more. She hoped Ana had gone back to sleep.

As she flipped the journal closed, something caught her attention on the last page.

It couldn't be. Could it?

Friday? Day 5? of Autumn Term
Entry 2

Ceri looked at the first entry she had read earlier; the most recent one in the journal. It was still there on the page before, but how could she have missed this one?

She scanned through the words, and then something remarkable happened.

A new line appeared at the bottom of the text in his own hand.

Leo was alive, and wherever he was, he was writing in this very journal right now.

Chapter Twenty

ANOTHER PLACE—OR TIME

Leo

Leo stood in the center of the High House courtyard just as he had moments before the lightning struck. Well, not quite exactly as he had. There were some minor differences.

For one, it was no longer storming. The sky was perfectly clear, the air was dry and slightly chilly, and the wind that had nearly knocked him over moments earlier had calmed to a gentle autumn breeze.

For another, it was no longer night. The sun was almost directly overhead, in fact.

Leo pinched his left forearm. He didn't know if it would provide a definitive answer as to whether he was sleeping or not, but it was what people always seemed to do in books in these situations.

"Ow!" he said. Nope, likely not sleeping.

Perhaps dead, then? It seemed possible. The last thing he remembered was being struck by lightning, after all.

Although he wasn't struck directly. It was the watch that had been struck. It was there on the ground in front of him, its glass casing cracked and blackened, with branches of burnt grass stretching out beneath it in all directions.

All of the objects were there, in fact, exactly where he'd left them, and the magimeter and his journal as well. At least there was that. Whatever was going on, he'd be able to write it down.

Leo reached in his breast pocket for his fountain pen, but it wasn't there.

Perhaps he truly was dead then, and this was hell. What could be worse than experiencing some kind of magical event with no way to properly record his observations?

Leo gathered the objects together and returned them to his satchel for safekeeping. The first order of business was finding a pen. If he could write down what was happening, perhaps he could make some sense of it.

Leo crossed the courtyard towards the library entrance. He glanced back at the Norminster Yew—that was strange. The iron fence Groundskeeper Tomasar had erected around the base was missing. Not knocked over in the storm, missing entirely.

An observation worth noting, definitely, once he had his pen.

The library was empty, which wasn't entirely unexpected. The entirety of the student body had been within the dining hall and was likely still there, although it was strange that no one was out cleaning up after the storm.

Not that there was anything to clean up. The only evidence the storm had come at all had been the lightning burns on the grass.

In fact, the ground hadn't even been wet, had it? The objects were, but the journal was dry.

Oh, all the observations and nothing to write them with! Torment. Genuine torment.

Leo braced himself for the library's customary greeting—a smack to the head from one of its many tomes—but it didn't come.

"In a good mood today, are you?" he asked.

The library did not reply.

All the better. Perhaps he could use this space unbruised, for once.

He spotted a pen lying on an empty table. It was one of the college's standard issue models, nothing that would be missed.

Finally.

He took a seat at one of the tables meant for studying, placing the bag on its surface where the objects within it rattled and clanged.

He flipped open his notebook and—

The lights went out.

"That's more like it," said Leo to the library. "Nice to see you too."

It was no matter. Although it was too dark within this particular part of the library to write, he could just move to one of the tables near the windows. It was a bright and sunny day, after all.

But when he gathered his things again and stood, his stomach growled. He'd skipped dinner that night during his preparations. He had a notion of going to the dining hall instead. Now that the library had noticed him once more, he'd be better off elsewhere.

And there was something a bit too quiet about this place that was unnerving, if he was being honest.

Of course, the greatest risk was running into Professor Idris. If Idris had already checked his supply closet, he'd be furious with Leo. But that would be true regardless of when Leo ran into him, so he might as well get it over with.

As Leo left the library, something caught his eye in the hallway. It was the statue of the phoenix near the entrance. It was wrong, somehow, but it took Leo a minute to realize what it was.

It had two wings.

Leo had first come to the college six years ago as a fresher. That same year, the statue had been broken, leaving one of its wings shattered on the floor. Dean Whittaker had been distraught, but no one came forward to take credit for the damage. It was all anyone talked about for the better part of a week.

Was it possible? Could he have gone back in time?

And if he had, where was everyone else?

He needed to take some measurements and record his observations quickly, but as his stomach growled even more, he knew he'd be better off if he ate while doing so.

He hurried down the corridor to the dining hall. The 'lectrics flashed as he went by—another odd occurrence.

As Leo had somewhat suspected, the dining hall was not boarded up for the storm or filled with students. The doors were open as if it were an ordinary lunchtime, but there was no one in sight.

The tables were full of food on plates: some half-eaten, others untouched, and some just crumbs. It was as if everyone had vanished at exactly the same moment, leaving things exactly as they were.

Curiouser and curiouser.

Leo found an untouched plate with one of the college's more palatable meals: creamy pasta with mushrooms in a wine-based sauce that suited his sophisticated Gallic tastes, still warm. It could have used more salt, but then, most things could. It was perfect fuel for research.

Leo opened the journal and flipped to his last entry, but as he turned the pages, he noticed something odd.

There were pages missing. Several of them. Crudely torn out, too.

Leo would never have torn pages in that manner. If he'd had to remove pages, he would have employed a ruler and a knife.

But the journal hadn't left his sight. How could that possibly be?

A question for later. First, he must write.

Friday? Day 5? of Autumn Term
Entry 2

What has transpired since my last entry only hours ago is so bizarre that I cannot begin to describe it. Except, of course, that I must, as it is my duty as a researcher. I will record all occurrences, no matter how incongruous, as authentically as I can in the hopes that I may find some manner of explanation hidden between the lines, for none is likely to be apparent to me within them.

As I held the magimeter to the watch, I felt a strange thrum of 'lectricity as if there was great potential between them, and I was serving as a conduit to bridge their divide. Unnerved by it, I placed the watch on the ground and hurried to record the reading in these pages before the rain soaked through them. Then, as had happened quite recently in the laboratory, a great bolt of 'lectricity came, but this time, I was not directly struck. It happened too quickly for me to confirm, but based on the incredible sound and shockwave which sent me flying backwards, I believe it to have been a lightning bolt from the storm.

When I reopened my eyes, which to me felt as though it occurred the very next moment, I observed that it was daylight, with no signs of the storm at all. The objects were with me, as were the magimeter and the journal (obviously), but I was left without my ink pen.

I entered the library in search of a writing implement, but I did not receive my usual greeting. However, after I located what I sought and prepared to write, the lights went out. While this is a common occurrence, the strange disturbances in 'lectrical flow have been observed again in the corridor and even now in the dining hall—

The 'lectrics had flashed twice more since he began writing. After he was done, he ought to go check the panel.

—but this is not the strangest thing that has happened.

No, the strangest thing would have to be the statue of the phoenix, which seems to have grown its wing back. Or the missing fence around the Norminster Yew. Or perhaps it is the peculiar absence of any other people, despite the seeming appearance of there having been people in this very dining room only moments before, judging by the state of the meals.

Or perhaps it is the state in which I've found this journal, with pages torn—

Leo's eyes caught some sort of motion further down the page. It looked like the spreading of an inkblot, although it made little sense as the pen he held was not leaking.

No, not a blot. Letters.

Letters written in a different hand were appearing on the page.

Leo was so startled he nearly threw the journal across the room. His pulse raced as he read each word as it was written.

Leo? Is that you? Are you alright?

Someone else was writing in his journal at the same exact time.

Impossible. Improbable.

Magic.

Leo fought the urge to record it; it was there on the page already, so it was hardly necessary.

It's Ceri. Are you there?

Leo's heart stopped. Well, it didn't stop, but it certainly skipped a beat or two.

Oh Gods, not her. Had Ceri read—no, no, no, no. Oh Gods, she did. She must have.

The sickening realization hit him all at once. Ceri had found his journal, which somehow still existed in the world he came from and in which he very clearly no longer was, and she had read it.

She had been the one to tear out the pages.

He flipped through frantically, piecing together from the pages that remained which entries were missing.

All of the ones that had mentioned her.

No, not all of them. But the ones where he'd…confessed. Where he'd written too much, where he'd had to redact some of his thoughts for the sake of posterity.

Those were the entries that were missing.

This seems silly, and perhaps I have it all wrong, but it seemed like you were writing just a moment ago. I guess I'll keep trying; maybe there's some kind of delay? I found your journal in the courtyard. I saw the flash of lightning and thought it struck you, but you were nowhere to be found. The only thing that was there was the journal.

Leo could not breathe as she wrote. What could he possibly say to her?

I lied to the others and said I found nothing. I wanted to—

The writing paused. The only sound in the room was the relentless beating of Leo's pulse in his ear.

—look it over first. I thought there might be things you wouldn't want everyone to know. Private things. I hope you don't mind that I've removed a few pages that felt—

Another pause. Another terrifying pause. What was she thinking? What had she thought of what she read? Did she expect it? Was she angry? Shocked? Disgusted? She'd removed the pages—that was kind of her. Or maybe it was due to her own humiliation. Maybe he had been entirely too obvious. Maybe she thought she'd spare him, and herself, the embarrassment.

—personal.

Yet another long pause. Waiting was absolutely torture. When he'd nearly given up and brought his pen to paper again, to write *something*, Gods know what, she finally continued:

Were those things true? What you wrote about me? Assuming it was about me. Assuming I'm LBB. Did you mean it?

Leo wanted to crawl under the table and never come out. He wanted to walk back outside and juggle his objects until lightning struck him dead. His ears felt as though they were going to burst into flames. What could he say?

What could he possibly say?

Yes, hello, Ceri. I'm alright.

Great start. Really great.
Positively inspired.

Chapter Twenty-One

MESSAGES BETWEEN WORLDS

Ceri

Ceri had returned to the toilets with a pen she'd found and another candle. There were a few others awake in the dining hall, but as it was still the middle of the night, none of them bothered to check on the princess with apparently serious digestive troubles.

She couldn't believe she had been so bold as to ask him outright if he'd meant what he'd written. It seemed there was little point in denying that she'd read it. From his own words, he could see that the pages had been removed. It seemed like the journal was in the same state between both worlds.

Perhaps she could have played dumb and avoided mentioning the issue altogether. Perhaps she should have.

It was too late now.

She waited on Leo's reply with bated breath.

*First of all, thank you for finding the journal and be-
ing so kind as to think of removing things of a more
personal nature. I suspect that if you hadn't, the entire
thing would have been read in an effort to find me, and
that would have been quite humiliating.*

*It seems as though I'm no longer in the same world
that you're in. If you've read this latest entry, you'll
know that there are things both familiar and unfamiliar
about where I am. However, I don't appear to be in any
immediate danger, which I hope will be a relief to any
of those looking for me or who are concerned with my
welfare.*

*I believe you must let the others know about the jour-
nal. I will do what I can where I am to find a way to
return to where you are, but I'm certain we'll have more
success if more people are able to assist in the research.
From what I recall, some of the entrepreneurs have been
through something of a similar experience. I had hoped
to ask them about it in more detail, and perhaps I'll still
do so when we are reunited.*

He was in good spirits, at least. Ceri couldn't help but
notice that he'd avoided her questions though.

There was a long pause before he began writing again.

*As to whether I meant what I wrote: I am a researcher.
I record in this journal observations, and I'm not in the
habit of lying about what I've observed. There would be
little point in doing so.*

Another torturous pause. Ceri gripped the journal in her hands so hard her wrists began to hurt from the tension.

I don't know how much you were able to read about LBB. I know I scratched out much of it. But what I wrote about LBB—what I wrote about you—I meant it. It was true.

Ceri's chest was tight from holding her breath. She scratched her response in a single word:

Good.

And then she thought of one more thing she needed to know:

LBB?

Lovely beyond belief.

It had been the answer she was hoping for, and also the one she had dreaded. She had come here to start over after a disastrous summer that was truly just the cherry on top of several awful years. She had wanted to change for the better, to focus on her studies and on being a better person and friend. The year had only just begun, and already she was off course.

Wasn't she?

Things had gone very well in her first week of classes. Her first assignments in Loegrian and Numbers had just come back with top marks, although they were more to see what everyone knew coming into the course than anything else. She had made at least one friend (if you didn't count Leo). She hadn't lied to Ana, not except by way of omission in order to spare her feelings, which felt like the right thing to do. And even if it wasn't, she was trying to do the right thing, at least.

She had helped with the research. Leo wasn't the only one who had been impressed with her ability to do so. She had cut back her time in the laboratory since classes began, but she'd gone there at least once a day and spent a couple of hours helping set up experiments or running numbers afterwards.

Isn't that exactly what she hoped to achieve?

She hadn't lied to Leo, either. Well, not after their first encounter, at least. She hadn't tried to manipulate him or guilt him into spending time with her. In fact, it seemed as though his initial feelings for her may have exceeded her own. Or at least they'd exceeded the ones she had been willing to acknowledge.

The truth was, she was scared. It wasn't something she would have confessed to Leo in person, but she doubted any of what they'd just shared would have been shared in person. Perhaps eventually, but likely not for a long time.

There was something freeing about the journal. There was something freeing about the college.

There was something freeing about Leo.

I wanted to say something to you, but I was afraid. I am still afraid. I have been hurt before. And I have done the hurting. And most of it—all of it—was my fault. I'm not a good person, Leo. I pretended to be selfish and cruel because those are the traits my father values. I pretended for so long I became them.

I am a liar. I am manipulative. I am vain. I am petty.

I am trying to be better.

The things you said about me. You meant them, but they aren't true. But I want them to be. I want to be the person you see me as.

And I want to get to know you too. You're brilliant and funny and you are just—

Was she bold enough to say it? Here, crouched in the dark in the toilets alone, writing by candlelight?

—so ludicrously gorgeous. It's unfair.

I will do whatever it takes to get you back here.

I still need to try that tea coffee of yours. I am convinced it will be awful, but I must find out for myself.

She had done it. She had put herself out there for him to take or leave. There were no lies in what she wrote. No trickery or malice. No desire to trap him into a confession for the sake of mockery.

She didn't know if she could do this.

But she wanted to try.

Ceri, I am speechless. Wordless? Is there a Loegrian word for not knowing what to write?

We all have a past. I am not certain if I believe your interpretation of your own. Often, we are our own worst critics. But either way, it does not concern me. From what I know of you, all I know is that I want to know more. Your past, your present, your future. The good and the bad. Whoever you are and will be.

I hope we will have that chance once I return.

P.S. It is simply insane that you, of all people, would call me "ludicrously gorgeous." If I am so to you, I'm certain it's only because you are lucky enough to see me through perhaps the most beautiful eyes in existence.

P.P.S. Tea coffee is divine.

Ceri knew she should probably leave it at that for the night. It was very late, or perhaps very early. The candle was nearly out, and she was exhausted.

And she probably would have, but she realized there were a few more things she should tell him, for the sake of his safety.

Do you have the ring with you that you took from Idris's office? Idris said it's extremely dangerous, especially with your other objects. I'm assuming they're with you. Idris's friends went through some kind of ordeal tonight that seemed to be connected to them or possibly to something in the college. I'm not sure if it would be the same where you are, but

you might want to store the objects if you can, separately, just in case.

It was a long time before Ceri received a response, so long that Ceri worried the candle would burn out.

Funny you should say that. Whatever it is, it's here.
I'm hiding in the toilets.
Tear these pages out and keep them in case they're of use. But please, tell the others about the journal.
Please, I need hel—

The writing stopped right there.

Chapter Twenty-Two

AN EARLY MORNING CONFESSION

Alison

Alison awoke to the sound of Ceri's voice as she shook Idris awake.

"Idris, wake up! I know you can hear me. I need help!"

Alison's neck hurt from the night spent on the floor. It was still dark when she opened her eyes, but it was difficult to tell if that was because it wasn't yet dawn or because the boarded-up windows let in so little light to make it seem like it was still nighttime.

From the sounds on the roof, it was still raining, but it seemed the worst of the lightning and thunder had passed.

"Idris. Please wake up. I lied. I did find something outside, only I was too embarrassed…it doesn't matter. Leo is in trouble."

"What do you mean, trouble? What did you find?" asked Idris groggily.

Alison heard the others stirring around them. She stood up (Gods, her back hurt; she was too old for this) and pulled the pair of them back to the corner they'd occupied earlier, where hopefully they wouldn't disturb the others trying to sleep.

Ceri held something out to Idris. He lit a tiny flame on the end of his fingertip—it looked like he'd slept long enough to get at least some of his magic back—and looked at what she held.

Leo's journal. She was certain Idris would recognize it as well; Leo was never without the thing.

"What does it say?" asked Alison.

"I don't know," said Ceri. "I warned him about what happened to you tonight, and he said something is after him too where he is."

"Where is he?" asked Idris.

"Here. But not here. He said it's like here but different. It's daytime there."

"You're able to communicate with him?" asked Alison.

"Yes, through this. It seems to be the same in both places."

Idris examined the journal. "There are pages missing."

Alison could guess at the meaning behind Ceri's guilty look without her explaining it.

She had removed the pages. Probably because they were about her, which is why she hadn't come forward with the journal immediately.

If Idris also reached the same conclusion, he didn't mention it. "I feel nothing unusual about it," he said. "Nothing which suggests dark magic, at least. If he's there with those objects and the items missing from my closet, he needs to separate them immediately. If he can put them back into their containers, all the better. We may be able to help him decurse some of them, but it will be harder with us here and the objects there."

"I tried to tell him all of that," said Ceri. "He stopped responding. I don't know if he's still there or if he even has the journal." She sat down at the closest table and checked for a response, but there was nothing there.

Idris sat beside her and held the flame nearby so she could see.

"Do you have any idea how to get him back?" Alison asked him.

"Not yet," said Idris. "I'll need to read what he's written about where he is. How was it that you escaped from that vine situation again?"

"Keir had to let me go over the falls. It was how he thought Charlotte had died."

"Some sort of acceptance lesson?"

"Yes, we think so."

Idris turned back to Ceri. "Are there any lessons you know of that he needs to learn? Other than not taking things that don't belong to him or messing with dangerously cursed objects without permission?"

"Most of those objects belong to him. You are the one who took something that didn't belong to you first."

"I took them for safekeeping, and after tonight, perhaps you can see why I did."

"Any response?" asked Alison.

"Nothing yet," said Ceri. She yawned.

"Have you slept at all tonight?" asked Alison.

"No," said Ceri. "How could I?"

"I'll wait to see if Leo responds," said Alison. Ceri looked like she was going to object. "Just for a couple of hours until you've had some rest. I'll wake you if anything happens."

"Promise you'll wake me," she said. "It would be nice to get a little rest. I imagine it's going to be a long day in the library trying to figure this out."

Oh Gods, the library. There was a disaster in there to be addressed before any research could be done at all.

"I promise I'll wake you," said Alison.

Ceri hobbled away, clearly inches from falling asleep where she stood.

"What do you think?" Alison asked Idris once Ceri was gone.

"I think he's in a great deal of danger, wherever he is." He read some of Leo's description of his surroundings over Alison's shoulder.

"The same place but with no people," said Alison. "That does sound like the vine world. We were at the waterfalls near Weldan House. I had never been there before, but it was exactly the same when I visited after. The only people who were there were Keir and me and our neighbor who had gone in by mistake. But we were acting out a specific scene, a memory. It was almost impossible to break free from it. It doesn't seem like that's happening to Leo."

"Maybe, maybe not," said Idris. "He mentions some differences. The statue and the fence. We should ask the dean if he remembers when the statue was broken."

"Or ask Groundskeeper Tomasar about the fence."

"Good luck with that. He always seems to be in a rage whenever I see him."

"Oh, I think he's just grumpy. He has a very cute dog. Even Willow is a fan."

They sat and watched the empty page after Ceri's reply for a couple of minutes.

"You don't have to wait up," said Idris. "It's my sister's…whatever he is to her. I can keep an eye on it. If I had taken more time to teach him about the curses, we might not be in this mess."

Alison had thought Idris had been a bit hard on Leo, but that didn't make this his fault. "I don't think Leo is the type who would have listened even if you'd warned him of the danger. Some lessons you have to learn for yourself. I'll wait up. I'm awake now anyway, and I don't think I can bring myself to get back on that floor."

Idris stretched as he got up. "Tell me about it. I'll admit that I'm curious about Leo's research. My own magic can't be maintained when I'm asleep, and I've spent years researching why that is when clearly many curses endure across lifetimes. I'd give anything for the ability to turn those awful sheets into a bed that would last the night."

"I'd offer to help, but I'm afraid we'll need my powers for the library tomorrow," said Alison.

Idris groaned as he walked away.

Alison was glad she didn't have a sibling.

Chapter Twenty-Three

THE AFTERMATH

Ceri

Ceri awoke to the sound of chairs scraping on the floor. It seemed she had slept longer than she had intended, longer than most of the others, many of whom were already at the tables eating a cold breakfast.

The 'lectrics were still out, then. Ceri looked around the room and spotted Alison at a table. Alison saw her walking over and shook her head.

"Nothing yet," said Alison, handing Ceri back the journal.

"Don't worry," said Rinka. "Idris filled me in. I'm sure he'll start writing again soon."

Ceri wasn't so certain, but there seemed to be little else she could do for him at the moment. She helped the others clear away bedsheets and rearrange the room until Dean

Whittaker rapped his hand on the head table to get every-one's attention.

"I've just received a pigeon from town saying the worst of the storm has passed, but we should expect more rain in the next day or so. So far, there appears to be minimal dam-age to the school. Some broken windows here and in town, some downed trees in the forest, some flooding down in the Quadrangle dormitories. We'll be keeping our Quad friends here for a time while we clean up." He nodded to a table of older students, who looked less than pleased with the news they'd be staying with the freshers for a while longer.

"Unfortunately, our largest problem at the moment, other than the lack of 'lectric power, is the bridge. The sec-ond bridge nearer to High House survived unscathed, but the first bridge has been washed out."

There were quite a few groans and whispers at that news. There was only one road into High House: how were they meant to get into town?

The flagball team was in an uproar. "What about flagball?" Harry Charlton yelled out.

Ceri rolled her eyes.

"Quiet, please," said Dean Whittaker. The room slowly calmed. It was funny how the dean, who often seemed un-assuming and in over his head, could still command respect when he needed to.

"I'm told the engineers are already on site to prepare for the construction of a temporary replacement, but it won't be able to accommodate carriage or motor carriage traffic. The flagball team and anyone else that needs to get into town should be able to take a carriage from the other side once the temporary bridge is installed."

"What about the schoolhouse?" whispered Lady Sibba from a few seats down. "I should have left before the storm arrived. Those kids need me."

Weyland squeezed her hand. "I'm sure we'll find a way to get out of here as soon as we can. If they can get the long-talkers back up, we can call Gwenla and ask her to send a letter to Duncan."

"I could take you," whispered Ceri. "I can get you into town. I can fly, remember?"

"Could you? Even if you could just get us over the river so we can walk the rest of the way, that would be a massive help, princess," said Lady Sibba.

She was right. Ceri could do something no one else in the room could: she could fly. King Derkomai would not have approved of the princess using her dragon form in that way. For Ceri's father, the purpose of becoming the dragon was defense and intimidation. It was to be used to display power to keep the people in line.

But Ceri could help. There was an opportunity here to do what she'd set out to do if she took it. She rose to her feet nervously. Dean Whittaker waited for her to speak.

"I can fly," she said weakly.

"What?" someone called from across the room.

Ceri lifted her head higher. She wasn't standing in the shadow of her father or even her brother anymore. She could make her own decisions about what she wanted to do. And she wanted to help.

"I can fly," she said, her voice carrying across the room. "I can help bring things and people back and forth from town until the bridge is rebuilt."

"Flagball's back, boys! Woo!" yelled Harry.

"Flagball comes *after* anything needed to help in the emergency," said Ceri. She couldn't help herself.

"Oohoo," said Harry. "They said you were spicy. Your wings, your rules, your highness. We're at your command."

"Yes, thank you for the generous offer, your highness," said Dean Whittaker. "I'm happy to put anyone willing to help to good use. We must all come together. High House has stood here for centuries, and we'll do what it takes to preserve it."

"Father would have hated that," said Idris as Ceri sat back down. He was brimming with pride.

"Why didn't Dean Whittaker mention Leo?" Ceri asked him.

"We told him what we knew. There's still going to be a search in a bit before the dean releases everyone back to the dorms; Alison and Keir think there's a chance we'll find his sleeping body somewhere around."

Ceri didn't like thinking of Leo as a "body." She checked the journal again, but the last lines were in her handwriting.

She lowered her voice so that only Idris could hear her. "I need him to be safe, Idris."

"I know," he said. He put his arm around her shoulder, and Ceri sighed, relaxing into his embrace.

It was good to have Idris back, even if he could be a royal pain in the arse.

The dean was true to his word on putting people to work: the flagball team was enlisted to help Groundskeeper Tomasar and the servants remove the boards from the dining hall windows and clear up the shattered glass; students from Professor Marin's classes helped set up the solar prototype and several other test devices in the courtyard to recharge the power-savers; and most of Idris's friends, Ceri included, spent the day cleaning up the library, with Ceri breaking from her task every few minutes to check the journal.

The library was still a disaster by the time they arrived to help, but many of the books had flown their way back onto the shelves themselves.

"Very good, thank you," said Ms. Redclaw as she reached over her wheeled chair to collect a book that seemed to be trying to climb up the sides. "The books like to help at times, but they aren't as meticulous about the order they go in as I'd like. If you wouldn't mind checking the shelves where it looks like they've replaced themselves…"

"Of course," said Alison, turning a book around that had hopped into the shelf spine first. She had collected a stack of books on a nearby table that might help in their search for a way to bring Leo back. Ceri couldn't wait until they could go through them.

With everyone helping, it only took a couple of hours to straighten the library back out. Ms. Redclaw was incredibly grateful, which made Ceri feel a bit guilty because it was at least somewhat her fault that the library was in the condition it was in.

After the library was sorted out, and with no further news from Leo, Rinka asked Groundskeeper Tomasar if they could borrow his dog for the search.

"If he's here, Barney'll find him," he said, giving him a treat. "He needs something to scent. Do you have anything of his?"

Ceri offered Barney a long sniff of the journal.

Willow the cat took a sniff as well. "It's good to refresh my nose. It's not quite as keen as Barney's here, I'll admit. I'm convinced he could speak—"

"Woof!" said Barney.

"—if he wanted to, but every time I try, he does that."

"Keep trying," said Rinka, bending to pet her. "Alison told me that Dinah has two words now."

"Isn't she just so clever? I do miss her."

Ceri followed Rinka and Groundskeeper Tomasar, who followed Willow, who followed Barney, out into the court-yard where Ceri had seen Leo last.

"He's got the scent, at least," said Rinka.

Groundskeeper Tomasar frowned at the browned grass spreading out from the center of the lightning strike.

"Better the turf than the tree, I suppose," he said, tugging his thumbs on the straps of his overalls. "Ol' Norminster lives to see another day. She'll outlive us all."

The yew had lost a limb or two but seemed otherwise unaffected by the storm. It had undoubtedly seen many more like it in its thousands of years.

The storm had succeeded in one thing: sweeping any last remains of the summer firmly away. The air it left behind was much colder, and the leaves on the trees up the mountain were noticeably more yellow, with some red and orange coming through.

Ceri wondered if it was autumn where Leo was.

She checked the journal again (still nothing) and followed the animals as they led to the dormitory door on the other side of the courtyard.

"In here?" asked Tomasar. Barney barked excitedly in reply, his fluffy brown tail wagging.

He was pretty cute, Ceri admitted. She'd never had a pet—King Derkomai felt they were unclean—but she'd admired her Aunt Chloe's various pets from afar. Perhaps when this was all over, she'd get herself a dog. Or a cat, although they seemed less like pets and more like friends.

Not that she minded the idea of making more friends, either.

Ceri smiled a little at the thought. Maybe there was something to what Leo had said about being too hard on herself.

Ceri realized as they moved through the dorm that they were on her hall. The dog stopped in front of her room, asking to be let in.

"Do you know it?" asked Tomasar.

"This is my room," said Ceri.

She unlocked the door. Ana was inside remaking their beds.

"Oh, hello, puppy!" Ana cried, running over to Barney. She swept her pink hair out of her face and let him lick her cheek. "Who's this? Who's a good boy?"

"This is Barney," said Willow.

"Hello, Barney!" said Ana.

"Leo's trail led us here," said Rinka. "Willow, was it recent?"

Rinka shot a glance at Ceri, who blushed. She was asking if Leo had been here before, and he had. But there had been nothing scandalous going on. He had simply walked her back a couple of times when they were in the laboratory late at night.

Of course, those nights also corresponded to some of the folded pages in Ceri's pocket, which perhaps wasn't a coincidence.

"It's recent, but it's odd. I lost it several times on the way. I believe Barney, but I can't smell anything in this room."

Barney had run into the bathroom. He was barking at the sink.

"There's nothing here, buddy," said Tomasar, "but good effort." He gave him a treat. "And a little bit of cheese for you too," he said to Willow.

They checked in the bathtub, under the beds, and in the wardrobe. Leo wasn't small enough to hide anywhere else.

Nothing. And nothing in the journal.

"It was a good idea, though," said Ceri. "Thanks for trying."

"Anytime, your highness," said Tomasar, tipping his cap to Ceri. "C'mon, Barn. We'll come back if you find anything else."

"I think I'm going to get changed while I'm here," said Ceri. "It's getting cold out there, and I've still got to make a few flights this afternoon."

"We'll be in the library," said Rinka. "Did you want me to keep an eye on the journal for you while you're flying?"

"Please," said Ceri. She hated to hand it over, but she couldn't bear the thought of missing him while she was in the air.

Ceri closed the door to the bathroom and leaned over the sink to collect her thoughts.

Where could Leo have gone? Ceri thought through all the stories from last night: the whispers, the fire, the blood, the hands that choked Idris. Could the hands have gotten to him? Or the fire? There was no one where he was to save him.

Could he have died in some other world with no one around and no way of them ever knowing?

Ceri wiped the tears from her eyes and splashed water on her face. If something had happened to him, there was nothing she could do, but she wouldn't give up hope yet.

When Ceri looked into the looking glass, she screamed.

It was Leo.

He was there behind her in the looking glass.

She turned to look, but he was gone. And when she turned back around to check the looking glass again, she saw only her own reflection.

"What's wrong?" asked Ana. "Are you okay in there?"

"I saw him," said Ceri. "He was there in the glass. Just behind me."

Ana looked skeptical. "Are you sure? I don't see how anyone could have gotten in here. We checked, remember?" She started checking again, just in case.

"I don't think he's here, not in this world. But I think he's here in his. Maybe Barney could smell him somehow."

Ceri looked away from the looking glass and looked back.

Nothing.

She ran to her bed and checked the journal again.

Nothing.

She grabbed the clothes she'd planned to change into and brought them into the bathroom.

Ana shut the bathroom door to give Ceri some privacy.

Ceri slowly undressed in front of the looking glass. If he was here, surely he'd have to respond to this particular action.

She stripped down to her undergarments. "They're Gallic," she said, teasing the strap of her brassiere.

Oh, dear. She'd gone insane.

She felt like a fool doing a provocative dance for no one into her looking glass.

Ceri redressed, putting on her warmer stockings and jumper. "I'm going to have to fly around in my school uniform again," she muttered to the looking glass. "And that's not half as absurd as talking to a damn mirror."

As Ceri left the bathroom, she swore she saw another glimpse of him smirking in the looking glass.

But by the time she'd turned back to check, there was nothing there.

❦

Ceri flew across the roaring river at least a dozen times, sometimes carrying supplies ('lectrical equipment, medicine, and several heavy buckets of anchors for the upcoming installation of the temporary bridge) and sometimes carrying people, who were generally terrified by the experience.

The last of the people to leave for the day were Weyland and Lady Sibba. Weyland was so large Ceri nearly dropped him into the rushing waters; he looked thoroughly shaken as Ceri deposited him on the other side. Lady Sibba, on the other hand, was one of the few passengers of the day that had enjoyed the ride.

"I would do that again," called Lady Sibba over the rushing water. The rest of the group had come out to say their goodbyes. "If you'd have me, of course, Ceri."

Ceri, still in her dragon form, knelt forward and bowed.

Lady Sibba squealed with delight.

"I hope you find him soon," said Lady Sibba. "I'm sorry we can't stay."

"We'll send a pigeon when we get to Gwenla," said Weyland.

Weyland and Lady Sibba were taking with them the latest schematics for the prototype and the power-saver. They still weren't perfect, but they were close enough to begin production. Hopefully, once the 'lectrics were restored to High House, they could finish the testing.

Although it would be difficult without Leo.

"Good luck!" said Lady Sibba as they were on their way.

Ceri took off for the final flight over the river for the evening. She soared high up into the air, taking in the damage.

There was a path of destruction through the woods that looked as though a giant had rolled down the mountain, toppling every tree in its path. It had narrowly avoided High

House—they'd gotten lucky. A force strong enough to fell that many trees would have done a lot of damage to the school.

The town below had been lucky too, apart from the slowly receding waters of the river.

The breeze up high was cool and dry as Ceri flew, the last of the rain finally having moved on. It was such a beautiful afternoon, she considered making a few laps around the mountain. Maybe she'd stop at the observatory and—

"Ceri! Ceri, it's Leo. He's writing!"

The pinprick that was Rinka was shouting far below.

Ceri dove.

She changed back the moment she hit the ground and grabbed the journal from Rinka's outstretched hands.

"I'm never going to get used to that," said Rinka.

Ceri didn't hear her. She was reading.

Saturday? Day 6? of Autumn Term

Apologies for my absence. I hope you weren't too worried.

I believe I'm still in some trouble, but I have an idea. Let me start with how I got here...

Chapter Twenty-Four

THROUGH THE LOOKING GLASS

Leo

Leo didn't have long to savor Ceri's confession—and how wonderful it felt to confess himself—before the whispering started.

It seemed to be coming from just outside the door of the dining hall. Leo took his things with him to investigate. Regardless of what it was, he needed to find some place to store each object separately, per Ceri's instructions. He figured he'd try Professor Idris's office first. If he was wrong about this being a different time, he'd find the storage boxes there.

And if he was right, well, he'd have to make do with spreading the items around the school. Since Idris's office was a good distance from all the places he'd likely need to go, he'd leave the ring, the most dangerous object, there.

As Leo reached the door, the whispering resolved into speech.

"*Come closer,*" it said.

It was a woman's voice. For a moment, Leo thought it might be Ceri, but the voice was too low.

"*I need you. Closer.*"

Leo hesitated, his hand over the handle to the door. Something rattled within his bag.

Leo looked down to see what it was, and the doorknob began to turn back and forth.

The door wasn't locked or even lockable as far as Leo could tell. Why wasn't it opening?

He reached into the bag. The locket was humming with some kind of energy. When he withdrew it, the door rattled violently in its hinges.

"*CLOSER!*" the voice screamed.

Leo took off running. He ran into the toilets.

They didn't have a lock.

He ran into a stall and locked it behind him.

He took out the journal and furiously scribbled a message to Ceri, begging for help.

The whispering was here.

He was trapped in here. He had to get out.

He burst open the toilet stall (nothing there) and ran from the toilets, through the dining hall to the door into the courtyard as the door burst open behind him. He didn't have the nerve to look back, but he could sense it back there: something large and fast and angry.

Leo sprinted across the courtyard, past the yew, and into the dormitory on the other side.

He didn't know where he was going. He didn't know if he was still being chased.

He ran up the stairs and down the corridor to Ceri's door.

It wasn't her door, really, not yet, but it felt like the right place. He didn't know how, but he knew it would be open.

He was right.

Leo slammed the door shut and locked it. He could hear movement in the hallway beyond and the clinking of metal in the bag as the locket tried to free itself again.

He sank to his knees in front of the door, peering through the keyhole.

As he saw what was chasing him lumber forward, he froze in fear.

It was a tarasque. A creature of myth with the head of a lion and an armored body that breathed poison and ate its enemies whole.

It had haunted his dreams since childhood. His parents had a book of Gallic children's stories they liked to read to the young ones, and most of Leo's siblings had loved it.

But not Leo.

The image of the tarasque terrified him then and now.

The poison breath, he realized.

He stripped the sheets from the bed and stuffed them under the doorframe and into the keyhole, his hands shaking.

Could it hear him? Could it hear the locket?

Did it know he was here?

In the hall, the tarasque roared. Leo heard it gallop up and down the corridor, scratching and banging at the doors.

Finally, it reached his.

It crashed into the door.

Once. Twice. Again and again.

Leo backed away as silently as he could, reaching behind him until his collision with a side table nearly gave him a heart attack.

And then, just as quickly as the tarasque had come, it left.

Leo collapsed onto the bare mattress. What the hell was happening here?

When his nerves had calmed enough to allow him to sit up, he emptied the bag onto the bed and raised the magimeter to the locket.

The reading was off the scale.

He pointed to each object in turn. Low readings on everything else except for the ring, which swung the needle to the high end of the meter so quickly, Leo was afraid it would break it.

He took out the pen to mark it down, but then he realized the problem:

He had left the journal in the dining hall.

∙╮╯∙

It took Leo the better part of the day to work up the nerve to return for the journal.

The tarasque hadn't been back, although he'd heard the whispering again a couple of times.

Leo didn't understand it, but it seemed the whispering woman and the tarasque couldn't sense him in this room. Were they one and the same? He wasn't sure. The tarasque had come after the whispering began, but the whispering had happened on its own as well.

Leo kicked himself for leaving the journal. Although he supposed he'd need to return to the dining hall at some point to eat, regardless.

He went into the bathroom to have a sip of water from the sink. Leo had never been in Ceri's version of the room, but he imagined the razor and beard shavings in the sink were unlikely to be hers.

He reached for the towel to dry his hands, and when he turned back, there she was in the looking glass.

"Ceri?" he called, looking around the room in confusion. She was gone.

But she was just there. He had seen her. He was certain it was her. Perhaps this room was a connection of some kind between his world and hers, just like the journal was.

He tried scratching a message onto the wall with his pen.

It's Leo. I'm here.

"Ceri, I'm here. Can you hear me?"

He was afraid to raise his voice higher than a whisper.

No response.

He lay back down on the bed, thinking hard. The objects were still together, and Ceri had said that was a problem. But they were also active, at least some of them, and Leo worried that if he did what he wanted to—which was flush as many as he could down the toilet and chuck the rest out the window—that he would need them again and wouldn't be able to find them.

They seemed to be somewhat safe in this room, at least. Maybe if he left them here, he'd be able to retrieve the journal without attracting the notice of whatever was out there.

Could that really be a tarasque? The monster in the story book had been roughly the size of a house. It had destroyed entire villages and was practically unstoppable because of its armor.

But the tarasque Leo had seen had fit in the hallway and had failed to even knock down a door.

Maybe it was a baby.

Or maybe it was Leo's worst nightmare come to life. There were few in Loegria who had ever even heard of tarasques, as he'd discovered while playing a drinking game with some of the other doctoral candidates last year. This place seemed to have been made for him in some way. Could it be that the tarasque was made for him too?

For what purpose?

Leo had read about curses that bent reality. He felt it was fair to say he was experiencing that. But while the rules may have changed, he believed there still must have been rules.

The tarasque of legend had been tamed by a woman who doused it in water blessed by the Gods. She'd then been able to put a collar on it, and she kept it as a pet.

Maybe this tarasque could be tamed the same way.

He had no blessed water, but maybe the blessing had been less important. He retrieved the horn from the bag (its reading was marginally higher than earlier, or maybe he was misremembering) and filled it at the sink.

As he left the bathroom, he thought he saw Ceri again, but maybe it was only what he wanted to see.

He needed the journal. It was his only hope of getting back to her.

He listened at the door. There was nothing nearby.

He opened it and crept into the hallway.

The sun was going down by the time he reached the courtyard. It seemed time, however different it was in this place, wasn't frozen.

No tarasque in the courtyard. He stuck close to the wall on the side that was still intact anyway.

He could enter the library here rather than cutting across the courtyard to the dining hall door. The library hadn't fought him before, and the stacks offered more protection than the open courtyard did.

He opened the library door.

No tarasque. No whispers.

No, there were whispers. But they were different.

It was a language Leo didn't recognize. There were several voices of varying age and gender. They seemed—kind? Leo wasn't sure. It could be some kind of trap. Maybe the whispering woman had realized he was too frightened of her to go along with what she wanted and had changed tactics.

Leo walked away from the whispers. They grew more urgent for a moment, but then subsided.

He made it into the hallway outside of the library with the statue of the phoenix, still unbroken.

It wasn't far now. Just one more corridor and then—

There it was. The tarasque.

Leo ducked behind the statue. Had it seen him?

The only sound was the pounding of Leo's heart. Could he manage to make himself take a look?

Hesitantly, Leo peered out.

The tarasque was gone.

Not gone.

Behind him. It was right behind him.

Leo yelled and ran, tossing the contents of the horn over his shoulder.

He heard a strange squeal and the thunder of six heavy paws crashing into the wall.

He dared to turn and look.

The wing of the phoenix statue was shattered on the ground. Could he have been the one to break it?

There was no time to consider it. The tarasque was there on the ground too, crouching. It didn't seem to be able to move, but for how long would it stay that way?

He wanted to run away from this object of his childhood nightmares, but it looked so sad and small there, its lion head bent low. It had been reduced from a creature of pure terror to something Leo pitied.

He understood then why Martha had reached out to it to tame it. He'd always wondered why she didn't kill the monster and take its head like they usually did in stories, but now he understood.

Leo reached out his hand.

The tarasque lifted its head in surprise. Then it nuzzled against Leo's arm.

"Would you come with me?" asked Leo. "I think I'm in danger here. I could use a protector."

The tarasque leaned back and stood, assessing Leo.

Leo knew he didn't look much like a hero of legend. He didn't cut an impressive figure. He wore no suit of armor. He carried no sword.

But neither had Martha, and she'd conquered the tarasque.

No, not conquered. Befriended.

The tarasque walked beside him, waiting.

"Is that a 'yes'?" asked Leo.

By way of response, the tarasque knelt to him.

Maybe he could do this. Maybe Leo could survive this and find his way back home, back to his research. Back to Professor Marin. Back to the family he should really write to more often.

Back to Ceri.

⁓⊙⊙⊙⁓

Leo heard the whispering woman on the way back from the dining hall with the journal and a bag full of the food he'd found that would last several days (bread, dried meat, hard cheese, and raw fruits and vegetables. It wouldn't make for fine dining, but beggars couldn't be choosers.)

But with the tarasque at his side, Leo was nearly un-afraid. He ignored the whispers and was able to make it back to the room without incident.

He hesitated at the door. Should he bring the tarasque inside? Would that alter whatever protection it offered?

The tarasque was licking its armored paws. He couldn't just leave it out there.

He brought it in and spread one of the sheets he'd ripped from the bed on the other bed for it.

It accepted this offering, curling up into a ball on the bed like a cat.

A very large, armored, poisoned-breathed cat.

With the notebook finally there, he first left a message for Ceri. He told her everything that had just happened: the whispering woman, the forgotten journal, taming the tarasque, and the whispers in the library, and then he shared with her his idea.

I believe both the ring and the locket are at work here based on the readings (with the occasional input from the horn, but its readings are so low by comparison, I'm uncertain).

Based on the readings now with the tarasque in the room, I believe the ring is tied to it, which means the locket must be tied to the whispering woman.

I believe the ring has the power to make our fears become reality, and I think I can use this to help find a way home—

Not your fears. Your nightmares. It brings your nightmares to life. You have to get rid of it. It makes all the other objects more dangerous.

Ceri. It was so good to see her writing again.

Nightmares? That's even better. I can try to guide my dreams. Some elves do nothing else every time they sleep.

Admittedly, I haven't quite mastered it, but it's worth a shot. I can dream of coming home.

It won't work. Idris says it has to be a nightmare.

What if I were to dream of coming home—but without my pants?

That doesn't sound like a nightmare to me.

Leo didn't know what to say to that.

Alison thinks you should try it. Try to dream of coming home pants-less with all the objects in tow.

It's night now here. I'll give it a try. Wish me luck.

I wish to see you pants-less.

If you keep writing like that, I'll be having a different kind of dream entirely.

Leo tried not to think of Ceri's innuendo. It truly could have the power to derail his process of entering into an elvish trance.

Especially since he wanted very much to think about what she had in mind.

Leo lay down on the bed and closed his eyes. At least he felt safe in here with the tarasque.

He had always had trouble entering the state of meditation required to trance. He'd tried all the usual techniques—counting breaths, feeling his body, reaching out and connecting with the ancestors—and he'd just come away more anxious than before, often with new anxieties about whether he was breathing right or whether he'd somehow been born without a spiritual sense.

Perhaps it was just the exhaustion from an unnaturally long day, but the trance came easily to him this time.

He guided his thoughts to the lab in his time. He walked past the library on the way there, seeing the broken statue to ensure he didn't just end up moving rooms in this time. He pictured himself there in the lab with the objects spread out on his desk. The others were standing around.

He dared to picture Ceri, but he did not let himself think of her.

And then he looked down.

Bare, pale legs.

And no underwear.

He covered his shame as the others pointed and laughed.

Then he fell into a deep, dreamless sleep.

⚜

When he woke, he was still in Ceri's room.

Godsdammit. It hadn't worked.

Or had it?

Leo reached for the lamp beside the bed, but instead he found a candlestick. He was alone in the room.

The tarasque had gone.

Leo was sad to see it go, but clearly something had happened. He checked the objects: both the ring and locket were missing.

Then he checked the journal.

I have some news: we think we know what's happening to you, at least some of it. It's the same thing that happened to Idris and his friends last night. We don't know what each object does, but we do know that the doll is tied to a child that will cause choking. It's the most dangerous after the ring, but Idris thinks we can help you decurse it. He's trying to find a way to do it without magic, unless you know how to use magic and just never told us?

There was also a fire (the lighter, we're guessing), and the dagger must have caused a trail of blood. Neither of those things had an actual impact on our world, but we have no idea what they will do in yours. It's less clear what the locket and the horn do, but we're still trying to figure it out.

It's getting late here. I hope the nightmare works and I see you tomorrow. If not, we'll find a way.

All of that is deeply alarming.

I'm still here, but the tarasque, ring, and locket are gone. Check the lab. Hopefully the tarasque has not come, but if it has and it's no longer tame, I used water to tame it.

The room is different. The beds have changed, and it seems like the 'lectrics are gone. I don't see any lamps or outlets of any kind.

I think I may have gone even further back.

The lighter is reading higher than the other objects now. Thoughts on whether that's related to the time shift?

I'm going to explore today. If the ring was causing the danger, and it's gone now, I'm hoping I'll be in a better position to do something about my predicament.

P.S. It was hard not to dream about you last night.

Leo closed the journal. He hadn't made it back, but he had proved at least one thing: he had some power to affect this world.

There were strings here to be pulled on.

All he had to do was find the right one.

Chapter Twenty-Five

THE MAN IN THE MIRROR

Ceri

Ceri was exhausted. She'd gone from hauling people back and forth across the river to frantically pouring over books in the library with the others, trying to find something to make sense of the world Leo described, and all of it on only a few hours of sleep.

The best they could come up with for a locket that caused a woman to whisper for people to come closer was some sort of scorned lover situation. Because Rinka had turned from it when she encountered the same thing, they couldn't know what she would do if she got ahold of Leo.

Ceri guessed it was nothing good.

She wrote to him what she knew and took a nice, hot bath. The 'lectrics had finally come back.

She crawled into bed and was fast asleep before she even thought to check the mirror.

When she woke, she checked the journal and was disappointed to see his message.

Not that she didn't want to hear from him. She'd just been hoping he would be back here instead.

She dressed in the bathroom, pulling on another jumper and tidying her hair in the mirror.

Leo was there.

Ceri froze. She was terrified if she turned around, he would vanish.

"Can you hear me?" she whispered. Ana was still sleeping in their bedroom.

Leo shook his head. Alright, he couldn't hear her, but he could see her.

Ceri wished she'd learned sign language. He was right there, so close that she could see him, but she couldn't speak to him.

He stepped closer.

In the reflection, it looked as though he was right behind her.

He mouthed her name, and though she couldn't hear it, she could feel it deep within her.

He brushed his hand at the hair on her neck. She couldn't feel anything.

She brushed away the hair herself, revealing the soft skin underneath.

The Leo in the mirror wrapped his arm around her waist and pressed her to him. She could almost feel the sensation.

She leaned back into it.

He leaned over and pressed his lips to her neck. She felt the phantom touch on her skin, like the moments after he'd touched her for the first time in the library.

She sighed.

In the reflection, he touched the jumper she'd just put on. She pulled it over her head.

He kissed the strap of her brassiere. She pushed it off her shoulder.

She pressed herself back against him. She felt him there or maybe imagined it. Maybe both.

This was somewhere between dream and reality. A liminal space where the veil between worlds was thin.

She wanted him. She could feel he wanted her.

She couldn't turn around.

She had to turn around, had to see him, to give herself to him.

She couldn't. She must.

She turned.

Nothing. There was nothing.

He was gone.

Ceri ran across the room to the journal.

"What's going on?" asked Ana, her head still on the pillow.

"Nothing important," said Ceri. "Go back to sleep."

"You got it," said Ana, beginning to snore again almost immediately.

Leo had already written something by the time she opened the journal.

I don't know for certain if what I just saw was truly you. I hope that it was.

I want you, desperately.

I want to tell you what I'd do if I was there.

Do you want me to?

Did she want him to?

Yes.

Gods, yes, Ceri replied.

Then she watched the page fill, and she added in some of her own ideas as well.

And when they were done, she ripped it from the journal and placed it with the other secrets.

❦

Leo's next entry was far more fit for public consumption.

Ceri had noticed him writing it while she was having her breakfast, and she'd let him continue without interruption: she knew how much the observations in the journal meant to him, and the more detail he was able to provide them, the better.

Sunday? Day 7? of Autumn Term

I'm finding it difficult to keep an accurate accounting of the time in this place. I went to sleep at night and awoke during what appears to be the afternoon, although I can't imagine more than eight hours had passed. Ceri, if you're able to add the approximate dates and times in our world to my entries, that would be most helpful for the sake of future reference.

The school is much as it was before, but the 'lectrics are entirely missing. The Norminster Yew has some fragments of its heartwood remaining where none exist in our time, and, most interestingly, the ruined western side of the cloister is in intact. If I recall correctly from my fresher orientation, that part of the school was severely damaged in a fire some fifty years ago or more.

I find it hard to believe it merely a coincidence that the lighter is most active under such conditions. Indeed, I believe it likely that this is the very lighter used to start the infamous fire. Although I'd very much like to observe the western cloister as it once was, I have avoided the area for this reason.

My last and truly most remarkable observation is that I am not alone here. I first spotted the young dwarf walking around the courtyard from the bedroom window. He appears to be harmless, merely walking around the yew and whistling, but I thought it best to avoid him. I took the longer route through the eastern buildings to reach the library, hoping to refresh my memory on the circumstances of the fire, but of course that book has yet to be written.

As I left the library, I noted the dwarf walking into the western cloister and the building beyond. I continued to avoid it and the courtyard, entering the dining hall from the eastern corridor. There is once again fresh food and drink on the table, although I'll note that it is severely lacking in seasoning compared to what I'm accustomed to. It seems I shan't starve while I'm here, except for the starvation of my palate for the variety it so craves.

I feel much more at ease now that the ring has gone. Although I don't doubt the power of the remaining objects, it feels as if I can prevent much of their danger by carefully avoiding the circumstances that surround them.

I have a theory that these movements in time are related to the watch in some way. It is a simple explanation, but the simplest explanation is often the most likely to be correct. Unfortunately, without further data points, it's impossible to determine how, exactly, that the watch is responsible for the transitions. The first occurred due to what seemed to be a natural lightning strike. The second possibly occurred due to the influence of my dream. I'm hoping I can measure the watch's activity during the next transition, assuming there is one. I have tried to wind it manually, but it won't budge. Perhaps the lightning fused its gears in some way.

I shall try the library again tomorrow once the sun is up. I had forgotten how difficult it is to conduct research by candlelight. And although I never thought I'd say it, I miss whatever magic the library in our world possesses that enables it to suggest books, no matter how temperamental and insulting it may be. Its absence is more of a hindrance than I'd imagined.

"He's right about the watch," said Idris once he'd finished chewing his toast.

"You think he's traveling in time?" asked Rinka.

"No, not in the sense that it's the same timeline we're on or that he can impact it in any way. I think the things he's seeing are more like echoes of things that happened related to his objects. You said he'd found them all in town, right?"

"At charity shops in town. Maybe he found one of them in the school; it's in here somewhere—" said Ceri, flipping through the pages.

"I bet they all were here at the school at some point, and he's living through those memories," said Idris. "The watch is what's carrying him from one to another."

"Do you think if he breaks it, he'll come back here?" asked Alison.

"Possibly," said Idris. "Although it seems as though it's already broken. It also could leave him trapped where he is. I think what's more likely is he needs to do something with each object, possibly during its own time, to move between them. It seems like getting rid of the locket took him out of its time. I wish the nightmare had brought more of the objects back, but maybe it could only bring back what was active. I still think the best bet is to try to neutralize each one. Whatever he's meant to do with them should probably be avoided."

"But would it even hurt him?" asked Keir. "If, say, he became trapped by the fire like I was. The fire was clearly an illusion of some kind. Was there any true danger in it? In the vine's world, Alison fell to her death, and it just restarted the loop."

"But I didn't die," said Alison. "Charlotte didn't die."

Idris rubbed his neck where he'd been choked. That danger at least had seemed real enough. "Keir, the curse you created was not born out of the kind of malice I detected on those objects," said Idris. "I asked Dean Whittaker last night about any fires connected to the school, and the dwarf that set that fire died in it."

Ceri thought of the dwarf Leo had seen. ***Do not approach the dwarf,*** she wrote as Idris continued.

"I don't think the world he's in is like the world you inadvertently created. I think it's a world born out of the malice of those cursed objects, and I think it's very dangerous indeed."

"But if that's the case, why has he been safe in my room?" asked Ceri. "Why can't whatever's there approach him when he's inside?"

Idris frowned. "No idea. I guess we'd better go find out.

☙⚬◉⚬❧

Ceri had worried there would be some sort of embarrassing answer tied to their flirtation, but the true answer, it turned out, was Ana.

"There's fairy magic here, or something exactly like it," said Alison when she entered the room. "It has that same feeling of invitation I felt a few months ago."

"Oh, that was me," said Ana shyly. "Just something my dad taught me. I don't really know how it works, but he said it's for keeping me safe, and I should perform the ritual everywhere I sleep. It's a little bizarre. You have to rub this serum over the doorway and chant something in the fairy tongue. It's really hard to pronounce; it's kind of like speaking backwards. I'm actually excited that I did it right. He's going to be really proud when I tell him."

She handed a vial of sparkling liquid to Idris, who opened it and gave it a sniff.

His eyes bulged from the strength of it. "At least ten different flowers and a lot of alcohol."

"It's keeping Leo safe?" asked Ceri.

"Probably. Fairy magic is beyond me," said Idris.

"Thanks, Ana!" Ceri gave her roommate a hug. She was still a little awkward at it, but showing affection was beginning to feel more natural.

"Are you heading to the library?" asked Ana. "I've got a paper to start for Ancient Languages. I could come with you and help during my breaks."

"That would be wonderful," said Ceri. She sighed with relief; although she was still worried about Leo, it felt like they were starting to get somewhere.

Everything felt a little more possible with the help of friends.

Chapter Twenty-Six

POETRY IN MOTION

Alison

The fireplaces in the library had been lit by the early
Sunday evening, and it was a good thing too: it was
getting so cold in there, Alison's hands were shaking
trying to keep the books open.

Keir helped her move the pile of books and sketches
Weyland had done of Leo's objects to a well-worn couch
and coffee table right in front of the fire where Willow was
already sleeping. Then he'd brought them a heavy tartan
blanket he'd packed from home and a steaming hot cup of
tea for good measure.

There were men, and then there were *men*, and Keir was
the latter.

They had split their time during the day between Professor Marin's lab, where they were able to transport all of the
power-savers for further testing now that the 'lectrics were

back, and the library, where they continued pouring over books, looking for answers to Leo's predicament.

They hadn't been able to come up with much regarding the lighter. Dean Whittaker had answered some questions for them in between supervising repairs, but he hadn't been present for the fire itself and knew little more of it than they did.

They'd had a little more luck with the doll thanks to Professor Marin, who had recognized it from the sketch as the kind that had been popular when she was a girl hundreds of years earlier. It gave them a place to start.

The language in the books from that time was nearly incomprehensible, even with Professor Marin's help. The professor of Ancient Languages wasn't available, unfortunately. He was down in Norgate lending his strong orcish muscle to the flood repair cause. Ceri's roommate Ana had only just begun her studies and wasn't able to offer much help either, although she had attracted the attention of the star flagball player, who had overheard their conversation and wondered if she'd help him with their paper. Alison had enjoyed watching the young couple flirt from a distance even if Ceri disapproved.

"I don't get it," said Ceri as she joined them by the fire. "I don't see the appeal."

"There's nothing wrong with having different taste," said Rinka, pulling up a chair. "If he were older…"

"Don't tell me I'd have to compete with a flagball player for your affections," said Idris.

"Just because your father is so insufferable about sports that you two hate them doesn't mean they aren't good fun," said Rinka. "I, for one, am looking forward to the first game."

"Anything new from Leo?" asked Keir as he passed around more cups of tea.

"He's in the library too," said Ceri. "I told him the books the library had suggested for us, and he's going through them as well."

The library had been less useful than usual in its recommendations. It kept hitting Alison with poetry books, and while she appreciated its encouragement, she couldn't seem to get it to understand that it wasn't her top priority at the moment.

The book Alison was currently reading—or perhaps skimming, since the language was so difficult to grasp—was a grimoire from roughly four centuries earlier, the time when the doll was popular. It had been copied from an even earlier manuscript and unfortunately had not been fully translated into even early Modern Loegrian.

The pages were illuminated with painted images varying from the ornamental to the macabre, lovely floral patterns on one page and then dark, demonic shapes on the next. The magic within its pages all seemed to involve strange herbs and animal parts mixed together under various phases on the moon, long continuous pages of instructions with little rhyme or reason.

Perhaps it was for this reason that one page in particular stood out to Alison.

It reminded her of the pamphlet they'd made. Each of the poems she'd written had appeared with an accompanying illustration by Weyland, and that was exactly how this page looked as well: like poetry.

Poetry.

"Wait," said Alison. Everyone looked up at her as if they weren't sure what they were meant to be waiting on. *"To quieten an curse.* I think this may be it. Oh Gods, how could I be so stupid! The answer was poetry all along."

"Come again?" said Idris.

"I'm not sure what the rest of this says, but I think it's a spell of some kind. Some of these old spells are just poems. I don't know why I didn't see it before. It's the piece that has been missing from my magic. The reason I can't do it consistently. You don't need it, but I do. I need poetry."

"Let me see that," said Professor Marin. She had been sitting some distance away from the fire but still within earshot. "This is not my mother tongue, but I can still recall it." She read from the book in a strange accent:

To quieten an curse, speke þese lynes þries:

Breke þyn bonde, breke þyn chayne,
Leve till oonly goode remayne,
Bi lighte o moone & fyre o sunne,
Lete us ende what hast ybigun.

"Can you understand it?" asked Alison.

"Can I see the journal? I can write down what it means."

To quiet a curse, speak these lines thrice:

Break thy bond, break thy chain,
Leave 'til only good remains,
By light of moon and fire of sun,
Let us end what has begun.

"It doesn't sound like much to go on," said Idris. "We've never needed words to do our magic. But maybe this magic is different."

"Could you try it?" asked Rinka. "On the locket, maybe?"

"Perhaps the ring instead," said Idris. "We don't know what the locket does, and that ring is more trouble than it's worth."

"I'm willing to give it a go," said Alison.

Idris rose to retrieve the ring, taking the secret passage back to his closet.

"What do you think about trying it outside?" asked Keir. "*By light of moon and fire of sun.* Maybe you need one or the other."

"Maybe both," said Alison. "Although I suppose they're nearly the same thing. It's cold out there, but I'm sure the library would prefer it if we didn't try it here."

The library dropped a book in response: *The Beauty of the Great Outdoors.*

"Message received," said Alison.

They met Idris at the entrance to the secret passage and entered the courtyard from the door Ceri had used during the storm.

The full moon was just beginning to rise over the mountains. A cold wind blew through, forcing Alison to wrap the blanket tightly around her.

"Do you think I just say it?" she asked Idris. "Does it need to be in Middle Loegrian, or can I use the translation?"

"No idea," said Idris. "I have no idea if this is going to do anything at all. But as long as I get the ring stored safely again before anyone falls asleep, there should be little risk in trying."

Idris removed the ring from the heavy box it was stored in and placed it on the ground in the middle of the brown patch where the lightning struck. "Might as well see if Leo had the right idea about this place. I can sense power here."

Alison held the journal up and read out the translated text three times.

Nothing happened.

"I didn't feel anything from you," said Keir. "I think you need to channel your power into it somehow. Or mine."

"But what power can Leo channel?" asked Alison.

"One thing at a time," said Keir. "Let's see if we can get it to work first."

Alison read the text once again, this time pulling on her power and Keir's in the way that occasionally did something.

The ring shook on the ground.

"That's doing something," said Idris, holding his hand over the ring to feel the power. "Keep going."

Alison read the text a second time. This time, the ring screeched.

Everyone put their hands over their ears.

"Read it again, quick!" yelled Rinka over the noise.

Alison read it a final time, struggling to concentrate over the sound, but it seemed to have worked: the ring fell silent.

"I can't believe it," said Idris. He picked up the ring and shook his head. There was no magic on it. "I've managed to decurse a fair number of things in my time, but usually there's some kind of trick to it. Some sort of negotiation or even a duel with a hostile force. It probably won't work on everything—basically nothing does when it comes to magic. But if it can work on anything, it's worth a try."

Alison shivered. "It's a beautiful ring, really," she said, taking it from Idris to feel the lack of magic on it for herself. "A shame someone did that to it." She handed it back to Idris, who stored it back in its box just in case the curse removal was temporary.

As they returned to the library, Idris pulled her aside. "Do you think you'd be willing to try it on me?" he asked her.

Alison could see immediately how serious he was. He was trying to appear nonchalant, but he couldn't quite look at her. She was used to the Idris that always had a joke or a jibe for any occasion. It saddened her to see him so vulnerable.

"Of course we can," said Alison. "We can try it right now if you like."

"Maybe once the others have gone to bed," said Idris. "I'd rather...I'd rather they didn't know. Just you, me, and Keir."

Alison didn't ask why he wanted to keep it from Rinka and Ceri. She guessed that maybe he didn't want to have to see their disappointment if it failed.

Ceri gave Leo the instructions on how to use the spell, although they still didn't have much of an answer about where he should draw the power from.

"The fairy queen Mab told me everyone has magic within them," said Alison. "I don't know if he'll be able to learn to wield it without any help in such a short time, but I could feel an energy in the spot in the courtyard. Maybe it could be enough on its own."

"Tell him to try to decurse the items one by one, starting with the doll," said Idris. "It's too much of a risk to take them all out of the fairy magic sanctuary at once."

"Coming to bed?" Rinka asked Idris, yawning. "I think that's enough for one night. I'm exhausted."

"I'll meet you there," he said. "I'm going to ask Ana if she can cast that same ward on my closet. It never hurts to have multiple layers of protection from curses."

Rinka nodded and left, with Ceri following behind her. Professor Marin had slipped away earlier without a good-bye, which was a move she used often and one that Alison envied.

"You probably should ask Ana to do that," said Alison to Idris once the others had gone.

"I hate to interrupt her 'studying' with apparently the most desirable man in the school, but I think I will do so," he replied. "I'll meet you both outside in a moment."

"What are you up to?" asked Willow, stretching. It was time for her to wake up now that it was dark outside. "What did I miss?"

"Nothing much," said Alison. "Just a minor break-through in why my magic has been failing all this time and also the possible answer for keeping Leo safe until we can bring him home."

"Oh, good," said Willow. "I was afraid I slept through something important."

"Do you really think poetry is the key?" asked Keir. "Do you think you could do something with poems you write yourself?"

"I'd like to try," said Alison. "It makes sense, in a way. I started writing it for the coin, but it eventually became how my mind works. It's sort of like a puzzle with words. I think if I can find a way to combine my poems with my magic, both of them will be better for it."

"They're both wonderful already," said Keir. He kissed her on the lips, which Willow took as her cue to take off. "You know, there's a fantasy of mine that takes place among the stacks."

It was very cozy here on the couch now that everyone had gone.

"I'm not sure if the library would appreciate that," said Alison regretfully. Or maybe it would, and she wasn't sure which was worse. "But maybe we should stop at Weldan House on the way back. I recall you having an impressive library there. Come on. It's time to decurse Idris."

"Do what?" asked Keir, but he followed her nonetheless.

"Idris asked me if we could try the spell on him," said Alison once they were outside. "So he can fly again, I suppose."

Idris was waiting in the same spot in the middle of the courtyard.

"Ceri took the journal with her," said Alison. "But I think I have it memorized. I said it so many times just now."

"Let's get this over with. It's bloody freezing out here," said Idris, pacing around to keep warm.

That seemed more like him.

"Do you think we join hands or something?" asked Keir.

"Sure, and let's all sing it together," said Idris. "It'll be just like nursery school."

"Gods, you're insufferable," said Keir. "I hope this works so you can fly off and leave the rest of us in peace."

"And miss out on all of the nagging and brooding? Not a chance."

"Will you both be quiet? I'd like to get back inside before I freeze my tits off."

Idris laughed as Keir said, "Alison!"

"What?" said Alison, looking at Keir's shocked face. "It's really bloody cold."

Alison took Keir's hand, ignoring Idris's childish laughter, and recited the spell exactly as she had done before.

Something was happening.

Alison couldn't tell what, but she felt the air change.

"Are you doing that?" Keir asked Idris.

"It's not me," said Idris. "I can feel something. Keep going."

Alison recited the spell two more times. Then she and Keir stood back.

Idris transformed into the red dragon with a loud crack and the smell of brimstone. He tried to flap his wing, but Alison could see it: it was still broken.

"I'm sorry, Idris," she said. "It really felt like it worked."

He changed back just as quickly. "Maybe it did," he muttered. "Thank you."

"What?" asked Alison, but he was already rushing off inside.

Alison and Keir followed him into the guest wing of the dormitory.

"You saw that, right? He can't fly," said Keir. "So what in the name of the Gods did he mean?"

Chapter Twenty-Seven

BACK AND BACK

Leo

Armed with the spell, the doll, and the instructions, Leo took off towards the courtyard at nightfall.

The dwarf had been hanging around the yew again during the day, but he had vanished once more by the time Leo reached the spot in the middle where he'd taken the fateful measurements that sent him falling through time.

Leo lay the doll down on the grass and took a measurement with his magimeter. There was no storm in sight this time, and if he was going to try to work magic for himself again, he might as well see if he could get some decent readings from it.

Leo had never had success with magic before. As a researcher of it, he'd tried it a number of times, of course. But if he had any sort of affinity for it, it seemed to have been buried somewhere deep, likely during his upbringing, which had been filled with more kooky superstitions and silly rituals than genuine magical practice.

At least, Leo thought it had. It would be fun to go back home with the magimeter someday, if he could bring himself to do it.

Leo opened the journal and began to read the incantation under the light of the full moon:

"Break thy bond, break thy chain,
Leave 'til only good—"

He heard the slam of a door. The dwarf was there, running across the courtyard from the library.

Leo grabbed the doll and took off in the opposite direction. He ran into the cloister and opened the door into a hall he didn't know, slamming it behind him.

He was in the western building. In his panic, he had run directly into the one place he was trying to avoid.

He looked around. It was dark in the corridor, with little moonlight reaching through the unbroken cloister to shine into the windows. He felt around for the light switch instinctively before remembering there wouldn't be one.

There was a sinister laugh somewhere nearby.

Leo raced through the hall. He'd seen from outside that there were other doors into the cloister. If he just kept going, he was sure to reach them—

He smelled smoke.

There was that laughter again. It was closer to him now.

Leo kept running. The doors were there. If he could just get back to the courtyard, he could maybe outrun the dwarf and make it to Ceri's room—

The doors were locked. Leo pulled on them helplessly.

He couldn't see in the hallway. The smell of smoke grew stronger.

He could pick the lock, he realized. He knew how. He needed something to apply torque and something to pick the pins within it. If he bent the magimeter, maybe it could apply the necessary torque—

He could see the fire now in the hall, spreading fast.

Did the doll have something he could use to rake the pins? He was running out of time. He coughed from the smoke. How could he have been so stupid to come in here?

He reached in his pockets, coming up empty.

Then he had it: his spectacles. If he could just bend the loop at the end of the arm—

Through the smoke, he saw the white face of the dwarf coming towards him.

"No!" he yelled. "Stay back!" He waved the magimeter towards him. Its meter was reading off the charts.

The dwarf kept coming. Leo threw the doll at him. The dwarf knocked it into the fire.

Desperate and not knowing what else to do, Leo screamed the lines of the incantation at him:

> *"Break thy bond! Break thy chain!*
> *Leave 'til only good remains!*
> *By light of moon and fire of sun!*
> *Let us end what has begun!"*

The dwarf reached for him and grabbed him. He was incredibly strong. Leo fought and thrashed against him, but to no avail. The dwarf dragged him back down the hall, back towards the rapidly approaching fire.

Leo shouted the lines of the spell over and over. *S'il vous plaît, mes Dieux. Aidez-moi !*

The dwarf said nothing. He dragged Leo along in silence.

This was it. The fire was so close now Leo could feel the terrible heat of it. There was no escaping this.

The laughter filled the hall until it became a scream. It wasn't coming from the dwarf. Not this dwarf, at least.

The dwarf threw the door open and threw Leo out into the courtyard.

The edge of Leo's journal had begun to catch fire. He threw it to the ground and stomped the flames out.

The dwarf was behind him. He fell to the ground and rolled, extinguishing the flames on his face and his shirt.

Leo looked at the dwarf. He'd thought this dwarf was the one who had set the fire, that's what the others had said, but it seemed like he'd saved him.

The dwarf looked up, and Leo was struck with recognition.

"Groundskeeper Tomasar?"

"Who are you? What were you--?"

Leo's world lurched backwards. He fell to the ground.

It felt as though the entire planet had come off its axis. It felt as though he could fall into the sky.

It turned and twisted and finally sent him crashing back into the ground as if he'd just fallen a dozen feet.

With the wind knocked out of him, he tried to pull himself up onto his elbow to look around.

The dormitory was gone. In its place was a plaster structure with dark wooden beams and a thatched roof. A child was crying somewhere in the distance.

The world lurched backwards again. It took him several minutes to recover this time.

The ground beneath him was dusted with snow. It was daylight again, the cloisters were gone, and the building that had replaced the dormitory was gone as well.

In its place were the stone walls of a castle.

The young Groundskeeper Tomasar was nowhere to be seen. The journal was still with him—thank the Gods—as was the magimeter.

Leo pulled himself upright. It was freezing cold out here. He needed to find shelter, quickly. Ceri's room was gone, but could the magic still be in that space? There was a tower in its vicinity.

Were the rest of the objects still there? He'd left the lighter behind, but it seemed that the dwarf that had started the fire had gotten it anyway. Perhaps if he went to the wrong place in the castle, it wouldn't matter that the objects were within the fairy magic ward.

What else was left? If the doll had been destroyed—and it seemed like it had, judging by the skip backwards in time—it would be just the dagger and the horn.

And maybe the lighter, although Leo wouldn't mind it right about now.

Leo entered the tower through a door at its base. On the way in, he noticed the yew: all of the heartwood had returned, and the diameter of the trunk had shrunk a small amount. It was still an enormous tree, but it seemed as though Leo must have gone back centuries.

Of course, the castle was a decent clue to that itself.

Leo followed a narrow spiral staircase up into the tower after pausing a moment at the lowest hearth to warm his hands. There seemed to be no one around, but Leo didn't count on that to last.

There was a landing and another hearth with a single bed beneath the staircase. On the floor, Leo saw the horn, the dagger, and the bag of food.

He placed the objects back into the bag. He knew it was a risk, but if the world kept changing, he worried he might lose them.

Then he collapsed onto the bed. His lungs still ached from the smoke.

Groundskeeper Tomasar saved him from the fire. Had that been the way he'd gotten his scars?

Was this version of this place somehow connected to the past? It seemed impossible—not just because time travel was impossible, but also because this clearly wasn't the full version of events. Where were all the people? Why could he see some and not others?

As if the world could hear him, he heard sounds from outside.

There was a small rectangular window that peered out into the courtyard, or the bailey, as it would have been called in this time.

There was smoke from beyond the dining hall.

Leo heard something tinny in the distance like sword fighting.

It *was* sword fighting, Leo realized.

Leo opened the bag and measured the dagger.

Oh, yes. It was definitely the dagger's turn.

There was still the spell. He didn't know if it had worked before, or if it had been the fire that managed to destroy the doll.

He looked down into the bailey. The ground was covered with snow now, but he could tell the location of the spot he'd used before from the location of the yew.

He heard a crash and saw dust and stone go flying from the ramparts across the way.

The castle was under siege.

Leo grabbed the bag and the thin woolen blanket from the bed and ran back down the stairs, sprinting across the bailey with what was left of his energy.

He made it to the spot. He placed the dagger on the ground, and as he did so, the ground rumbled.

A battering ram? Leo heard voices shouting in a language he could not understand.

He tried the spell.

Then he tried it again.

It was no good. Nothing was happening. The dagger read as high as ever on the magimeter.

"Inward!" a voice shouted from entirely too nearby.

That was a word Leo knew.

There was a thundering sound of armored knights entering into the bailey.

They were elves, Leo realized. His own people. Some of them likely still lived.

They didn't seem to recognize him.

Leo grabbed the dagger and the bag and ran for the tower, screaming.

A whipping sound flew past his ear: an arrow. They were bloody shooting at him!

"I'm an elf! I'm an elf!" he shouted at them as he ran. He realized his modern school apparel and Modern Loegrian language probably weren't helping his case any.

"Elfe! Ye olde elfe!" he yelled. The only thing he knew about Middle Loegrian was that it had a lot more "E"s in it.

An arrow pierced the wood of the tower door, and then another.

If he kept running for it, they'd hit him for sure.

Leo cut back and forth across the bailey, trying to move as unpredictably as possible.

And then, in the corner opposite the yew, he spotted his salvation.

A forge. Leo could see the fire burning within it through the large window in front of it.

Leo reached into the bag for the dagger as he ran, hoping to get it by the handle.

Or the blade. He'd take the blade at this point.

"You see that?" he said to the dagger once he had it in his hand. "That's where you came from. You're going back there."

An arrow struck his bag. Another grazed his long ear.

He was nearly there now. He leapt over the windowsill and took cover underneath it. They would be on him in seconds; they were as fast as he was, and they were wearing armor.

He said the incantation three more times—who knew if it helped?—and threw the dagger into the fire.

Oh Gods, they were still coming.

Leo crawled around on the floor, trying to get under a table.

He'd nearly made it there, nearly made it, when the world lurched backwards again.

❦

When Leo awoke, there was no castle to be seen.

The ground was clear and dry. Tall trees loomed overhead, their yellow leaves falling gently.

He heard movement nearby.

He sat up on pure instinct. He was exhausted, but his impulse to survive refused to let him give up so easily.

A woman emerged from behind a tree. She was wearing strange furs, and behind her were a pair of white, feathery wings.

She said something to Leo in another language he didn't know.

He scrambled to his feet, nearly falling over from the effort.

"Please. I need a break. Can we have a break before you do whatever it is you're going to do to try to kill me?"

The woman shook her head.

Leo sighed.

"Come on with it then," he said. He stretched out his hand in expectation.

The woman gestured to someone else behind the trees. It was another woman, this one older.

In her hands was a horn. It was just like the horn in the bag.

"I guess that makes sense," said Leo. "What are you going to do with it? Gore me?"

The women shook their heads and said something to each other in their language.

The older woman held out the horn to Leo, keeping a careful distance from him.

Leo reached for it. Might as well get it over with.

The horn was filled with water.

"Water?" asked Leo.

The women shook their heads, but they gestured to him to drink.

Leo smelled it. It smelled of nothing, but for all he knew, it was filled with deadly poison.

He took a sip anyway. He was too tired to fight it, and Gods, was he thirsty.

It was water.

More men and women emerged from behind the trees. Leo tried to move away from them, but they came over to him slowly, gently, like they were approaching a frightened animal.

They brought some of the furs, and they wrapped them around Leo's shoulders.

He shivered and pulled the furs closer to him.

The strangers touched his ears and whispered in their strange language. One of them tied something soft, a plant of some kind, to his ear that was bleeding from the arrow wound.

Then they led him into the trees. He followed them up a ramp and into a hut.

Inside was a set of furs for sleeping.

Leo looked at the strangers. They gestured for him to lie down.

He didn't know what to do. He was scared and exhausted and had no idea whether to trust these people.

They gestured to the bed again. A child ran in, laughing, to show him how to lie down. She must have thought he didn't know how. Then she got up and fluttered her wings to land on her father's shoulders.

They weren't going to hurt him. They wanted to help him.

Leo slowly lay down on the bed and cried.

Chapter Twenty-Eight

REFLECTIONS

Ceri

Ceri woke on the day of her matriculation—her formal induction into the student body of Winwold College, a ceremony that had been rescheduled on account of the storm—to the journal in a state of hellish disrepair.

What the hell is going on? Where are you? The journal is burnt, and it has a hole in it. Ana said it looks like it was pierced by an arrow! Are you okay? Please, Leo. Answer me!

Ana did her best to console her as they dressed, donning their academic robes and mortarboard hats, but Ceri could not stop picking up the journal and checking it.

"It's a good sign that there isn't any blood on the arrow hole, isn't it?" asked Ana.

Ceri blanched at the thought.

"Sorry, I didn't mean—"

"No, you're right. It's probably a good sign."

Finally, after the ceremony was complete and they had been dismissed for their first classes, there was writing:

Monday? Day 8? of Autumn Term

I'm fine. I wanted to start with that because I can see why you would be concerned, but I am completely fine. I am safe now.

Ceri interjected before he could continue:

Oh, thank the Gods. Where are you? Or when?

I'm back as far as I can go, I think.

Leo explained to Ceri what had happened when he'd tried to decurse the doll, how he'd managed to destroy it and to skip back to the dagger's time, only to come under attack and be forced to destroy the dagger as well.

I don't know what happened to the lighter. You may want to check around the cloister; it's where I found it originally. I imagine it may still pose a threat.

As far as where (or when) I am now, I appear to be in a fairy village of some kind. The fairies appear to be the size of ordinary Fullings, which is somewhat surprising as I've only encountered their Eighthling forms in our time. They are peaceful and only curious about me so far, not hostile or suspicious. I cannot understand their language, nor can they understand any of mine. (I've tried Loegrian, Gallic, and the broken bits of Elvish that I could recall.) Perhaps you can ask Ana if she knows any of the fairy tongue, though I imagine it has changed quite a bit since this time.

It appears I have come back thousands of years, long before the time of my parents or even my grandparents. The Norminster Yew is present but very young. Less than 100 years at best, I'd guess. It stands on the edge of a small clearing the fairies seem to use for ceremony, the very same spot I used to come here. It seems that particular place has had special significance for thousands of years.

The fairies are most curious about my magimeter, my clothes, and my journal. But nothing has enchanted them more than my pen. I was terrified they were going to empty it of its remaining ink, but instead they showed me a similar ink they use to record their ceremonies. I have never seen symbols like the ones they use in their writing. I will copy some of them here for future study.

Please tell the others that I greatly appreciate what they have done to help me. I did try using the incantation, though I'm uncertain whether it had an effect.

But it has given me an idea: perhaps if the incantation can be used to decurse a cursed object, which essentially removes or releases its stored power, a similar one could be used to store power in the first place.

The primary obstacle in the usage of our mithril-iron design is the damage done when the power-saver is depleted. The cursed objects have a way of maintaining low levels of power for hundreds of years without affecting future usability. I'm not suggesting we curse the power-savers, but perhaps a protective enchantment of some kind could work similarly.

I believe one such enchantment exists on the horn, which reads quite strongly in this place, as you might have expected. The fairies here use similar horns for drinking and ceremony. I am hoping by continuing to observe them, I may learn of the nature of the enchantment.

Ceri was relieved to hear Leo was safe, but she was also a bit upset with him. How could he remain so calm after everything that had happened? Why wasn't he begging her to find him a way back?

Did he even want to come back?

You didn't mention coming home.

Ceri, please don't mistake my attempt to make the best of a difficult situation as apathy about ending it.

There is <u>nothing</u> that I want more than to return home to you.

I'm doing what I can to see if there's some kind of answer here. I know the fairy magic is incredibly powerful, but the communication barrier has to be addressed before I can ask for their help. I hate to ask more of you, but as I no longer have access to the library, I can't continue the research there.

I am open to all ideas. But I also want you to know that I am safe here, at least for now, and I don't want you to miss out on your time at school or your education on my behalf.

That being said, one of the very first things I did when I woke was look for something that could be used as a looking glass on the off chance I could see you in it.

There is a small pond nearby. I shall be as the doomed hero of old, staring endlessly into my reflection.

But it is not myself that I hope to fall in love with.

Ceri spent so long in the bathroom that night staring in the looking glass, poor Ana had to leave and use the common one downstairs.

Chapter Twenty-Nine

BREAKTHROUGHS

Alison

The days slipped by as autumn took hold of Winwold, sweeping the college and the town up into a whirlwind of reconstruction, flagball games, and even an adorable autumn carnival which Keir insisted they attend to give Alison a much-needed break from her tireless research. (He won her a stuffed bear at a ring toss game. The game had been rigged, so he felt no shame in using a little bit of magic to defeat it.)

The relief of knowing that Leo was safe and that they could take their time with finding him a way home had been considerable. As Alison understood it, he was making some progress in communicating with the fairies, in part thanks to letters exchanged with Aras, Alison's neighbor. They'd written to Ana's father on Turtle Island as well, but at the rate it took for the post to cross the ocean, they'd be lucky to hear back from him by the Winter Solstice.

They also enlisted the help of the Ancient Languages professor, Professor Zerod. In exchange, he asked them for one thing: help with the annual SERSHO (Society for Equal Rights for Smallfolk, Humans, and Orcs) bake sale.

Everything was delicious: Keir made buttery shortbread, Ceri tried her hand at the egg tarts Leo had made her (the dough was harder to make than it looked), Idris made traditional Formosan mooncakes, and Alison called her mother and got the sticky toffee pudding recipe her dad had loved. (She also called Ms. Varma from Andsaz Industries for her gulab jamun recipe and was amused to hear that they had underestimated just how much work she had done around there and hired not one, not two, but three people to replace her.)

But it was Rinka that stole the show with her chocolate-chip banana bread. It was unbelievably moist and rich with just the perfect amount of sweetness. Alison bought a couple of slices for herself.

(It also didn't hurt that Ana dabbed a bit of the fairy "grey goop" on everything at the end, making every dessert into the best thing that anyone had ever eaten. SERSHO raised enough coin to cover their expenses for three years.)

While they hadn't made much progress with a plan for getting Leo home, his suggestion to enchant the power-savers combined with Alison's intuition about the power of her poetry had made for some interesting experiments. There did seem to be some kind of potential there, but the issue was endurance: as Idris had noted, spells that continued indefinitely were considerably more difficult to achieve.

At one point, they had considered trying to architect an "accident" similar to the vine that had nearly swallowed Herot's Hollow, but the breakthrough finally came from a call on the long-talker with Gwenla.

"You know, the dwarven blacksmiths once carved runes into their blades and hammers. The young folks think runes are old-fashioned, but I wonder if there wasn't something lost when we stopped doing it. Maybe if we took the enchantment you created, translated it into our runes, and carved it into the power-savers, it might last."

"Do you think human magic will work with dwarven runes?" asked Alison.

"I can't imagine it would hurt to try," said Gwenla. "If it doesn't work on the power-savers, maybe it'll work on these kids. Gods know we need some way to get them under control."

"You're going to carve runes into the kids?"

"Oh no, not carve. But there's a man around here that does tattoos. At this point, I think Yordin would prefer tattooed, docile children over the hellions that he has."

Alison laughed. She had seen enough in one night to know that was true. "Any thoughts on whether you'll be bringing Finnli back with you?"

"I'm going to have to. He keeps trying to grow vegetables in the dark down here. You've never seen such stretchy tomatoes in your life, and not a flower in sight. I have to do it for the plants' sakes. It would be cruel to leave them alone with this little black-thumbed maniac."

Alison had already known what Gwenla's answer would be, but she enjoyed hearing Gwenla trying to justify what

Alison knew to be the simple kindness that her dwarven friend could not avoid showing if her life depended on it.

Later that same night, as Alison read in the familiar spot by the fire in the library (this time with Willow in her lap), she came across a book on Samhain rituals.

"Listen to this," she said to Keir. He was leaning back with his feet propped up, having spent a long day down in Norgate helping deliver a baby (a healthy orc girl). "*On Samhain night, a bonfire is lit to open doorways between worlds. It's thought that passage between fairy realms and the mortal world is possible.* Passage between worlds, Keir."

"Interesting, but I don't see how that could connect to the horn," said Keir. "All of the times Leo visited had something to do with the item in his possession."

"Sure, but he didn't interact with all of them. He skipped the locket and the doll. Maybe we've been too focused on the horn. What if we could bring him back with a ritual on Samhain? It's just a week away."

"You're suggesting we light a bonfire and do what, exactly?"

Alison hadn't actually thought of them being the ones to light the bonfire, but it wasn't a bad idea. "I was going to say that Leo could do something in his world, but maybe it would be better if we did both. Maybe if we light a bonfire here and they light one there, and if we copy whatever their ritual is, it'll open a door."

"And what if it sends us to his time rather than the other way around?"

"Then I think you're about to revolutionize medicine. Imagine teaching three-thousand-year-old fairies about anesthesia."

"I was thinking more of you without your 'lectrics. I'm not even sure how I'm meant to get you back to Herot's Hollow after weeks with hair curlers and 'lectric lamps."

"Ah, but what we really ought to do is bring them a power-saver. Maybe by the time we made it back, the world will have advanced so much we'd be living on the moon."

"Now that's a place that's more suited to you. Being made of cheese, after all." Keir tugged playfully on Alison's plait. "I do like your idea, though. Either we manage to bring Leo back, or we just have a nice bonfire on an autumn night and try something else later."

"With a bonus ancient ritual that's sure to have at least three professors losing their minds," said Alison. "I do worry that Leo's usefulness for their research may lead to their sabotage of our efforts to bring him back."

"I wouldn't be too concerned," said Keir. "There's absolutely no way Ceri lets that happen."

He had a point. If there was one thing Alison had learned, it was that nothing could stand in the way of Ceri. Not curses, not school rules, not her royal status.

Not even time itself.

Chapter Thirty

SAMHAIN

Leo

On the morning of Samhain, Leo found an unexpected visitor lurking among the trees.

He had seen the shadow of it for several days, but the fairy villagers kept scaring it off. From what they had shown them in paintings they had done on their huts, there were a number of fearsome beasts stalking about in the woods, many of them incredibly dangerous judging by the violence of the images.

And this visitor was unquestionably one of those, or it had been once.

It was the tarasque. Leo had no idea how it had gotten there. Had it followed him through all of his journey? Was it bonded to him somehow? He didn't even know if it was real or just some strange remnant of magic that only existed in this place because of whatever was keeping him there.

But he was happy to see it, nonetheless.

The villagers flew down with their spears in hand as Leo approached it.

"*Tak,*" he said to them. It meant "no." He held his hand up. "Friend," he said.

"Friend?" asked the grey-haired matriarch. She was their leader and the person who had been the most interested in learning Loegrian.

"Yes, friend," said Leo. He reached out a hand to the tarasque. It licked him with its lion tongue, which felt a bit like it was taking the flesh off his hand.

The matriarch gestured to the others and spoke some words Leo had learned related to food.

They brought out a slab of deep red meat: the hind-quarters of an aurochs, a fine cut that honored Leo's declaration of the beast as a friend.

Leo bent his head in gratitude at their offering. He had learned that many of their interactions involved subtle gestures of the head and wings, and while he couldn't replicate the wing movements, he mimicked the head movements as closely as he could.

The tarasque took a sniff of the meat, looking at it skeptically.

Then it devoured the entire thing, a slab roughly the size of a goat, in a single bite.

The fairies murmured in their language.

"Friend?" asked the matriarch again.

"Friend," Leo reassured her. Truthfully, he wasn't certain that the tarasque posed no threat to them, but he seriously doubted their ability to defeat it even if it did, so he saw more promise in diplomacy.

Leo led the tarasque back to his hut and reread the description of the Samhain ritual he'd written into the journal. It had taken a great deal of convincing to get the matriarch to divulge the ritual in advance. They had been happy to have him watch, but they weren't as keen on having him participate. But insisting that he really wanted to had been the only way to get the matriarch talking, and in the end, their culture respected the wishes of guests too much to refuse him.

Leo had been tasked with beating a certain drum, a task that he suspected was generally given to children due to their laughter when they saw him practicing with it, but either way, his hands wouldn't be free to use his magimeter.

Once, the missed opportunity to take measurements would have filled him with anxiety and pre-emptive regret.

But he'd found that the more he tried to explain this place, the more he tried to pin it down like a butterfly to a corkboard, the more it eluded him.

Before he dressed, he set about writing what he desperately hoped was his final note to Ceri:

As I prepare to (hopefully) say goodbye to this place, I must take a moment to acknowledge the wonder of it and the privilege it has been to experience something with my own eyes that no one living has ever known. While my journey began in fear, these past few weeks have been incredible in the literal sense: an experience beyond belief. I have done my best to document it, to measure it, to understand it, but I have realized that perhaps there is something more to it beyond that which can be readily explained or understood.

Do not misunderstand me: I do not now think the pursuit of knowledge is a fool's errand. I still believe in the incredible power of science to transform our understanding of both the natural and supernatural worlds, and I believe that the never-ending quest for knowledge will be forever our best weapon against the forces which would consume us. There is no surer path to violence, hatred, and despair than ignorance.

And yet, perhaps, there is a beauty in the unknown. There is something to be said for not having all the answers. There is something to be said for the humble acknowledgment that although the pursuit of knowledge is pure and should never be abandoned, some things may simply be beyond our comprehension. I don't know why I've come here, but I know that it has forever changed me. And maybe that's enough.

Another thing I know is that I could not have done this alone. I will forever be indebted to everyone who has helped me in this journey, and there have been so many. I hope to be there to give them each my thanks in person soon.

But of all the people who have helped me, none of them helped me more than you, Ceri.

You, who believed in me.

You, who were my life raft while I was lost at sea.

No matter what happens tonight, you saved me.

And I will never, ever forget it.

Je t'adore. À bientôt, mon miracle étoilé.

The Samhain bonfires had been lit in the same spot in two different worlds and countless others across time and space.

As the sky turned to dusk, the fairies gathered, each of them wearing a special mask honoring a forest spirit or a soul of the dead. The masks had been crafted from dried vegetables and animal skins, and their appearance in the flickering light of the bonfire was lifelike enough to startle Leo. The children found this great fun, taking turns sneaking up on him and screeching with their little crow faces.

At the beginning of the ceremony, a goat was slaughtered. This had been the most difficult part of the entire ritual to replicate back in Leo's home world because, unsurprisingly, the thoroughly modern faculty of Winwold objected to the ritual sacrifice of a live animal in their courtyard. They settled for the pouring of pig's blood onto the altar by Professor Marin, who was a regular enough customer of the butcher shop in town that it didn't seem too much of a strange request.

Following the sacrifice, the fairies made offerings to a nearby altar for the dead. They presented gifts of fruit and grain, crafts and wreaths made from straw and dried summer flowers, and painted portraits and written messages to those who had passed on. Leo understood that a similar altar had been crafted in the High House courtyard, and that students had come by all week leaving portraits and letters to lost loved ones.

Finally, the matriarch had placed the heart bone of an aurochs on the altar, beginning the chant. Dean Whittaker had called the zoological department at King's College and managed to obtain a similar ossified structure of an ox heart used in anatomy lessons, the aurochs having gone extinct some centuries earlier.

The chant began with a low single note sung by the matriarch's partner. Then the matriarch joined in, singing a simple lilting melody in their language. Her voice was layered in harmony by the others, and then finally the drums began. Leo had been unable to fully transcribe the words of the chant, but he'd learned enough in his time there to guess at the meaning: "forest," "dead," "spirit," "bread." The song explained the significance of the ritual and begged the spirits to take their offerings and walk among them once more. Alison had taken the general ideas and created a simple verse and melody for them to sing:

> *O come ye spirits to this night,*
> *Among the trees in pale moonlight,*
> *To join us here in feast and fire,*
> *Now lift the veil and leap the pyre.*

As the chanting continued, the dancing began. Some of the fairies took flight, circling the bonfire like moths, while others danced with their drums on the ground. Leo joined them, doing his best to mimic their movements. As he danced, he began to hear strange sounds. Whispers in the fairy language and in Loegrian. Laughter and shrieks from far away.

And out of the corner of his eye, strange images appeared. Glimpses into other versions of this world, places he had come from and some beyond his comprehension, pasts and futures colliding.

The sounds and images were overwhelming. It was as if a million points of time had collapsed into one, and Leo had no idea how he was meant to use this chaos to get home. Had this all been a mistake? What if he followed the wrong path and ended up somewhere far worse?

And then he heard her voice.

Ceri, her voice sweet and clear, if a little out of tune. She was singing the song Alison wrote. But as she sang, the tune began to change. The songs merged, joining together into a harmony that was neither past nor present but somehow a blend of both.

Leo called to her. His wasn't the only voice calling a name in the din, and he worried she wouldn't hear it.

But she answered. "Leo!" she shouted from a thousand miles away.

And then he saw her through the fire. It was the Ceri from the mirror, the image of her reversed and shimmering in the flames.

He knew it would be insane to step into the fire to reach her.

But he also knew that he must. He could not explain how he knew it. It went against every bit of logic and reason that he possessed. It went against his instincts, his most primal fears. It was a great leap into the unknown.

Leo made the leap.

He felt a blaze of heat. Fear clutched at his heart as he doubted his decision. Could he have been wrong? Had he gone this far to fail at the final test?

And then there was nothing. An inky black void, a space between worlds.

Silence.

Above him, a thousand million stars. They spread across the sky, shooting like meteors, exploding like fireworks, filling the darkness with their twinkling light, surrounding him.

He spun around to look at them all. How could there be so many? He felt the infinite vastness of it. He was adrift in a sea of stars, tiny and alone.

But he wasn't alone.

Ceri was there. The stars had come together and made her. She burnt with their fire. He could see them flicker in her movements, could see the trails of them spinning as she reached out for him.

He took her hand.

She pulled, and he followed. She pulled him closer to her, moving galaxies in her wake. She held his face. He could see a nebula reflected in her blue eyes, worlds being born and collapsing into dust over and over in an endless cycle.

She kissed him, and the worlds collided.

He felt the same lurch as before, but forward, not back. He fell with her through the darkness, tumbling and turning, on and on and on, and then in the final moments, drifting like the floating of a feather onto the ground.

When he opened his eyes, he was home.

Chapter Thirty-One

JOURNEY'S END

Ceri

Ceri opened her eyes on the ground, feeling that same sense of falling into the sky that she'd felt weeks before on the blanket next to Leo.

Next to her, he grabbed her hand, pulling her back down to solid ground.

They had done it. He was here.

She kissed him. It was filled with more than the weeks that had been between them, between the first moment under the stars and this one. It was a kiss that spanned centuries, millennia. It was the ecstasy of one hundred lifetimes in a moment.

"It's nice to see you too," said Leo when they parted.

Ceri shoved him playfully as he laughed.

He pulled her to her feet and kissed her again. This time, he wasn't laughing. As he pulled away from her, he whispered in her ear, "Thank you."

"Leo!" shouted Professor Marin from the other side of the bonfire. She ran to him and embraced him warmly, kissing each of his cheeks in the continental style. "You absolute imbecile. I'm so happy to have you back."

Ceri stepped back to give Leo room to accommodate all the hugs, well wishes, and mockery he had coming to him.

And then someone screamed.

"Oh Gods, what is that thing?"

The bonfire crowd split in two: those that ran towards danger, and those that ran from it.

Ceri and Leo stood their ground.

Bounding around the bonfire was a lion. No, not a lion. It had the mane of a lion, but its body was armored like a turtle. It was weirdly familiar.

"My friend," said Leo. "You came back with me."

It was strange, but Ceri felt she had seen it before. Or perhaps felt it.

"What is that?" asked Alison. She approached it cautiously as Willow ran off in the opposite direction saying "nope" over and over. "It's so familiar to me."

"To you too?" asked Ceri.

"I've felt its presence in the woods and the halls. Something stalking me just out of sight. I swear it's the same. I've felt it since I came here."

"This is the object of all of my childhood fears: the tarasque I described from my first night in the other world. I thought it had gone when the nightmare ring left me, but it returned today before the ritual. Don't worry, it's quite tame." The tarasque licked Leo's arm and then took to chasing a moth near the bonfire.

Ceri held her breath as Barney the dog ran across the courtyard barking at the tarasque.

"At least I think it's tame—" began Leo.

The tarasque lay down in front of Barney, bending its armored paws. Barney walked around sniffing it. Then he barked his approval and ran to join Willow under the Norminster Yew.

"I don't care how nice it seems," Ceri heard Willow saying to the dog. "I have all the friends I need already, thank you very much."

Alison left to go comfort the cat.

"What are you going to do with it?" asked Ceri.

"I have no idea," said Leo. "It seems to be trying to protect me. I guess I'd better let it."

"Not on school property, please," said Dean Whittaker, eying the tarasque suspiciously. "We've had enough excitement for one year, and the autumn term isn't even halfway done."

"I don't know," said Harry Charlton. Ana was lurking shyly nearby, watching his every word. "The team could use a new mascot. Imagine the faces of King's College if we showed up with that thing in tow."

Harry grabbed a sausage off of the altar and tossed it to the tarasque.

It swallowed it whole.

Harry cheered.

"I don't get paid enough for this," the dean muttered, walking away.

"Welcome back, Leo," said Idris, extending his hand to shake.

Leo took it nervously, looking for a catch.

Idris pulled Leo closer to him. "If you ever put my sister through anything like that again, I'll have your head," he whispered. "So nice to have you back," he said at normal volume, patting Leo on the shoulder.

"Don't worry," said Ceri. "Idris is all talk."

It wasn't completely true, but there was no need to worry Leo unnecessarily. Ceri had no intention of letting him out of her sight anytime soon anyway.

As the bonfire wound down, Alison found them again to update them on the research.

"We've had some promising results in the lab. Professor Marin says the charge retention is much higher than the original design. We'll be stopping in with the dwarves on the way home to see how they're doing with replicating the enchantment. Did you want to come see the numbers?"

"Of course," said Leo.

"Later," said Ceri. She shot a meaningful look at Alison, who smiled.

"Tomorrow morning, then, before we leave," said Alison.

"What did you have in mind for tonight?" Leo whispered once she'd left.

Ceri pulled the torn journal pages from her pocket. "Something like this," she said, and pulled him by the arm towards the dormitory.

Chapter Thirty-Two

ENDURING MAGIC

Alison

In the morning, after they'd shown Leo the inscribed power-savers and gone through all of the numbers with him, Alison and Keir said their goodbyes before their journey home.

"I'm glad you enjoyed your stay here with us," said Dean Whittaker as he helped them to their carriage, which they had to meet on the other side of the river due to the bridge construction. "It's been…eventful."

"Thank you for having us," said Alison. "We gave our regards to Professor Marin last evening, but I hope you'll reiterate them for us when you see her next."

"We'll be back at Herot's Hollow as soon as the term has finished," said Rinka, pulling Alison into a tight hug. "Idris says there's a chance King Derkomai will come to see how the 'lectrics are coming along, but it's the peak of the flagball season, so he might accept Idris and Ceri going in his stead."

"We'll make sure the cottage is ready for visitors," said Alison. "Not that you have to only visit. There's still a room there for you if you want it."

Rinka looked at Idris. "He's had an idea about that. I don't want to say too much too soon because a lot will depend on the king, and you know how he is. But there was an abandoned port town we went through in the summer where the Burning Ash pirates hide out in the off season. The king is very interested in both stopping them and developing Wilderise, and Idris thinks there's a chance he'd support Idris investing in the area. There's a ruined monastery nearby he thinks would make for a nice college."

"A college in Wilderise?" asked Alison. "How far is it from Herot's Hollow?"

"Ten, twenty miles maybe."

It was still a good distance, but it would be nice to have Rinka closer again. "How long would it take to build?"

"Years, I'd guess," said Rinka. "Although you know what the king is like. If they come to him and say it'll take five years, he'll give them six months."

They were just past the three-month deadline he'd given them themselves, but the good news was that the bulk of the work had been done. With any luck, Alison and Keir would be making the voyage home with the first solar generator shipment.

"Give my love to Gwenla," said Rinka, hugging Alison one more time. "And Lady Sibba and Weyland and Charlotte and Strelka—"

"And everyone, got it," said Alison.

The saddest goodbye of all was between Willow and Barney. "You make sure that tarasque doesn't eat him," Willow told Leo. "He's a good boy. He's not dinner."

Alison had seen Barney and the tarasque playing together, but she didn't mention it. "We'll come back and visit," promised Alison.

"We'd better," said Willow. "Or you could bring Barney to visit us. I'd love for him to meet my friend Dinah."

Alison couldn't imagine Groundskeeper Tomasar leaving his beloved yew, but she told him he was always welcome nonetheless.

⁕

Riding the rail-wheeler back to Rodaz Mountain was a bit like traveling through time. The elevation change meant the autumn leaves, which were nearly gone by the time they left High House, were right at their peak in the valley where Gwenla's people lived.

It was lovely, like having a second autumn, and Keir told her they'd have a third when they returned to Herot's Hollow, which was much further north but also much nearer to sea level and likely had leaves just beginning to change.

The dwarves of the Rodaz Mountain Industrial Corporation were seeing the same success as Alison and the others had seen in the lab, but there with a small additional step required to replicate the spell Alison had cast.

"My uncle Dorrik is one of the oldest dwarves in our clan," said Gwenla, showing Alison into a cavern that opened to the surface they were using to test the generator. "He remembered that the runes must be imbued with the dust of diamonds to endure. That's supposing you don't intend to stick around and enchant every power-saver that comes off the assembly line."

"I don't," said Alison. The home of the dwarves was nice and cozier than she had originally expected, but she missed her cottage in Herot's Hollow. "Diamonds? Are they very expensive?"

"Oh, not at all," said Gwenla. "Diamonds aren't rare, and they don't have to use gem quality ones anyway. Yordin said the cost savings from not having to replace the entire power-saver will be substantial. He's already had two more orders come in for the power-savers. Alison." The elderly dwarf held Alison's arm and pulled her close. "We're going to be rich!"

Alison thought about Idris's idea for the coastal town and the college in Wilderise. "Have you ever thought about investing?" she asked.

❧

Alison, Keir, Gwenla, and Finnli refused Yordin's offer to use his rail-wheeler car or carriage during their journey back.

"We may be posh now, but we won't forget where we came from," said Gwenla.

Alison didn't want to count their chickens, either. There was still the matter of the installation of the solar generators once they arrived back in Herot's Hollow. Lord Ainsley, who had cleared off back to Arcas Dyrne until the entire construction project had completed on account of the noise, had donated an unused field at Weldan House to set them up. All of the numbers and tests in the world wouldn't matter if they didn't work in practice, but it would be a few months yet before they'd know for sure.

"When you lived in Arcas Dyrne, did you ever see the Winter Solstice displays they put on?" asked Gwenla. "All the pretty lights shining in the streets and decorating the houses? Yordin showed me pictures of it. Could you imagine something like that in Herot's Hollow?"

Alison could. She could just picture the snow falling, silent and still in the forest, with the warm glow of Herot's Hollow off in the distance.

But there was still more autumn to enjoy before then.

When the carriage came around the final mountain, filling the view with thatched roofs, rolling hills, and drifting clouds of leaves in spirals of gold, amber, and maroon, Alison felt at peace.

They were home.

Epilogue, Part One

Back at the cottage, Alison found a larder full of the autumn harvest thanks to Charlotte's hard work.

"Look at all of this! Have you ever seen so many apples? I'm not sure we'll need to go to the market at all this winter if we can get this lot canned," she called to Keir.

He didn't answer. "Keir?"

Alison left the larder and found him at the kitchen table. There was a small box sitting in front of him.

"You know, I had this whole speech prepared. I've been thinking about it for weeks, but now that the moment is here, it doesn't feel right," he said. His face was very serious.

"What do you mean?" she asked. He looked from her to the box.

"I don't know," he said. "It just doesn't feel like there are words good enough to describe how I feel about you."

"I know how you feel," said Alison. "You don't need to tell me again."

"I don't think you do," he said. He popped the box open. In it was a sapphire ring. "Will you marry me, Alison?"

"Is this the nightmare ring?" asked Alison, so surprised to see it she hadn't heard the question.

"Yes," said Keir. "I asked Idris for it when you said you liked it. He assured me it was perfectly safe. I thought you could have it until we can get you the one you want."

It was only then that Alison processed what he had said. "You want me to marry you?"

"Yes," said Keir.

Alison took the ring from the box. "I do really like this ring."

Keir looked like he was about to faint. "Do you not want to marry me?"

"Oh Gods, sorry, I was just surprised. Yes, of course I do. Yes."

Obviously. She was surprised he had to even ask.

"Oh, thank the Gods," said Keir. "May I?" He took the ring from Alison's hands. He was shaking.

Alison laughed. "I'm so sorry. I didn't mean to scare you. I thought you were breaking up with me there for a minute. I didn't even hear what you said."

"Well, that will probably go down as the worst proposal of all time. I should have stuck with the speech," said Keir. He shook as he slid the ring onto Alison's ring finger. "I wanted it to be special, but I was so terrified you'd say no that I couldn't work up the courage to even really try."

Alison took his hand. "Stop. I don't need anything special. Every day with you is special enough on its own. Of course I'll marry you, Keir Ainsley. I love you."

"I love you too, Alison."

He kissed her until they both laughed from all the silly nerves of it all.

"Look," he said, pointing out the window when they parted.

The first snow had begun to fall.

Epilogue, Part Two

"Look, it's really very simple," said Ana. She sat with Ceri and Leo in the stands of the Winwold College flagball stadium in Norgate.

In front of them, wrapped in a blanket in the Winwold College colors of crimson and black, Rinka was having a very similar conversation with Idris, who could not have looked more bored if he tried.

"When they blow the whistle, the flag runners will run for the flag in the middle of the field. And the ball kickers will try to move the ball to the goal. But they can't score unless the flag runners are either holding the flag or have planted the flag in one of those posts on their side of the field. If they score without the flag in their possession, it's a point for the other team. The flag runners have to protect the flag or try to steal it, but they can't touch the other runners or it's a penalty. They can also use the flag to try to get the ball in the goal themselves, but no one can touch the ball with their hands. If a flag stays in a post for five minutes, they have to reset, and everyone runs to the middle of the field. If you don't get there in ten seconds, that's a point for the other side too."

"And you think that's simple?" asked Ceri.

"Just watch," said Ana. "You'll get the hang of it. Here they come. Go number four! Woo!"

"Do you get this?" Ceri asked Leo. "Please tell me you don't get this."

"There were many games in my home—there were enough of us to make several teams—but not this one, no. It's very popular in Gallia too, though. I think there it's more of an excuse to drink."

He handed her the vacuum flask of tea whiskey. She was glad he'd brought that instead of the tea coffee. He'd finally made it for her the morning after they returned, and she had been…unimpressed.

"An acquired taste, perhaps," he had admitted.

Ceri watched as someone in Winwold colors kicked the ball into the goal. She cheered.

"No, no," said Ana, quieting her. "They didn't have the flag. YOU MORON! DO YOU EVEN KNOW WHAT A FLAG LOOKS LIKE?"

She wasn't the only one yelling, but most of the others were saying things that were considerably ruder.

"I'm sure he didn't mean to," said Ceri.

"You can't play at this level and make mistakes like that," said Ana. "How humiliating. AMATEUR!"

Even apart from that mistake, Winwold was thoroughly outmatched. The School of Numbers was up 5-0 at the half, and the Winwold crowd was thoroughly defeated.

"We could always help things along," said Idris, creating a magical breeze with his fingers.

"That's cheating!" said Rinka. "Absolutely not. They've got to learn from a loss like this if they ever hope to beat King's College."

It seemed pretty unlikely to Ceri that they would, given today's showing.

But then, a miracle happened.

"That's it. That's better," said Ana. Harry had the flag now, and he was running for the goal with the ball kicker kicking the ball just behind him. They dodged a mean tackle from a School of Numbers defender, the ball kicker kicked, Harry deflected with the flag, and then: "GOAAAAAAAAAL!"

The crowd erupted. Even Ceri was on her feet screaming.

And then came the heartbreak. The referee was holding up a handkerchief, which Ceri felt was rather odd.

"NO!" screamed Ana. "There's NO WAY that was off-sides!"

"Offsides?" asked Ceri. Ceri took it that the handkerchief was bad news.

"I'm not even going to try to explain," said Ana, looking at Ceri as if she was hopeless. "It just means he's saying it doesn't count. The goal doesn't count."

The stands started singing a song that was frankly deeply insulting to the referee's mother. Then the Winwold coach and another referee came out to argue.

"Wait," said Ana. "They're overturning his ruling. It's good!"

The crowd cheered again.

"This is a lot of emotions to go through in just a few minutes," said Ceri.

"That's what makes it great!" said Ana.

Ceri wasn't so sure, but even she was excited when Winwold managed to pull a draw out of the game in the end.

"That means we're only a point behind King's College in the rankings. If Winwold beats them in the rescheduled game, they win the season!"

Ana went to meet Harry afterwards as Ceri and Leo took the long walk back to High House.

In the forest, the tarasque was chasing after deer. "No ruining your supper," called Leo. His bag was full of the butcher's special of the day: lamb. "Meet us in the courtyard."

They fed the tarasque, watching him bound around and warning him not to get too close to the Norminster Yew before Groundskeeper Tomasar had his hide. When they had finished, they went into the library.

With the cursed objects gone or safely stored, the library had made peace again with Leo. As they curled up together on the couch, Ceri with her assigned reading and Leo with his research, the library made one final suggestion.

Living Quietly: A Guide to the Tranquil Lifestyle.

"Thanks, library, but no thanks," said Ceri.

"Forget that," said Leo. "Where's the fun in life without a little good trouble?"

They set the book aside and settled in for a long night by the fire.

About the Author

Amy Yorke is an author of light and cozy fantasy and lover of all things magical and romantic. She is half English, half American, and she offers her sincere apology to readers of both languages for her idiosyncrasies in word choice. In her spare time, she enjoys gardening, playing video and tabletop games, and chasing after her cats.

Join her mailing list to receive news, updates, and promotions, including free advanced reader copies prior to new releases: https://www.amyyorke.com.

Read on for a preview of *The Silent and the Silver,*
Book Four of the Wilderise Tales

Prologue

Charlotte did not build up the nerve to approach Weldan House, her childhood home, until the third Winter Solstice after she fell over the nearby waterfall to her supposed death.

In the first weeks after she fell, she had thought of the whole thing as a bit of a joke.

Not that she hadn't been terrified when she went over. She had, of course. Not of dying—that was something that happened to old people, people who were at least thirty, not to little girls. No, she was afraid of getting hurt, of breaking her arm again and having to wear a sling for weeks. She was afraid that the trees she so loved to climb would be out of her reach, that she wouldn't be able to pay ball with the other kids in town.

She did not think of drowning, not until it happened.

Charlotte had been able to swim for years. Her brother Keir took her down to the lake beneath the manor and out into the water before she'd even started school. They had learned to swim from the Lady Willana, an elf from the town on the other side of the woods. The old lady was uniquely beautiful and graceful, and having no young children of her own, she had taken an interest in caring for Keir and Charlotte whenever she had the opportunity. Charlotte couldn't picture her own mother, her having passed shortly after Charlotte was born. But when she read about mothers in children's books and heard about them in nursery rhymes, it was Lady Willana that she pictured.

Lady Willana had taught them well despite not having the most captive audience. Charlotte had been more interested in splashing her brother than listening to the elf's instructions or her stories of life in the city. But Lady Willana had persisted, and ultimately, both of the children learned all their basic strokes.

So when the water from the falls plunged her down into icy darkness, Charlotte did as she had been taught—she kicked and thrashed her arms, reaching for the surface.

But the surface didn't come.

Charlotte's eyes stung as she pried them open under the water. The air burned in her lungs as she fought the urge to take in a breath. Lady Willana had warned her about this feeling. She said that giving into the temptation to breathe would be the death of her. That if she found herself trapped under the surface, she must do anything she could to reach the air. That she could not wait for someone to save her. She would have to save herself.

Lady Willana's advice had been well intended, but it had also been wrong.

Someone did come to save Charlotte in the end. Charlotte was drifting out of consciousness by the time the tiny korrigan pulled her from the depths and to the shore, so she never saw which of their number was her savior.

But she guessed it was Nolwynn. All of the korrigans were brave and kind, but none so much as Nolwynn. The woman barely came up to Charlotte's waist, even though she clearly had decades on the little human girl, but she had the biggest heart of anyone Charlotte had ever met.

She was infinitely patient as Charlotte struggled to come to terms with what had happened to her, not just when she fell, but what had been happening to her for the years that preceded it.

Charlotte knew her childhood wasn't ordinary. She hadn't known her mother, but she had grown up in the grandest house for miles around, so it wasn't a surprise to her to realize that the other children in the village lived very different lives from hers. But it took being given the option to live somewhere else for her to realize that her life wasn't just unordinary.

It was wrong.

By the time Charlotte had recovered from her near drowning, the search for her had begun. Keir had looked for her himself first. Charlotte hadn't seen him, but the korrigans told her when she woke that he'd been up and down the shore, above and below the falls, shouting for her. He'd waded into the water at the base of the falls and had come so close to going under the surface, the korrigans thought they were going to have to save him too.

But he'd eventually given up and gone back to the house for help. Charlotte could hear them in the forest around her, calling her name. Not "Charlotte," her true name, the name she had taken for herself. Her other name, the one she had been born with.

"Danny."

The korrigans had seen the way Charlotte had reacted to the voices searching for her. They had seen her fear, a feeling Charlotte couldn't name for herself.

And so they hid. They hid themselves and Charlotte with their magic, a magic that made them blend into the streams and the reeds and the woods. The men and women from Weldan House and Fossholm came within inches of Charlotte without ever seeing her.

And so she stayed with them as the weeks turned months turned into years. They seldom asked her questions about her life in the manor. This, Charlotte came to realize, was their way. Many others came to live with the korrigans during her time with them. Some stayed only for days, others for decades, but the korrigans rarely asked questions. The korrigans understood that there were some things in this world that didn't need to be spoken of. That there were some pains too great to share.

It took Charlotte many years to share hers. The innocence of childhood had offered her some degree of protection from it. Keir's efforts had offered her even more, although she wouldn't realize that for decades. She saw him sometimes, months after she fell. He seemed half of the boy he had been even as he grew taller. He walked the grounds and the woods silently, far too sullen for his years.

Charlotte couldn't understand then why that was. The Keir she had known had hated her. He had resented sharing with her, had taken things from her, had ruined her games and spoiled her fun. Worst of all, he had forced her to keep who she was secret.

Charlotte's fascination with dresses and dolls had been a cute little quirk of hers in the eyes of most of the household from around the time she could walk. But her father had no patience for it. He would not listen to reason about how normal it was for a child to try different things. He flew into a rage whenever he spotted Charlotte wearing a bonnet or pretending to embroider pillows as her mother had loved to do.

Keir had told her that, about their mother. He was young when she died as well, but he knew a few things about her, and Charlotte made him tell her the stories of their mother over and over again, every night before bedtime.

That was how she came to know that her mother had been certain that she was a girl when she was still in her belly, that she'd been so certain she had named her and bought her a doll. Keir told her the doll's name was Charlotte, the name their mother would have given her if she had been born a girl.

Charlotte could not explain it then, but later she would understand the feeling she had when she heard the story: she knew, deep down, that her mother had been right. She *had* been born a girl. Her true name was Charlotte.

Charlotte began to play games of pretend with imaginary friends who knew her true name. That was how Keir found out who she was. He caught her out near the river curtsying to a fairy prince, introducing herself as the Princess Charlotte of the Riverlands.

Keir hadn't been angry. But he had been afraid. He had looked all around, making sure no one had heard her, and then he had grabbed her by the shoulder. "You can't say that," he'd said. "You can't let Father hear you. Don't ever say it again."

Charlotte didn't understand then that Keir was trying to keep her safe. She had cried and shouted at him. Keir hadn't shouted back—he rarely did—but he would not budge. He didn't understand what it meant to her. They would get into the same argument again and again for years, right up until the day she went over the falls wearing a dress.

So when Charlotte saw Keir mourning her, she didn't understand it. She thought he would be happy she was gone.

On that Winter Solstice night more than three years later, it finally seemed like he was. A carriage had arrived the day before, and Charlotte had spotted them—Keir and their cousin, Rory—playing in the fields outside of Weldan House.

She had heard the shouting first. She raced to the edge of the woods, keeping herself close to the trees to let the korrigan's magic hide her as they had taught her to do. Winter had come early that year; the snows had started right after the harvest and had rarely let up since. Out in the yard, the boys were having a snowball fight.

Charlotte listened to the boys shouting and playing, their laughter echoing over the frozen ground, and felt a powerful sense of jealousy and loss.

She should be there with them.

She watched them for hours. She couldn't see them clearly from such a distance, but she could picture them. The rosy red of Keir's cheeks. Rory, breathless, crouched behind a tree, lying in wait.

If she had been there, she would have scaled the great old oak and pelted them both before they even knew what had hit them.

But she couldn't join them, not now. It had been too long. How could she explain what she had done? How could she make Keir understand why she had to leave, why she couldn't go back to the house even though she was so close?

He would be angry. And Father would be angrier. He might hurt the korrigans for helping her. They were good at hiding, but people spotted them sometimes. She couldn't risk their safety for her sake.

So she reluctantly dragged herself back into the woods as the sun set. Hours later, she heard the chime of the dinner bell on the breeze. She had eaten already with the korrigans, but as delicious as their fish stew was, she longed for a taste of the traditional Solstice roast.

She would settle for just seeing it. She crept back through the woods to the spot from which she'd watched the boys earlier. There was no need to sneak—the korrigans would not be angry with her for going—but she did so nonetheless. Perhaps it was herself she was hiding from.

The windows of the manor were lit with flickering candlelight. Smoke poured from a dozen chimneys, leaving a hazy cloud over the great building.

It was so warm, so inviting. The cold barely touched her now that she had lived among the korrigans for so long, but she was still tempted by the promise of a night spent beside a roaring fire, a cup of hot cocoa in hand. It was almost enough to make her forget what had happened to her in that house.

The dining room faced the eastern courtyard where the boys had been playing. It was such a grand room that it had no fewer than eight windows. The heavy curtains had been drawn over them, but there was a gap between them on the third window from the left.

Charlotte crept over the fresh snow, passing through the bushes and climbing onto a thin ledge of stone to peer inside. The gap was narrow, but it gave Charlotte a good look at the end of the table.

Keir was there, and so was Rory. They had bathed and dressed in their finest attire. Keir was thirteen then, and this was likely his first Solstice dinner at the adult table. He was doing his best to mind his manners and look the part of the future lord of the house, but she could hear his gentle laughter at some joke he shared with Rory, could see him fighting off the fit of giggles that desperately wanted to escape.

Charlotte's breath caught in her throat as she watched. It was so…ordinary, so joyful, in a way their family dinners never had been.

She realized it then: she was right. They were better off without her.

Keir lifted a glass of amber liquid, and as he took a sip, he caught Charlotte's eyes for a moment.

Charlotte stood still as she watched the color drain from his face. He froze there, the drink still touching his lips, his eyes wide open and staring straight ahead.

As Keir lowered his glass, Charlotte bolted.

She leapt from the windowsill onto the snowy ground, not noticing the pain of the impact. Not daring to look back, to see if they were coming for her, she tore across the moonlit yard into the night.

She crossed the river—the river that had nearly killed her—effortlessly. The water was as familiar to her now as her old room in the manor, as much her home as any other place. But she didn't want to be at home. Not now.

Her feet carried her through the woods, past the korrigan's camp, up and up, to the edge of her father's land where it met the road into Herot's Hollow.

With everyone at home enjoying the Winter Solstice feast, the roads were silent and still, the only sound the quick crunch of her feet through the freshly fallen snow. Charlotte knew where she was heading.

What she didn't know was what she'd do once she got there.

Across the river, there was a line of shops with living quarters in their upper stories. Charlotte passed the tailor and the apothecary and stood in front of the third shop in the lane: Mrs. Knox's Bakery.

Charlotte looked into the window: the shop was dark, but she could just make out the empty shelves behind the counter. It looked just the same as it had the last time she had been there over three years earlier, the same simple wooden tables with the chairs stacked on top, the same hand-drawn sign, tucked in the corner:

1dz Solstice biscuits 1s
½ dz Mince pie   1s5c
Solstice log   2s
Fruit cake w/o brandy   2s
*   w/brandy   3s*

The bakery was her favorite shop in Herot's Hollow, but she wasn't the only one who loved it. Next door, above a venture that had changed several times over the years (Mr. Blair's Antiques and Collectibles, Mr. Blair's Flowers, Mr. Blair's Fine Furnishings), candlelight flickered in the leftmost window of the upper story.

Julian was awake.

His family's Solstice dinner must have finished before she got there. Shadows moved at the back of the shop—Julian's father coming up with another wild scheme to make some coin, perhaps. Charlotte crept carefully along the front of the house, worried her hair (once brown, now korrigan silver) would catch the light from the streetlamps, alerting Julian's father to her presence.

Charlotte and Julian had been playing together since before Charlotte could remember. They'd run up and down the streets of Herot's Hollow, climbing the walls and the trees and generally causing mayhem.

The only thing that would get them to sit still for a minute was Mrs. Knox's chocolate biscuits. They were crumbly and rich, covered in a thin layer of dark chocolate which Mrs. Knox pressed into a swirly pattern that made you dizzy if you stared at it too long.

Not that you would have been able to. The biscuits were so delicious, especially with a big glass of cold milk from her icebox, that they seldom lasted more than a few seconds in the presence of any of the children in town. Or any of the adults, for that matter.

Charlotte hadn't had one of those biscuits in years. She wondered if Julian still stopped by the bakery on the way home from school. She wondered if he ate a biscuit (or two, or three) at one of the little wooden tables on his own now, or maybe if he'd made another friend to share them with.

Charlotte wondered if he thought of her sometimes. He must have heard what happened to her. She wondered if he believed she was dead like everyone else did, or maybe if he thought she'd run away like she often spoke of doing. Maybe he thought she'd gone to join the pirates in the Sallin Sea. Maybe he pictured her with a wooden leg and golden tooth, wielding a saber with a flourish as the stormy waters raged around her.

Or maybe he never thought of her at all.

Charlotte knelt to the ground in front of the shop. She felt around the cobblestones of the street until she found it: a perfect little pebble.

She turned it over in her hand, considering.

Should she see him again? Could she walk away, now that she was here?

No, she decided. She could not.

She launched the pebble upwards, striking Julian's window with a *tap*.

She held her breath as she waited. His shadow stirred within the room, rising from the bed and heading to the window, the silhouette of the boy growing smaller and more distinct as he approached the paned glass.

It was him. He was taller than she had expected, and his hair had been cut closer than she knew he liked it, but it was the same boy she had known.

The same boy she had grown up with. Her best friend in the world.

At least, she hoped he was. She hoped that whatever he thought of her—if he thought of her—that it didn't make him too sad.

She hated to imagine him sad.

Charlotte hesitated for a moment more. He was looking around—any moment now, he would spot her.

Then she took off and ran before he could.

Whoever he was now, he was better off without her. She was sure of it.